THE BAKER'S GIRL

Meg just wants to keep her family together. Her mother is desperately ill and her sister is still in school, so it is up to her to support them.

All Meg knows to do is bake and desperation leads her to Ted Lund, the miserly owner of a local bakery. In a moment of uncharacteristic kindness, he takes pity on Meg and offers her a job.

But Ted's charity ends there. He'll save money at any costs, cutting corners by using sawdust in his bread, ignoring vermin in his flour, and paying Meg a pittance.

But despite her mistreatment, Meg can see what the bakery might yet be. Using her baking skills, can she turn the shop around?

SPECIAL MESSAGE TO READERS

THE ULVERSCROFT FOUNDATION
(registered UK charity number 264873)

res... ...or
...ases.
...e

- ...
- ...
- ...at
  (...
- ...ment
  a...ersity
  c...
- ...titute
  c...
- ...halmic
  ...
- ...

Y... ...tion
b... ...ery
con... ...d like
to... ...ther

THE ULVERSCROFT FOUNDATION
The Green, Bradgate Road, Anstey
Leicester LE7 7FU, England
Tel: (0116) 236 4325

website: www.ulverscroft-foundation.org.uk

GRACIE HART

THE
BAKER'S GIRL

Complete and Unabridged

MAGNA
Leicester

First published in Great Britain in 2021 by
Simon & Schuster UK Ltd
London

First Ulverscroft Edition
published 2022
by arrangement with
Simon & Schuster UK Ltd
London

A catalogue record for this book is available
from the British Library.

ISBN 978-0-7505-4942-4

Published by
Ulverscroft Limited
Anstey, Leicestershire

Printed and bound in Great Britain by
TJ Books Ltd., Padstow, Cornwall

This book is printed on acid-free paper

For my very understanding editor,
Molly Crawford.
Thank you for your time and patience and for
publishing my titles in such trying times.

1

Leeds 1894

Seventeen-year-old Meg sat by the side of her mother as she lay in her bed unwell. Agnes had been getting progressively worse with each day, but despite her ill health, she always kept cheerful and planned for the future of her much-loved children. She instructed Meg daily not to waste her life and to count every day as a blessing and Meg in turn tried to reassure herself that things were not as bleak as both knew they really were. Meg's father had died eleven years ago, killed in a pit disaster at Wheeland Pit. She could barely remember his face or voice, and now she feared she was going to be left to raise her younger sister, which was a task that she did not relish unless her mother's health improved. She had already been helping out with earnings from doing errands for the market stall-holders between looking after her mother and raising Sarah but she now knew she would shortly have to look to make real earnings in order to survive.

'Aye, I'm aching today, my pet. Your mother's not long for this world, I doubt.' Agnes turned and looked at her precious daughter; she stroked the side of her face and smiled. 'You'll have to make the best of your life, when I'm six feet under. But before I do go, I need to see you in employment and then I know that at least you can keep this roof over your heads and your bellies full because I've nowt to leave you. Life has not been good to us, my sweet, and I wish I could

1

have done better by you both. And you must promise me that you'll take care of Sarah. I know she's young and headstrong but she'll soon grow up.' She sighed and tried not to show the worry and pain that she was really in.

'It's all right, Mam, you've always been a good mother to us both,' Meg replied. 'We've both wanted for nothing. Love's more important than possessions, and we've been shown plenty of that. You'll have a better day tomorrow but you are right, with you being ill, we aren't able to take any washing in. It's too much work for you, and I haven't the time to have my hands in soap suds every day and worry if I'm going to get it dry and ironed before it's needed by our customers.

'I wondered whether to ask Ted Lund if he needs help in his bakery. I can go early in the morning, he's always got the ovens going by four in the morning, and he's closing his doors by noon, so that would work out well for me while I'm looking after you and Sarah.'

Meg looked around the small bedroom that she and her sister shared with her mother. It was damp and cold. The wet dripped down the walls, leaving the once whitewashed walls black and mouldy, and the fire that burned in the hearth was only just keeping the creeping fingers of winter out of the bedroom. They had no money for the extravagance of extra coal to keep the bedroom and the kitchen fire alight, so Meg and Sarah had begged and pleaded the stall-holders in the busy market in the town centre for their used packing boxes to burn just to keep their mother warm. However, Meg knew she needed paid work yet at the same time, she had to be there for her mother and sister in their hours of need.

2

'He's not up to much is Ted Lund, he's as tight as a duck's arse,' Agnes told her. 'He's lazy and all, so he might just be willing to take you on if he thinks he can have a lie in his bed an hour longer — and at least you could bring us a loaf occasionally when he's not been able to sell it. I'm surprised he sells anything: his bread is that rubbish, he should have been shut down years since, but folk will eat anything to keep their bellies filled in these hard times.'

Agnes sighed and held her breath as another bout of pain made her feel faint. 'I need to see him. I'll get up out of this bed tomorrow and tidy myself up so he doesn't realize how ill I am. He owes me a favour; I've done his washing for years and he knows he's paid me short on many a time. He'll know that now he's taking it to Mrs Battersby's on York Street and it won't be as well ironed.' She held out her hand to be taken by Meg as she fought the pain and tried to smile. 'You are a good baker, he'd be thankful for your light touch with pastry and cakes — not that his bakery's that frivolous with fancy goods.

'Now, you fill me this bed bottle and go and have a word with him. I'll have myself forty winks while you are out.' Agnes passed Meg the brown stoneware arched bottle from her bed, which was giving her the only warmth in her life. She felt death drawing ever nearer each day that she awoke. 'I will, Mam, and I'll not be long. His day will nearly have come to an end so he should be nearly finished in the shop.'

Meg took the hot water bottle from her hands and looked at her mother as she pulled the patchwork quilt that had been made by them both over many months when times had been happier from offcuts of worn-out clothes. Each stitch had been done with a

3

smile and love as they had sat around the fire of an evening together. Now the love sewn into it was pretty much all that was keeping her mother warm, and she was glad of it.

She made her way down the wooden stairs into the main kitchen and living room in their small one-up one-down on the street known as Sykes Yard. She poked the dwindling fire and added a piece of coal onto it before placing the iron kettle on the stand over the fire, knowing it would soon boil. The kettle was always kept full and warm at the side of the fire and she waited for it in the Windsor chair where her father had always sat. She closed her eyes and tried to think of better times when her parents had both been hale and hearty and money had not been the worry that it was now.

Her thoughts were interrupted by the sound of people rowing next door. The noise coming through the red brick walls with clarity was nothing new. Twenty people were living there in a house the same size as theirs, a family with ten children, two grand-parents, and various lodgers who came and went with the shifts in the local flax mill and slept in the base-ment. There were frequent arguments to be heard at number 8, so the day was nothing unusual and Meg found herself feeling thankful for her lot as she heard the baby next door squealing yet again and the father raising his voice. Meg's family might be poor and share rooms but they were not as cramped or as poor as some of the families in the square.

Meg heard the front door of next door slam and glimpsed the father storming off down the cobbles, probably on his way to The Globe public house where he would find solace in a drink or two, then, depending on his mood on his return, would either return to his bed or to argue with his wife again. She heard his wife sobbing as the baby kept wailing and the children were turned out into the yard to play despite the cold north wind that was blowing along the Yorkshire streets.

It was always the woman that caught it, Meg thought as she went to the back door and emptied the stoneware water bottle down the back drain and lifted the now boiling kettle to refill it. There was no way that she was ready for marriage, not to be lumbered with a baby every year and a husband who drank. She was prepared to wait until a decent man entered her life, one like her late father. Or even better, she would make her own way in the world without the aid of any man, she thought, as she tightened the stopper on the bottle and made her way back up to her mother before heading out to visit the grumpy Ted Lund with her suggestion.

★ ★ ★

'Meg, Meg, have you any spice?' The oldest of the Hartley family from next door ran up to her in his rags and no shoes on his feet begging for some toffees as she pulled the front door behind her and wrapped her shawl around herself in protection from the sharp biting wind.

'Sorry, Harry, I've no toffees today. I wouldn't mind one myself.' Meg smiled at the crowd of young children. Within the year, ten-year-old Harry would be made to go and work at the local woollen mill like his older brother, but as of now, he was in charge of his younger siblings, and unlike her younger sister, had a lot of responsibilities on his shoulders. 'Are you all all right? Your mam, is she all right?' Meg asked with concern as she looked at the rag-taggle bunch that looked half starved.

'Yes, but my da's in a black mood. He threw his dinner plate at her and said he was fed up with bread and dripping for his dinner and that it wasn't fit to eat. He's buggered off to the pub, so my mam and we have a bit of peace until he comes back.' Harry put his arm around his sister and looked up at Meg with wide sorrowful eyes. 'Is your Sarah coming out to play?'

'No, she's up the backyard, pretending to dance like those in the music hall. She is a right madam is our Sarah.' Meg shook her head as she thought about her younger sister, whom she loved but who both she and her mam knew thought herself precious. 'You look after your mam, and the others behave and be good, and I'll see if I can afford you some spice in a day or two if I can find myself some work.'

Meg smiled and left the children playing around the gas lamp. They had tied a length of string to it and were using their feet to swing back and forward. She couldn't help but think her sister would be better mixing in with them than daydreaming about something that she could never be.

'You going to get a job, Meg? Where at? I can't wait to work at the mill and then I can make some brass!' Harry yelled after her as she walked down the cobbles.

'Hopefully with Ted Lund,' she turned and answered.

'That old bastard? He's a right skinflint, my mam says, you'll not be able to buy us any spice if you work

6

for him,' Harry shouted back and then went to organize his siblings as they swung around the gaslight.

Harry was right, Meg thought as she walked quickly out onto York Street where Ted Lund's run-down bakery was to be found. She stood and waited for a minute while she plucked up the courage to talk to the local baker; he was not known for either his manners or his generosity. She watched as he came out of the shop and picked up an advertising board and took it back inside his shop. She'd picked her time right — he was making ready to close, so he would hopefully have the time listen to her and be feeling tired. The offer of a willing pair of hands might be attractive as he thought wearily about the following day's preparation. Her heart beating fast, she walked across the street and into the small bakery.

'We are shut! Can't you read the notice?' Ted Lund nodded to the cardboard sign that he had just turned over in the window of the shop's door.

'I'm sorry, Mr Lund, but I have not come to buy anything off you.' Meg hesitated as she saw the scowl on Ted Lund's face.

'Well, I can do without folk like you bothering me. What are you standing there for then? Bugger off!' Ted moaned as he pulled the shutter down and then rearranged the morning's leftover bread to the front of his counter for resale as new the following morning.

'I was just wondering . . . I mean I'd like to ask you if there is any chance of me getting employment with you. My mam says you've got to come and talk to her about it but I can ask for myself without bothering her at the moment.' Meg had decided as she walked on her way to the bakery that she had a tongue in her head and she would ask for work herself. Besides, her mother was too ill to be bothered with grumpy Ted Lund.

'She's suffering at the moment, I hear,' Ted said, less gruffly. 'I miss her doing my washing — that woman further down the street charges more and doesn't take as much care.'

Ted looked at Meg. He'd known her all his life and knew that things must be bad if she was seeking work with him. 'What makes you think that I need somebody here at my bakery? I've run it by myself for years, so there's no need for me to take on a slip of a lass that I'd have to keep my eye on all the time.'

Meg looked at the leftover bread and quickly replied, 'You wouldn't have any of this leftover each day because I'd work long hours for you and I'll be good at sales. I could help bake in the morning and then you could have a sleep while I serve on. You could stay open until late then if there were two of us. I'd be able to work from early morning until one, and at least as long as my mam was all right, I could even come back and catch the mills turning out in an evening if you wanted me to.' Meg immediately regretted that she had offered her services so much but knew she had to say something to make him see his business would be the better for taking her on.

'I'll see,' Ted replied, and took a moment before continuing, 'let me think about it. I've been thinking the mornings are beginning to take their toll on me. Let me sleep on it. I will however come and see your mother: she can tell me if you can bake or not. It's no good taking on somebody who doesn't have a feel for the dough. A baker's not made you know, you are born a baker. My father was a baker and his father before him. This shop has been in our family for over fifty years; I can't let it go to the dogs if I take you on.'

Ted went to his cash drawer and started to put the day's takings into his pocket. 'I'll come around and see her about you tomorrow after I've shut shop. She'll be looking to make sure I'll treat you right if I do happen to take you on, if she is as bad as I've heard tell.'

'Thank you, Mr Lund, we will both be grateful and I'll be a good worker . . . and I can bake.' Meg was smiling as she was ushered out of the shop by Ted, who just wanted to get home to his bed.

'Aye, well, I've not said as much yet. We'll see after I've talked to your mother. She's a good soul, an' I'll not be easy to work with, I'll warn you. You'll have to do as you are told whether you like it or not.'

Ted scowled as he walked out onto the street with Meg and turned to lock his shop's door. The church bells tolled for the hour and everybody knew it was just one o'clock in the afternoon so if they hadn't caught the bakery on York Street it was too late because Ted was away to his bed, even if they wanted to give him their trade. 'Until tomorrow — and don't hold your breath, I might change my mind when I've had some sleep.'

'Thank you, my mam will be pleased, we will look forward to your company.'

The smile stayed on Meg's face as she walked with a spring in her step back down the street. The bakery was only small and Ted would probably pay her poorly but any money would be better than nothing.

'Have you got your job, Meg?' Harry asked, lifting his head at the sight of her returning as he sat on the unscrubbed steps of his home on his own in peace.

9

'No, not yet, but I will. Then I'll give you a farthing for some spice, I promise, Harry.'

Meg was still smiling as she walked up the pristine steps into her home. They might be poor but they had their pride and what they could keep clean they did. She prayed that Ted Lund would give her the job and that her mother would not be too ill the following day to see him. She loved baking. Her new position would be a godsend — it was made for her if Ted Lund would only take her on.

* * *

'They look good, our Meg — the money spent on them will be worth it if it persuades Ted Lund to take you on.'

Agnes smiled with pride as she eyed the batch of rock buns that had been baked in honour of Ted's visit. The recipe was one of the cheapest and tastiest that they both knew and eaten fresh there was nothing to compete with them. She sighed as Meg placed them on one of the better plates and put them down alongside the few pieces of good china that they owned ready for Ted to have tea with them. 'Now do I look all right, not too ill? I don't want that old devil thinking I'm on my last legs,' Agnes said as she sat in the chair as close to the fire as she could. She had no meat left on her bones and found herself always cold as well as wracked with pain. 'I'll away back to my bed once he's been and gone. I can't sit here for too long.' She wriggled in her chair and wished that Ted would hurry up.

'You look fine, Mam, a lot better than you did yesterday,' Meg reassured her. 'You frighten me when you

10

have bad days like that.' She looked at her mother. In her prime she had been quite buxom with long black hair and a good glow on her cheeks. Now she was skeletal, her hair grey and her cheeks sunken, only half the woman that Meg once knew. She hoped that she would be forgiven for lying for a good cause.

'Aye, well I frighten myself, my lass. I never thought this would happen to me. You think yourself immortal when you are younger and then Death points his finger at you and you know he's waiting around the corner.'

Meg pulled a strand of loose hair back away from her mother's tired eyes as they both heard a knock at the door. 'Let him in then lass, don't keep him waiting. Let's get on with the show. He'll wonder how he's ever survived without you by the time I've built you up.'

Agnes grinned as Meg opened the door to the scrawny shape of Ted Lund as he took off his top hat and peered in at Agnes, registering the smell of sickness, the odour of rotting flesh that he had smelt too many times. He knew instantly that Agnes Fairfax was suffering more than she was letting on as she smiled and greeted him, trying to rise from her chair but then sitting back down quickly.

'Stay where you are at, Agnes, there's no need to stand on ceremony, and I'll not be stopping long.'

Ted looked around the small room that was still spotless, a fire in the grate, and noticed that some of the ornaments that Agnes had been so proud of were missing. The room looked more sparse than he had remembered it from when he used to leave his washing with her. No doubt the pawnshop had benefitted from the dire straits they had found

11

themselves in. 'Now, your lass here, she says she can bake, is that right?' 'Aye, look at the rock buns she made this morning. Try one with a cup of tea, and then you can tell me what you think of our proposal. She'd be a good help and no bother. Her grandmother, God rest her soul, learnt her how to bake before she could hardly walk,' Agnes said, exaggerating the age that Meg had actually found a liking for baking.

'Well they look all right . . . You've even put sultanas into them instead of currants. That's a bit extravagant, I'd not be having you doing that in the shop!' Ted bent down and cracked the rock bun in two. It crumbled but held its shape well as he took a bite.

'Mmm . . . that's all right, but it is one thing making cakes and fancies. Can you make bread, lass? That's what I sell the most of in my shop.' Ted looked at Meg as he finished his bun but shook his head to a cup of tea as Meg started to pour a cup for her mother and then him.

'Yes, I can make bread. Why do you think we don't buy it off you? It's because we make our own,' Meg said quickly and glanced at her mother.

'Well cut me a slice of what you've made this morning,' Ted said, quickly looking across at the sideboard where a breadboard was placed with no bread upon it.

'I never made any this morning, I made these instead.' Meg sighed, frustrated that she couldn't prove her bread-making skills.

'She can make bread, Ted, she makes good bread,' Agnes put in. 'We just didn't have enough money to make both this morning and she'd made these before I could say owt. She needs a job, I need her in a job. Take her on, if only to make an ill woman happy. It's

12

your turn to do me a favour,' she pleaded and winced as she moved in her chair.

'You are not in a good way, are you, Agnes? I suppose I can try her for a week or two. It will give me a bit of a break, and aye, help you out. I'm not a millionaire though; she'll get paid what I think she's worth.' Ted looked at Meg. 'I'll expect you at my bakery by four every morning and you do as you are told, no shirking or questioning what I do and why I do it. I'll see how you work out and pay you what I think.'

Ted breathed in deeply and looked at the relief on both women's faces. 'I'm not promising owt, so don't count on me; if I find your bread baking is worth nowt, then you'll soon be on your way.'

'Thank you, thank you, Mr Lund, I'll not let you down, I promise. I'm a good worker and you'll not regret your decision.' Meg smiled at her mother as Ted made for the door.

'Get your mother to bed and I'll see you on Saturday morning, just for a half-day and then you can start properly on Monday if you are any good. Don't expect any leeway on your first day, I'll start as I mean to carry on. So don't expect any niceties,' Ted growled as he let himself out.

As he walked back home, Ted thought carefully. The rock bun he had tasted was excellent and if she made bread as good as her posh scones then she would be worth his money. Besides, her mother was in a bad way — she'd need some money coming into the house to pay for the laudanum to ease her pain which he had spied on the mantelpiece. He didn't know how much longer Agnes would be with her beloved daughters but of one thing Ted was sure: there was going to be heartache soon at 10 Sykes Yard.

2

Meg watched her mother as she slept, peering through the darkness, reassured by the sound of her breathing. It was not yet light as she heard the church clock chimes and she yawned as she dressed quickly and pulled her covers back in place upon her bed.

'I hope that you're not going to wake me every morning at this time when you go to work,' Sarah said sleepily as her big sister wakened her from her slumber. She pulled the covers back over herself.

'Shush, you'll wake Mam, and besides, you can go back to sleep for another hour or two. But when you do get up, remember what I told you last night: make sure Mam has everything she needs. Go to the market and beg some firewood, but don't go trailing out around the streets and leave her too long. You've to look after her and take responsibility while I'm at work,' Meg lectured her young sister, even though she knew Sarah usually did anything other than what she was told by her older sister.

Meg made her way down the stairs in darkness and sat down in the chair next to the fire that still had a few glowing embers. She pushed some dry sticks into the oven and she watched as it came back to life. As the light from the fire lit the room, she placed the kettle above the flames before slicing a thin slice of bread for both her and her mother. That along with a cup of tea that was going to be breakfast for Agnes, just in case her younger sister didn't show her mother the same care as she would have done.

14

She carefully and silently crept back upstairs, placing the meagre breakfast on the table next to her mother, as they'd arranged the evening before. She looked at her mother and breathed in heavily. She hated leaving her mother in Sarah's care, but somebody had to earn some money to help them live. What little savings Agnes had were now spent and there was little charity shown by the good and great of Leeds. If they weren't careful the poorhouse beckoned and nobody with any pride wanted to end up in there.

She returned downstairs, her stomach churning as she pulled her shawl around her shoulders. She took a quick sip of the weak tea and a bite of the crust of bread she had allowed herself and then stepped outside into the square. The smell from the midden that the whole row used to empty their chamber pots into assaulted her nostrils. It was always the worst first thing in the morning when the air was still and clear and she had to stop herself from retching as she made her way quickly out of the square by the light of the gaslight.

'Morning,' she said quietly to the knocker-upper with his long pole as he tapped on the bedroom windows of those who had paid him for their early morning call. She would have liked to ask him to have done the same for her, but it was an expense that she could ill afford.

'Morning, miss. It's a cold one this morning,' the elderly man said as he moved on to his next client.

'It is,' Meg agreed as she clutched her shawl around her and hurried on her way.

She must not be late for her first day with Ted Lund. Her stomach continued to churn as she approached the shop which had the bakery behind it. It looked to be still in darkness as she turned the door handle. The sign was still showing closed as she tried the handle to get in. Was there another way in that she didn't know about or was Ted not opening today?

'He'll not be here yet for another half-hour yet,' the knocker-upper called to her from across the street. 'He likes his bed too much does Ted, never mind that everyone is waiting for the bread before going to the mill.' He then moved on to his next port of call as Meg stood shivering on the step in the cold morning's light.

* * *

'What are you doing shivering there for?' Ted demanded a few minutes later when he finally appeared. 'You should have come and knocked me up, you know where I live. Folk will be waiting for us. You had better shape yourself better when you set about baking else I can do without your so-called help.'

Ted glared at Meg as he opened the door and walked quickly into the back of the bakery where he set about lighting the fires underneath the ovens that were built into the walls of the building.

Meg said nothing. She hadn't realized that awakening Ted was part of her job too. She watched as the baker placed kindling and coal underneath the huge arched ovens and closed the heavy iron doors of them to build the heat up within. Then with his coal-blackened hands, he carried a bag of milled flour into the small bakehouse, putting it down against Meg's feet and nodding to a huge mixing bowl. 'Don't just stand there. You are here to help me, so get mixing some bread. Think on you are making enough for nearly a hundred folk, so make sure you make enough. There are bread tins over there — fill forty of those and make some plaits and cottage loaves. Make sure you leave it to rise enough, I don't want bricks,' Ted instructed as he lugged another bag to her side and then brought her enough yeast to make sure the bread rose well.

Meg looked at both sacks and started filling the mixing bowl with more flour than she had ever handled before in her life.

'Nay, lass, mix it with some sawdust from the other bag before you start adding the yeast and salt and you'll need some water from the pump out in the yard. You go and get that and I'll add the sawdust.' Ted shook his head. He'd never made his bread with a hundred per cent pure flour for years and he wasn't about to now.

'You add sawdust to your bread — are you supposed to do that?' Meg asked as she reached for a metal bucket to get the water in.

'I can do what I want, there's nobody out there to stop me. I'm not a bloody millionaire and folk have never complained about my bread. You say nowt to nobody mind, else you'll not be stopping long with me. Besides, some bakers add plaster of Paris. That's worse — it makes the bread claggy and you can taste it. At least this sawdust is so fine you don't know it's in there. Now, stop gawping and get that water, else we are never going to have owt to sell today,' Ted said sharply and watched as Meg walked past him and out of the back door to the small yard where his water pump was.

Meg stood at the pump and looked around her. The yard was a mess. There were used flour bags and crates stacked up all around it and she nearly squealed as a rat ran along the wall top as she pumped water from the iron pump. The kitchen wasn't much better, she thought, as she lifted the bucket full of water from under the pump, spilling some on her skirts making them wet and cold. They'll soon dry, she thought, as she watched the smoke from the ovens rise up the chimney into the damp winter's air and felt the warmth of the kitchen as she opened the door with her bucket of water in her hands. How long had Ted been getting away with adding sawdust to his bread, she wondered as she watched him mix the concoction and mutter to her not to mix the yeast and salt together as they didn't like one another, before he added the water and made the huge amount of dough, which he then stepped out of the way for Meg to knead.

'Put your back in it lass — give it a good pummelling, it needs some air putting into it.'

Meg had never kneaded so much dough, and her arms and hands ached as she stood back and looked at the mountain of dough on the wooden table.

'Right, that'll do,' Ted told her finally. 'Now make your plaits and cottage loaves and I'll make the tin loaves. I'll have to, else we'll have no bread ready for them that work on the early shift at the mill. You should have worked faster,' he growled as he took half the dough away and started dividing it into the bread tins and covering them with the dirtiest tea towels that Meg had ever seen to enable them to rise in the now warm kitchen. Then he put them on a tray on the wooden shelves that surrounded the bakery's walls.

Meg divided the dough and started to roll a third into the larger round bun of the cottage loaf. Then she rolled smaller buns to be placed on top to make the cottage loaf.

But when she reached for a knife and started to

18

mark the bread with decorative lines around the larger bun, Ted stopped her. 'We will have nowt fancy on my bread,' he told her. 'Folk like it just as it is, no decoration. As long as it tastes right they'll not be bothered what it looks like and you are wasting time.'

Ted looked across at the lass with fancy ideas as she placed twenty cottage loaves next to his on the proving racks.

'My mam says you eat with your eyes and that food should look pretty,' Meg said as she went to what dough she had left and divided it again into three to plait into a loaf.

'Tah! Your mother and you talk rubbish. Folk isn't bothered about what they eat as long as their bellies are full. When you've done that, you can go and sweep the shop out and open it up. Yesterday's bread wants selling before I put the fresh batches out. They that are in a rush to get to work are usually not that fussy. I'll bake the bread once it has risen; I'm not trusting you with my ovens yet,' Ted said as he quickly glanced at the rising bread and stoked his ovens up.

Meg finished plaiting her loaves and then took hold of the brush which, like everything else at the bakery, had seen better days. It was nearly bare of bristles, she noticed, as she left the warmth of the bakery and went into the shop. She stood for a second in the gas light's shadow and wondered if her decision to work for Ted Lund had been sound. His bread was far from right. He was duping his own customers by adding sawdust, so no wonder his bread tasted of nothing and was not popular.

She looked at the stale bread that she was supposed to sell as fresh and screwed her nose up. Some of it looked and felt more like two days old. A couple of the loaves even had Ted's charcoaled fingerprints on them where he had picked them up with dirty fingers from the fire. Cleanliness and freshness were obviously of no importance to Ted, she thought, as she took hold of the brush and started to sweep the scraps and rubbish from the previous day from off the floor. That might be his way of working, but she had been brought up to do differently.

She made the most of the bristleless brush and turned the shop sign to say that the bakery was open for custom. In half an hour the mill whistles would be heard all over Leeds summoning their workers into the woollen, flax and cotton factories that made the city of Leeds one of the wealthiest in Yorkshire. The sound of clogs running on the cobbled streets would fill the air along with the chatter of the mill girls and the banter of the men trying to chat them up.

Ted would probably be proven right. If they were in a rush and just needed something to fill their bellies at dinner time they would be grateful for his stale bread. She was best saying nothing and just doing her job. After all, she was just a shopgirl — and a shopgirl who needed every penny she could earn so best she'd not say what she was thinking to her new employer.

Meg finished sweeping the floor and then went back into the bakehouse. The smell of freshly baked bread was beginning to fill the air and the warmth from the ovens made her see the bakery in a different light. Ted Lund could have a good business if he could only be bothered, she thought, as she watched him push another dozen or so loaves into his oven on a flat paddle. But who was she to think as much? She was new to the job and had to earn his respect if she was to stay working for him.

20

She watched as he pulled the first newly baked batch from the ovens. She realized that Ted had once loved and been a master of his craft from the efficient way he moved as he emptied the bread tins and left the bread to cool, once he had tapped each loaf on the bottom to make sure it was baked through. Why had he lost love for his work? She'd never lose her love of baking if the shop was hers, she found herself thinking as she gazed around the bakehouse.

'Stop your gawping. Put that apron on that's behind the door and go and stand behind the counter!' Ted yelled at her. 'Folk won't wait to be served.'

Sweat ran down his forehead from the heat of the fires as he kept them fed with fuel. 'Tin loaves and cottage loaves are a penny ha'penny and plaits are a penny. We don't do tick — they've to show their brass first or they go without.'

Ted watched the lass jump to his words as she put on the apron and vanished back into the shop without replying. He sighed, wiped his hands on his apron, and went to repick one of the loaves up made by Meg. It looked and felt good; she was going to be worth her money once she'd got used to his ways.

It was a shame that his own daughter and wife were no longer alive. They would have filled the bakery with the love that only women could put into baking and he would not have needed the lass. Perhaps the lass might give him a new injection of life or perhaps she could at least make his life easier on the days he didn't want to leave his bed when he hadn't the heart to take on the world. Time would tell, he thought, as he heard Meg serving the early morning rush.

★ ★ ★

21

'You're new! Has old misery guts taken you on to help?' Daisy Truelove looked Meg up and down and passed her a penny ha'penny for her bread and stood waiting for a reply.

'Yes, I'm on trial. I hope he keeps me on, we need the money.' Meg smiled at the young lass who was on her way to the mill for her day's shift.

'Well if you can, put me a loaf of fresh bread to one side for me in the morning. I know this will be yesterday's if not older,' Daisy said. 'The other week, my loaf had started to go mouldy. Lord knows how old it was! I wouldn't shop here but you are handy before I make my way to the mill. I'm a blanket weaver — the pay is poor but at least I help my family keep a roof over our head. A fresh loaf to look forward to would be grand.' Daisy smiled and took the loaf that Meg had wrapped up in white paper for her and placed it under her arm. 'I'm Daisy, by the way, I live four doors down.'

'I'm Meg, and I'll try and do that for you on Monday if I can.' The young lass looked about her own age of seventeen and guessed she was luckier than her — at least Meg wasn't working in the noisy, hot and dusty world of the mill. There, wool was spun into thread to be made into blankets by young lasses with quick hands and quick eyes in order to save fingers and lives.

'That'll be grand, I daren't ask miserable old Lund, else he'd stop serving me altogether. Grumpy old bastard.'

Daisy winked and then made her way out of the door as she heard the factory whistle blow once more to summon her to her life of servitude.

'I thought your mother said you were good at baking bread. I could build a bloody house with these loaves.'

Ted entered the shop with a board filled with the freshly baked bread. He'd heard the shop bell ringing continuously in the last hour and he knew that the old bread would nearly have sold out and now that the factory workers had cleared him of yesterday's bread he would need his new loaves for the regulars that shopped between eight and one when he closed. He looked at the scowl on Meg's face as she wondered whether to answer him back about her baking skills.

'I'm sorry, perhaps I'm not used to adding sawdust into the mix,' Meg said more sharply than she intended.

'Keep your voice down, lass, anybody could walk in. I told you not to talk about our secret. On Monday perhaps a lighter touch is needed,' Ted said as he filled his empty shelves up with the newly baked bread.

He couldn't let his new apprentice think she had the upper hand on him and his bread baking — but at the same time she had made his life easier. He had recognized over the course of the few hours she had been in his shop that it had made his load a lot lighter. Meg would be a boon to him once she had come around to his ways.

* * *

The morning flew by for Meg. First, there had been the factory workers in their rush to get to work, then there were the wives and daughters making sure that there was fresh bread on the table for their loved ones,

23

and then finally those that came in when they had decided they were out of bread or just wanted to idle the day and have somebody to share their troubles and woes with. All had been glad to see a new face over the counter of the bakery. Ted Lund had no time to hear anybody's woes, so a young lass with a welcoming smile and caring way was to be welcomed in the austere bakery.

Meg heard the clock on the wall above her head strike one. It was dinner time and the shop always closed at one, once the morning rush had finished. There were but a few loaves left from the morning's baking so Ted would have to be up and going sooner, she thought, as she turned the notice on the shop's door to Closed after hearing Ted yell at her to shut for the day. She breathed a sigh of relief. The time had soon gone but in the back of her mind when serving each customer she had been worrying about her mother and sister at home on their own. She quickly untied her apron strings and hung it up behind the bakehouse door.

'I'll be away now, Mr Lund. Or do you want me to sweep up and tidy the shelves? I've covered what bread is left and pulled down the blind.' Meg stood in front of her new boss and waited to see what he wanted her to do.

'Nay that can be done in the morning, the ovens are out now and I'm away to my bed. It's been a hard morning.' Ted yawned and looked at her. 'Be here on time come Monday and remember our secret: don't be going telling your mother about my ingredients,' he growled.

'No, Mr Lund, I won't and I'll be here on time. Do you want me to come and knock of you if it gets past five?' Meg asked as she watched him slip on his well-worn coat.

'If I'm not here you best had. You are taking up a bit of my time having to teach you everything and things have taken longer than usual with you being under my feet,' he said, virtually shoving her out of the shop as he locked the door behind them both without looking at what bread was left on the shop shelves. 'I'll see you on Monday morning, Myra, bright and early.' He didn't turn his head as Meg reminded him that her name was Meg, not Myra, as he walked down the street to his home and bed.

Meg shook her head. He couldn't even be bothered to remember her name and a little gratitude would not have gone amiss for the work she had put in that morning. He was no better than most employers — he just wanted as much work out of you that he could.

She wrapped her shawl around her and started to run down the street back to her home in Sykes Yard. Would her mother still be in bed or would she have managed to wash and dress herself? All had been left for her to make herself comfortable; the coal scuttle had been left filled as well as the kettle. As long as she had managed the stairs by herself she should be fine. She knew Sarah was at home and should show her mother some care but she also knew her sister to be selfish and easily led if there was something better to be doing than looking after her ailing mother.

3

'I'm home, Mam!' Meg yelled as soon as she opened the front door. 'Are you both all right?'

She was relieved to see her mother sitting in the chair next to the fire with a cup of tea in her hand.

'I am, lass, but I don't know about Betsy next door,' her mother said wearily. 'They wakened me as soon as you walked out the door, before light this morning. Shouting and yelling and carrying on, you've heard nothing like it. Now that no-good husband of hers has just slammed the door and she's up the backyard bawling her eyes out and her mother's taken most of the children with her when she turned up an hour ago.' Agnes shook her head. 'It's a rum do, all those folk in that house and they still can't afford to keep their children fed and shod. He just drinks it all and she's useless. Can't cook, doesn't clean, just keeps on having babies - and they can't all be her husband's, they all look to have a different father.' Agnes sighed. 'When I first came to this square it was so respectable, run-down but we all had our values and kept our noses clean.'

'Well, it sounds as if I needn't have worried about you this morning,' Meg said. 'Betsy and her clan have been entertaining you, and there was I worrying that Sarah might not even have managed to get you out of bed.' She went and put the kettle on to make herself a drink and smiled at her mother who always had liked a good gossip.

'Aye, she managed, but she soon got fed up with

26

showing her caring side. It didn't last long, especially when young Harry next door knocked on the door and led her astray with the idea of going around the market together. Neither of them is back yet; I hope that they are not up to no good, he's a young bugger-who is that'en.'

'I hope she comes back with some broken crates or something for the fire, else she'll answer to me. She might be only nearly eleven but she could help a bit more than she does,' Meg sighed.

'Now, Meg, don't be so hard on her. She's only young, she knows no different. Anyway, how did you go on with old Ted this morning? I bet he's a bugger to work for but at least you'll be warm and doing something you enjoy doing. Better than taking in washing especially on dreary days like today.' Agnes looked at her daughter as she stared out of the window that looked out over the terraces' backyards.

'He's all right, he's a mucky old devil. I'd like to give everywhere a good clean and sort out but I'll hold my tongue. After all, I'm just his lackey.'

Meg looked out at her next-door neighbour, Betsy, who was sobbing her eyes out and rocking herself with grief at what had happened in her house. 'Mam, I'll tell you more in a minute. Just let me go and see if I can do owt for Betsy, she looks besides herself with grief.'

'Aye, go and see what they've been up to — it's a wonder the peelers didn't turn up with the noise that they were making.' Agnes's curiosity meant her daughter's account of her morning could wait.

★ ★ ★

'Betsy, are you all right? I couldn't help but see that you are upset when I saw you from out of our kitchen window.' Meg stood and looked at her neighbour from over the red-bricked wall that separated the houses. She stood head in hands still sobbing, her blonde hair unkempt and her skeletal body shaking.

'Aye, I'm all right. I doubt my Jim will be coming back to me though. I don't know how I'm going to feed my children now, but it is all of my own doing.' Betsy sobbed and then raised her head to reveal her battered face. Her eye was bruised and her nose looked to Meg as if it was broken, with dried blood running from it.

'Has Jim done that to you? No matter what you've done, he shouldn't treat you like that!' Meg looked at the woman who was only five years older than herself but looked nearly as old as her mother. 'Can I do anything for you — have you some comfrey to help with the swelling?' Meg looked at Betsy with pity.

'Jim came back home and he caught me in bed with Henry, one of our lodgers. I thought he was going to kill him and kill me come to that. Henry's flown but he left me to face the music. I suppose I deserve every mark on my face but Jim never shows me any love . . . he'd rather seek solace in his beer. What's a woman supposed to do when she's no money from off her husband and no love shown to her either? I was just in need of both and Henry was there to give me 'em.' Betsy sobbed.

'Aye, Betsy, you'd have been better to keep your legs together, that's what my mother always tells me to do,' Meg said, reckoning her mam had got the right idea about Betsy. 'But I suppose it's a bit late to give you that advice and I know that urges can sometimes get the better of good judgement.' Meg hung her head thinking of the band of ragged urchins that were her next-door neighbours.

'Aye, my mother's lectured to me that and all, but what's done is done. Jim will come back to me once he's calmed down — he's nowhere else to go and nobody in their right minds will want him.' Betsy sniffed and wiped her nose. 'I'd better go. I can hear the baby crying. My mother's taken four of them and the older ones have gone roaming the streets until things have calmed down. I hope our Harry doesn't get himself into trouble, he's taken to pick-pocketing. I found a fancy hanky in his pocket the other day, that he denied all knowledge of, the thieving little devil, but he's only trying to help out bless his soul.'

Betsy tried to smile as she made her way down the yard and back into her home with Meg watching her and hoping that she would never be in such dire straits.

'If I can help, you've just to ask,' Meg shouted after her as she went back to her mother, worrying as she did so that Harry might be leading her younger sister astray with his pick-pocketing exploits.

'So, what's been going on then?' Agnes asked as soon as Meg entered the house.

'Jim's caught her in bed with a lodger, he's given her a good hiding, and she's in a right mess,' Meg said and sighed.

'It's six of one and half-a-dozen of the other,' Agnes retorted. 'So, how was working for Ted today? You were about to tell me.'

'It was all right. He likes his own way and he doesn't believe in himself doing hard work. I had to wait half an hour for him to appear this morning before he opened up. Then when we closed shop because he said we had been open long enough, he thought so much of my help he forgot my name and called me Myra!' Meg walked over to the near-empty cupboard and took out some oatcakes and cheese from within it and placed them on the table for her and her mother's dinner. She looked across at her mother as she caught her breath sharply as if in pain.

'Are you all right? Was that a bad spasm?' Meg looked with concern at her mother.

'No, it was Ted calling you Myra. He must have been thinking about his young lass that he lost. He's never been the same since she and her mother died. It was a tragedy and I know their deaths marked him badly. It was his wife Eleanor that ran the bakery like clockwork. There were fancy cakes and pastries in the window every morning and the bread would be fresh and scrumptious,' Agnes said with a sad look in her eye. 'It'll be over twenty years since they both drowned at sea. I know it was a good while before you were born.'

'I never knew that he'd been married and had a daughter. The poor man. Where were they going and how did they drown at sea?' Meg asked as she and her mother ate their meagre dinner.

'Eleanor was from Ireland and she and Myra were going to see her parents,' Agnes explained. 'They'd sailed from Liverpool but it was a really stormy winter's day when they had boarded. In fact, I think Ted had told them not to sail but she wanted to visit her mother after hearing that she'd been ill. Anyway, the ship was lost mid-channel as it crossed the Irish Sea. Nearly fifty folks were lost; some bodies were never found, Myra and Eleanor two of them. It was a tragedy, a tragedy that Ted has never got over. It left him heartbroken and bitter. I suppose he blamed himself for letting them go.' Agnes looked into the fire as she remembered Ted and his family in happier times.

'The poor man, I didn't realize, no wonder he's like he is,' Meg said, feeling pity for her miserable employer.

'Ted's a good baker if he puts his heart into it and he had customers from all over Leeds coming for his baking,' Agnes recalled. 'He can make much more than just bread — not that the bread he makes is anything like what he used to make. You wouldn't get me buying it, if I wasn't desperate some days. Besides you make ours and you can't get much better.' Agnes sighed.

'No, we will not be buying it in the future, not now I know what he does to it,' Meg said quietly. 'He's told me not to say anything, but Mam, he adds sawdust into his mix, I couldn't believe it when I watched him adding it to the flour.' 'He'll not be the first, and he'll not be the last,' Agnes replied. 'He'll be watching the money, and he always was a tight old devil. It's not helping him in the long run — there are no queues like there used to be when his baking was good. Eleanor must be turning in her grave.'

'I didn't know bakers did that, I couldn't believe my eyes.' Meg tidied what oatcakes were left away from the table.

'Oh, aye, it's common practice. It's time the government put something into place to check folk like Ted, it is a recipe for disaster, these bakers that add all sorts into their mixes. It's always best to make your own, that's what my mother used to tell me.'

Agnes closed her eyes. She was ready for a nap now

she had Meg back home and knew that she'd be there if needed. 'If I owned that bakery, I wouldn't do anything like that,' Meg told her. 'Folk are not daft: if it doesn't taste good you don't go back. Most of his bread is sold early in the morning to the mill workers and some of it is days old and not fit to eat. I promised one lass that I'd put her a fresh loaf to one side for her when she came into the shop this morning. It's only right that folk gets good food for their hard-earned brass.'

'Well, when his wife was alive, the bakery used to be open until the evening whistle at the mills blew, and then he'd have another wave of buyers. Eleanor knew how to make money and what folk wanted, but that is all gone now. Ted's heart is not in it.' Agnes yawned. 'Now, leave me be for a while lass, and let these old bones have forty winks in this chair. I'm not feeling too bad today but I soon get tired.'

Meg placed a blanket around her and smiled, then went up to their shared bedroom and sat on the edge of her bed. She thought about Ted Lund and the bakehouse. He must be still mourning for his lost wife and daughter; with them gone he had no purpose to live, it would seem. The poor man, she thought, as she got up and walked towards her mother's bed. Seeing blood on the pillow from her coughing, she quickly changed the pillow sham. The sickness must have reached her lungs she realized as she plumped the pillow and pulled the covers straight. She too would soon be broken-hearted and without a mother.

With the beds made and all tidy she stood and looked out of her bedroom window thinking about her new job at the bakery. The place could make a good profit if it was looked after properly, just like it had done in the past. If it was hers she would sell good fresh bread and pastries, scones and buns — all the things that the good people of Leeds needed every day. It was in a good position and would be a welcoming shop if looked after properly, with love and care shown it. However, she knew her daydreaming would come to nothing. It was Ted's bakery and she was just his servant lass. Perhaps if she ever had her way, she could improve on his bread because despite what he had said to her, the bread she made was far superior to his.

Meg looked down into the square. Standing outside number 8 was Jim, who was hesitating as he looked up at his house. Meg smiled as she saw Betsy run out to him and fling her arms around his neck, and he responded by kissing her in full view of everyone in the square. Well, at least they were back to normal for the time being, although Meg knew it wouldn't last long. It would only last as long as Jim kept off the drink and Betsy kept herself to herself, neither of which would ever happen.

Life was what you made it, but Meg was sure of one thing: she would never marry a Jim of the world. She would plough her own furrow in life if she had the chance.

4

'What have you been doing out on the streets of Leeds until this time?' Meg asked Sarah sternly as her younger sister slammed the front door behind her and slumped down at the table. 'Just look at you, you look like a street urchin and where's the wood for the fire you were supposed to be collecting?' Meg stood over her with her hands on her hips and a scowl on her face.

'There wasn't any today. It had all gone by the time Harry and I got up to the market. Besides I'm fed up with always going out and scrounging firewood. Why should I always do it? You even make me go around the market before school; well I'm not doing that on my own if you are going to be at work all the time. It's not fair, our Meg, you just bully me.' Sarah folded her arms and swung her bruised and scratched legs back and forward underneath the chair while pulling a petulant lip at her sister.

'You'll do what it takes for this family to survive and wandering off with Harry Truelove is not part of it. I suppose you've both been up to no good; I hope he's not been pick-pocketing like his mother thinks he has.' Meg looked long and hard at her young sister and noticed a flush come into her cheeks. 'No good will come of it if he has. You don't get led by him, are you listening? Now, what are we going to do for warmth tonight? We've hardly any coal. I suppose I'll have to go out up the market now. They'll be packing the stalls up so perhaps I can find one or two crates

34

that they leave behind if they haven't all gone. You keep an eye on your mother and don't go out again. It's coming in dark and lasses your age shouldn't be out.'

Meg reached for her shawl and shook her head. At least she would have a bit of peace the following day with it being Sunday, but she would still have to find a way of keeping everyone warm and fed whether it was the Sabbath or not.

'You'll not be long, will you? I could do with some supper, I'm starving,' Sarah said and put her head down on the table and sighed.

'There's some bread in the cupboard, but don't eat it all. I'll make us some soup when I return, it will warm us all up — and hopefully, seeing I'm having to go to the market, I'll be able to scrounge a few vegetables that the traders don't want to take home with them. Now stop moaning and listen out for Ma, she's suffering today.'

Meg wrapped her shawl around her and walked out into the dimly lit streets of Leeds, making her way to Briggate where on either side of the wide street traders were selling their wares. She walked quickly, ignoring the prostitutes, who, with the darkening of the sky, were beginning to walk their patches in search of punters. Meg kept herself to herself as beggars heckled her for a penny or two. Little did they know she was as poor as them but unlike them, she had her pride — and she would never lower herself to sell her body like the women of the night, even though she knew that it was desperation that made them do so. In the gas-lit street of Briggate, she looked around her and made for the vegetable stall, where she knew she'd be able to find offcasts for her soup from the jovial stallholder who she had become friends with and worked for whenever she could.

'Now then Meg, it's late in the day to see you out and about. Have you come to make things right with Mike over there? I knew once you found out what your Sarah and that no good lad that she hangs about with had got up to you'd have something to say about it.' Roger Ingram looked at Meg and saw the puzzlement on her face and shook his head. 'By the looks, you perhaps don't know. Me and my big mouth!'

'What are you on about, Roger? What has she and Harry been up to that I need to apologize for?' Meg felt her stomach churn as she feared the worst.

'Nay, it's not for me to say, I've already said enough. Go and talk to Mike, he's calmed down now. I've told him Sarah would not be to blame, that it's just the company she was with. Anyway, they were hungry — you can't blame them. We'd have done the same but our fathers would have tanned our backsides, that's the difference.' Roger sighed.

'She's stolen from the stall! Oh, my Lord, I'll kill her when I get home,' Meg said and looked across at the fruitier who was packing his stall up onto his cart in readiness of going home. 'I'll go and make it right, but I haven't any money on me to pay for what she stole.'

'That'll not matter. As long as Mike knows she'll not be doing it again, he will be right with you. Now, I've some broken crates — do you need them? Sarah didn't take them this morning when I offered her them and I've half a sack of tatties I was going to throw out because some are nearly rotten. You can have them and if you are quick with your business with Mike, I'm going your way so I'll give you a lift back home

36

on the cart,' Roger said as he saw the worry on Meg's face as she looked across at Mike on the fruit stall.

'I can't thank you enough, Roger. I'll take you up on all your offers. Once we get back onto our feet I will repay you for your kindness. But now, as you say, I've got to make things right with Mike. I feel so embarrassed. Just wait until I get home. I might not wallop our Sarah but she'll know my wrath.' Meg sighed and then walked across the cobbles to where Mike Flannigan was packing his stall away on his cart.

'So, you've come to make things right eh, Meg?' Mike said in a soft Irish drawl that was hardly recognisable after his many years of living in Leeds. 'If it had been anyone else she'd stolen off, the peelers would have been knocking on your door. She needs a good hiding and to learn to keep away from that Harry.'

'I'm sorry, Mike, she'd never said a word to me. Roger has just told me. What did she steal from you and how can I make it right? I've no money on me else I'd pay for what she's taken.'

Mike leaned against his cart and looked at Meg. 'Him and her took an apple each and then ran like buggery. In fact, Sarah fell over, and she'll have bruised her legs if not worse. It was the lad that was egging her on — she knew I recognized her and she knew she was doing wrong. She's too easily led. You have your hands full with that one, lass.'

'I'm sorry, she knows better than to steal. I'll give her what for and make her come and apologize,' Meg said, feeling heartily ashamed of her sister. 'She's pushing her luck at the moment. I think she's finding it hard seeing our mother being so ill but this doesn't help. To make things worse I'm having to go out to work so I can't watch her as well as I have been doing, but we need the money.'

Mike knew Meg was doing her best and was up against it when it came to making a good life for her family. 'It's all right, lass, it's only an apple. If she'd asked I'd have given her one — there was no need for her to steal if she was that hungry. Where have you got your job at? Not in a mill, I hope, those are soulless places to work in.'

'I'm helping Ted Lund in his bakery on York Street. I like baking, I should be all right there as long as he pays me and we don't fall out.' Meg smiled wanly and looked at the kind-hearted Irishman who stood at the market no matter what the weather.

'That tight old devil! I hope his bread improves because at the moment it's not fit to feed my horse let alone anybody else. I wish you luck there.'

Mike stood and looked at the young lass in front of him; he had a daughter the same age back home. Unlike Meg and her sister, she didn't go hungry and have to make do. He made a good living with his fruit stall on the market. 'Here take this bag of fruit, it's Sunday in the morning and by Monday it'll not be worth owt.' He reached over his stall and picked an apple or two and some pears that were past their best and smiled as he put them into Meg's hands. 'I expect an apology from that sister of yours and then it will be right. I'm sure she'll get a good tongue-lashing from you when you get home.'

Meg's eyes filled with tears. 'I can't thank you enough. Really it's me that owes you.' She smiled at Mike as she juggled the fruit in her hands.

'Aye, well if I can't show a bit of charity from time to time, I'd be worth nowt. There was plenty of folks

38

who helped me when I first came from Derry over forty years ago and there were them that would rather spit on me than talk to me. You don't forget the ones that help you and the others, well . . . they don't matter. Good luck with old Ted and you take care of your mother and tell your sister to behave her sen.'

Mike watched as Meg walked across to Roger who was standing waiting for his passenger. Both had talked about the family in Sykes Yard and agreed that Meg needed help if she was to bring her young headstrong sister up without incident. They would do all they could to help.

★ ★ ★

Roger drew up his horse and cart outside Meg's home and helped her down with the broken crates and her sack of potatoes, which now also contained Mike's fruit and a cabbage that Roger had decided he would give her.

'If you are working early hours in the bakery, you won't have time to come and salvage any disused wood from the market,' he pointed out. 'Here's not out of my way of going home — I'll drop off what I can every night. I'll ask the rest of the stallholders to put what they have on the back of my cart, it will make your life a bit easier.

'Now, I've been thinking, do you want me to have a word with Sarah? A fella's words might frighten her and make her think.' Roger held his impatient horse's reins and looked down at Meg as he waited to climb back onto his cart.

'You've already done enough,' Meg replied. 'I'll see to Sarah and rest assured she'll not be stealing from off any of you again. I know how she falls so easily under Harry's spell. He does have the charm of an angel, and I even feel sorry for him some days. However, I'll not be having her following him into the gaol, because that is where he will end up at the speed he is going. I can't thank you and Mike enough for all of this; I was worrying how I was going to keep my mother warm and fed tonight.'

'It's all right lass, it has cost us nothing and if it's of use then you are welcome to it. Now go and sort that sister of yours and tend to your mother. I'll spread the word around the market that old Ted Lund has a new baker and that she's a good one. He'll be thankful he has you working for him by the time I've finished. There will be queues for his bread all the way down the street.'

Roger winked, flicked his reins across his horse's back and set off down the cobbled street. Meg stood and watched him until he disappeared around the corner. She breathed in and listened to the raised voices coming from next door. Hers would be joining them shortly, she thought, as she opened the front door with her booty under her arms. She wondered what she was going to say to her younger sister. How she wished her father was still alive — he'd have soon put her in her place. If her mother was well enough to lecture her she would be grateful but as it was, it was up to her to place her sister back in line.

'I didn't steal anything — thick Mike is lying. He's lying, I tell you,' Sarah squealed as Meg tackled her. 'He's mistaken me for someone else — I never went near the market today.'

'Then how come Roger from the vegetable stall saw what you did as well? You are lucky that you didn't

40

get caught by the peelers; you'd be being shipped off to Australia by now if they had reported you both. You stop mixing with Harry next door — he can be a grand lad but he's not to be trusted,' Meg yelled at her sister.

'You don't believe me, you never believe me, and I hate you!' Sarah stood with her face wrinkled and ugly and with her long unkempt ginger hair hanging down her back.

Meg looked angrily at her young sister. 'You can say what you like. I know it was you. Mike said you fell and hurt your leg when you were running away from him — are you all right? Show me your legs.'

'No, I will not. My legs are grand, he's lying. I tell you it was not me,' Sarah said but was near to crying.

'Well, you needn't go near the market again for any wood; Roger is going to drop any unwanted crates and boxes off from the market every night. It'll keep you out of temptation's way. They've also given us enough vegetables for me to make some good broth for supper — we have got a lot to be thankful for because of them. Seeing tomorrow is Sunday, you can put pen to paper and sit down and thank Roger for his kindness and write a letter of apology to Mike. He's expecting an apology from you in person but a letter will do.'

Meg scowled at her young sister. She'd have walloped her hard if she had dared but she knew Sarah would have fought back and the scuffle would waken and upset her mother.

'But I didn't do it! Why don't you believe me?' Sarah yelled and slumped down at the table.

'Just hold your noise, Sarah. All three of us are not stupid, we know it was you. You need to wash that knee — by the looks of it you have gravel in the cut;

it will take bad ways if you are not careful,' Meg said calmly after spotting the cut on Sarah's knee with dried blood on it. 'Now, help me peel these potatoes and quieten down, there's no need to waken our mother with your squeals. But you will write those letters tomorrow if you know what's good for you and you'll stop running wild with Harry, no good will come of it. I'm sorry but I have to be bossy with you at the moment but nobody else is here for you or me, so behave and try not to give me more worries than I already have.'

Sarah said nothing as Meg placed a bowl of warm water poured from the kettle and grabbed a small piece of cloth for her then signalled Sarah to show her the hurt knee properly. Meg bent down and wiped away the blood gently and looked at the gravel that she washed out of the wound. 'You did go a pearler. Now think on no more thieving, write that letter tomorrow and that will be the last of it unless I hear differently.' She watched the tears start to trickle down her young sister's face. 'It's only because I love you that I lecture you. We need one another, Sarah, and Mam is not going to be with us forever.'

Meg put her arms around her young sister and kissed her on her head but Sarah said nothing. She was still fuming that her sister could boss her around. Meg would never take the place of her mam, no matter how she tried, and she had no right to make her do as she said.

★ ★ ★

It was Sunday evening; the atmosphere in the Fairfax home had been fraught all day. Sarah had only

42

spoken to Meg when she had to and although she had written an apologetic letter to Mike on the fruit stall, it had been under duress. Meg sat next to the fire, her mother across from her mending Sarah's dress for the following day. Sarah was already in bed. She'd taken a book up with her to read, deciding that she'd had enough of her big sister watching her every move.

'You've been quiet today, Meg, are you all right?' Agnes asked and looked at her eldest daughter with concern. 'I heard you chastising Sarah last night. I think the whole street heard.'

'I'm sorry, Mam, I tried to be as quiet as I could, and I didn't want you to worry about what she's been up to.' Meg put her mending on her knee and looked at her mother. 'She doesn't listen to me and I'm not respected enough by her. You must have heard that she'd stolen some fruit from the market with Harry; she can't do that, else she's going to get herself in bother.'

'If her father had been alive, he would have taken his belt to her. Although if he was and if I were well she needn't have stolen fruit to fill her belly. She was hungry, Meg. I know what she did was wrong but it is a terrible thing, hunger, and she had to prove herself to Harry, I suppose. You were just the same at that age, you had to do what your friends did. Can you remember me playing hell with you for trying to jump down that high set of stairs at the end of Mill Lane? You could have broken your neck and that was because you were playing with that Marjorie Goodall and others. All I'm saying is put yourself in her place: she's frightened, hungry, and doesn't quite know what's going to become of her, despite you being there for her after my death.' Agnes sighed and closed her eyes.

'Neither do I, Mam, I don't know if I can look after her and work, especially as she is so stubborn. I wish . . . I wish you were well, Mam, I don't want to lose you,' Meg sobbed.

'I wish I wasn't going away, lass, but the pearly gates get a little closer each day and I can't do anything about it. Be strong, follow your heart, and have faith. Sarah, I know, will be looked after by you, you'll look after one another eventually. Now let's stop this maudlin talk. You are back with old Ted tomorrow, he'll keep you on your toes. Don't you worry about Sarah and me. We'll both be fine, she'll get herself to school and if I don't feel like coming down here and getting dressed, I'll stay in my bed until you return. There's nothing to worry about except keeping on the good side of Ted Lund. His money when he pays you will be more than appreciated and if you have the fellas from off the market delivering us some wood every evening, you've no longer that worry. They'll do anybody a good turn, will some of those traders. Some folk look down their noses at them but they are a good lot. Perhaps Sarah did you a favour pinching that apple, she found us an angel.'

'I don't know about that, but it will be a good help. I'm sorry, Mam, I'll try and be more understanding with Sarah, it's just we are like chalk and cheese. Sometimes I look at her and wonder how she can be my sister.' Meg held out her hand for her mother's touch.

'Well she is and she needs you and you need her, so don't let the theft of an apple when she was hungry come between you. There will be many an apple pinched from off that market — it's like a red rag to a bull when you are hungry. It's just unlucky your sister

44

and Harry got caught. She will not be doing it again; Harry, well, he'll do what he wants because nobody does care about him and his siblings, poor little buggers. You two are loved and always will be whether I'm on this earth or in Heaven above and never forget that.'

5

'Meg, I'm sorry. I haven't slept all night for worrying, and I shouldn't have stolen,' Sarah whispered as her older sister left her side in the darkness of the early morning and pulled the bedcovers back over her.

'It's all right, just don't do it again. I know you were hungry. I am all the time. That's why I have to work for Ted Lund, but hopefully I'll earn enough to keep us fed if nothing else.' Meg pulled her stockings on and her dress over her head then turned to kiss her younger sister as she snuggled back under the covers.

'I'll go to the market this morning before school and give Mike his letter and apologize,' Sarah said sleepily, her mind easy now that she had made peace with her big sister.

'You do that and make sure Mam has everything she needs before leaving, but go back to sleep now. It's still early and it's raining.' Meg looked down at her sister and sighed. At least she had admitted that she was in the wrong after a good night's sleep.

* * *

The rain was coming down in torrents as she walked along the empty street to where Ted Lund lived. Lights were starting to appear in some of the terraced house windows but it would be another good few hours before the streets came alive. She felt like a drenched rat as she stood on the doorstep of Ted's house where no light was showing as she knocked on the door and shouted up at the bedroom window.

The bedroom window rattled open. 'Hold your noise, I'll be down with you in a minute. You're awakening the dead with your bellowing!' Ted yelled down then slammed the window back down, leaving Meg shivering on the step for at least ten minutes before he appeared out of the battered front door of his terraced home.

'You've made me come out with nowt in my belly, in your rush for me to open up. You can put the kettle on and make a brew as soon as we get to the bakery. I'm worth nowt until I've had a drink of tea and something in my belly,' Ted growled as he pushed past her and walked at speed along the street to the bakery.

'I'm sorry but you told me to knock of you; I was only doing as I was told,' Meg retorted.

'Aye, well, I'm not used to being roused in such a way. I'd forgotten that I'd asked you.' Ted jangled his keys in his pocket and fished them out to open the doors to the bakery. Once inside he lit a vesta from his case and lit the oil lamp in the shop before walking through to the bakery with Meg following him.

'Get the rest of the lights lit and fill the kettle, and I'll stoke up the fire and ovens,' Ted yawned. He looked dishevelled and half undressed as he dragged the dry kindling onto the fire and riddled out the old ashes left from the baking on Saturday out of the ovens.

The shop and bakery were cold and unwelcoming in the lamplight but in another hour it would be warm and full of the smell of baking, but an hour was a long time. Meg stood soaked through to her skin, hair dripping as she made her way out into the yard, with Ted not giving her a second glance as he

47

mumbled and groaned to himself.

Once filled, Meg hung the kettle on the hook above the fire that Ted had now got going and quickly warmed her hands for a brief second. Then she went into the shop to get a loaf of stale bread from out of the shop display, thinking that if she fed Ted, happen he'd not be as grumpy.

'What have you brought that through here for?' Ted looked at her with an annoyed look on his face.

'I thought you were hungry; I'd make you some toast before we start baking,' Meg said quickly.

'You can think again if you think I'll eat that. It's all right for them out there.' Ted nodded his head towards the shop. 'But you'll not get me eating that stuff. I've brought my own, there are two slices of bread with jam on it in my pocket, that'll do me. I take it you have already had something. Now, get a move on and get that mixing dish, flour, and the rest and this time don't forget the sawdust in your mix. I'll be watching you.'

Meg dried out as she followed Ted's instructions, mixing the ingredients then kneading the dough. She stood back and looked at her morning's work and felt pride in her job. Ted had not even given her a second glance this morning, so she presumed it was acceptable to him as she patted her hands free of flour.

'I suppose that looks all right. Now here, take this brush and give the shop a sweep and wipe the counter; you left it in a terrible state on Saturday. You tidy up after yourself today, do you hear?'

Ted shoved the brush in her hand then reached for the only comfortable chair in the bakery and sat down in front of the fire and closed his eyes. If it hadn't have been for Meg knocking on his door he would have still been in his bed, but he'd still have managed to get his bread baked in time for the morning rush. After all, it was only straightforward bread he baked nowadays. Gone were the days when he made spiced fruit teacakes, crumpets and scones, which lapped up lashings of butter when still warm. Folk never asked for them, so why should he bother himself making them.

Meg bit her tongue as she took the brush from his hand and watched him sit in his chair and warm his hands once again. He'd told her as clear as day not to bother sweeping up as she had left on Saturday. He was nothing but a cantankerous old man and he didn't deserve to be given the time of day. However, she would put up with his ways because she needed the money — not that any payment had been mentioned since she had arrived. She just hoped that come the end of the week, he would pay her what she was owed.

Meg put her back into sweeping the floor, reaching into every corner that had not been swept clear for months if not years. Crumbs and litter were abundant, and in one corner she found a long-since deceased mouse that had mummified because it had been there so long. There were obvious signs of more recent visitors, with mouse droppings on the floor, and she felt filthy and itchy as she swept the remains and the rubbish up onto a shovel before taking it into the bakehouse to show Ted Lund, who had now divided the dough and was placing the loaves into the warm ovens.

'You've got mice!' Meg said and showed Ted the remains of the mouse and all the rubbish that she had swept up.

'There will always be mice where there are bread

and flour, that's nowt new. I put down poison, but the little buggers still come back. What do you expect when folk live as they do? These back-to-back houses are full of vermin, and they are ideal breeding grounds. A dead mouse is nowt compared to some things in Leeds. The canal is the worst — they find dead horses in it regularly. Folk take them when they are dead and drag them in rather than take them to the knacker's yard. I often see them being dragged out,' Ted said as he shoved the next batch to be baked into the oven.

'But we deal with food, we should keep all clean!' Meg said and looked around her. 'We have got to stop the mice from coming in. I need to set some traps and to mop the floor; I think the shop will smell sweeter for a good clean and the mice gone.'

'You do, do you? I don't think so, as we've no mop and no traps. Poison see's to the vermin. Now throw that rubbish on the fire and go and serve on behind the counter and shift Saturday's bread before anything else. Do as I say — it's what I'll be paying you for if you are still with me by the end of the week.' Ted placed the last batch of bread on the long flat shovel and placed it into the oven to bake. 'Go on, that was the shop doorbell, folk is waiting for you,' he added, said sharply as the shop bell rang, stopping Meg from arguing with him as she watched the mouse being cremated on the open fire before turning around and making her way to the shop where a customer was waiting.

'I don't usually get my bread from here, but I've no option this morning. The bakery down Inkerman Street is where I usually go. His bread is a lot fresher and the place is cleaner,' the little woman who stood in front of Meg commented. 'I've had to come here.

My Jamie is ill this morning and I don't want to leave him for too long, I fear that it's scarlet fever, he's covered head to toe in a rash. Mr Brown would never forgive me if I brought him scarlet fever, but if Ted Lund gets it, it would be no loss to anyone. I didn't know he had you serving on!' the woman continued and then pointed to one of Saturday's leftover loaves, not giving Meg time to reply. 'I'll have one of those, I suppose it will be as dry as my bum, but my old man will have to make do with it if he wants something in his bate this morning.'

'Sorry, the fresh bread is on its way but not quite ready yet.' Meg reached for the best-looking loaf and wrapped it up for her customer.

'It would happen help if Ted got himself up in a morning; his wife must be turning in her grave, poor woman. She used to run this shop like clockwork. All would be clean and there would be doilies out on the shelves with all sorts of baking on them. She knew how to do business! She'd have sold this old stale stuff off cheap at the end of the day or given it to them that couldn't afford to buy it. She was a grand woman. Just what she saw in that miserable old bugger I don't know. A penny is it, or will you take a ha'penny seeing it's at least a day old?' The woman looked at Meg and waited for a reply.

'A penny please; I daren't charge you a ha'penny else Mr Lund will have something to say.' Meg looked embarrassed as she took the coin and put it in the till quickly, thinking of Jamie who had scarlet fever as she did so.

'Aye, well it was worth a try. I'm Jenny Pratt, I live further down the street. You must try and get the old bugger to smarten himself up and put a bit of pride back into this place. Everyone used to shop here. It can be a good business given a bit of love and care. Now you take care and I hope that I haven't passed on my Jamie's disease to you,' Jenny said, then hearing Ted coming into the shop, quickly made for the door before she had to talk to him.

'Was that Jenny Pratt? What's wrong with her, who's ill in her family today? She always has someone nearly on death's bed, a right hypochondriac she is,' Ted said with a sarcastic tone to his voice.

'She says her Jamie has scarlet fever; I hope not, else she will be spreading it to everyone,' Meg replied and looked at the loaves of bread that were now freshly baked and smelled wonderful, despite their added ingredient, as Ted placed them on the glass shelves of the counter.

'He'll not, so don't you worry about it. It's all in her head. She worries about everything. Everything that she shouldn't worry about. She should be worrying about where her husband gets to of an evening as he wanders the canal side mixing with the women down there. She needs to look at what diseases he'll be bringing home with him, instead of worrying about the ones that she hasn't got.' Ted noticed a blush come to Meg's cheeks as she finished placing the bread on the shelves. 'Remember the old bread goes first, no matter how they complain.' Then he turned and left Meg to serve the customers that would soon be with them as the light of day appeared over the houses and chimney tops and the sound of the machinery in the nearby mills filled the air.

Meg stood and looked around her. It was quiet yet, so she decided to look in the many drawers that were built into the shelves behind her, wondering what delights were within them. It sounded by what Mrs Pratt had said, that the long-gone Mrs Lund had indeed taken pride in her work. Perhaps there were still things that could be re-used in the drawers if she could persuade Ted to use them.

The first few drawers were a disappointment: the remains of empty packets of currants and raisins which even the mice had abandoned because they had gone old and musty. The following shelf of drawers was filled with spices, nutmeg, ginger, cinnamon, caraway seeds and cloves, all preserved and safely kept in small bottles. If they still smelt and tasted fresh they could be re-used, she thought, as she closed the drawers and reached for the stepladders that leaned against the bakehouse doorway so that she could climb to the top tier of drawers and see what was within them.

She carefully picked her skirts up and made her way to the top of the steps and started to open the drawers. Jenny had been right; there within lay delicate paper doilies that looked like lace. How pretty they must have looked when placed along the glass shelves with baking displayed on them, she thought, as she carefully picked them up and then replaced them. The next drawer disclosed handwritten signs delicately illustrated with birds and roses around the names of loved confectionery. Cream Horns, Eclairs, Scones, Caraway Cake, Shortbread; the little signs had obviously gone next to the goods that had been baked that day.

The bakery must have been wonderful in its heyday and the smells must have been heavenly, Meg thought as she fingered them before putting them back into the drawer. It felt like she was intruding into the past life of Eleanor and Myra Lund and perhaps opening

53

something that was as well left in the past, a distant memory of the bakery when it was supported and loved by everyone.

The shop bell went and Meg turned around quickly, nearly falling from off the top of the steps as her thoughts were interrupted.

'I'd be careful up there. Old Ted can look straight up your skirts if he comes and stands behind you. It'll give him a heart attack, seeing bloomers and ankles like those.' Daisy Truelove laughed and stood back as Meg cautiously climbed down the steps.

'You might be able to see my ankles, but you can't see my bloomers, or at least I hope not!' Meg said as she hastily brushed her skirts down and placed the steps to one side as she looked across the counter at Daisy who stood with her hands on her hips grinning at her.

'Yes, I was only joking, but you could see your ankles. Shocking, you know, you will be getting a name for yourself if you're not careful! Not that I'm bothered by what folk think. You should hear some of the conversations and sights that go on at the mill, the women are worse than some of the men.' Daisy grinned.

'Have you come for your bread? The newly baked has just come in, so I can give you a fresh loaf.' Meg reached for a new loaf and started to wrap it in tissue paper for Daisy.

'I'm more than grateful; his stale bread is not worth eating. What I really want to know is, what are the chewy bits that you sometimes get in old Ted's bread? Nobody else tastes like that and it lays heavy in your stomach unlike other bakers. It never used to be like that.' Daisy passed her money over to Meg and took hold of her bread.

'I don't know, I can't help you. He doesn't let me know what he puts into his bread, but I presume it is the usual flour, yeast and water — that's all it can be,' Meg said, feeling uneasy about lying to Daisy.

'Oh well, it must be the flour that he uses. I just wondered, that's all.' Daisy looked at Meg. 'You've decided to be a glutton for punishment and stay the course then. I don't know which is the worse: working in a mill or working for Ted — both of us will never get any recognition no matter how good a job we do,' Daisy smiled.

'Yes, I need the money, my mother's ill and I've got a younger sister who needs my help,' Meg sighed.

'No father then? I have, but I keep clear of him most of the time. He's usually too tired to bother with any of us, he's working down on the cut, loading the barges. That is when he's not having a drink. My ma says she should never have married him and wouldn't have done it if my brother Joe hadn't have been on the way. She always blames him, although he's a good'en is our Joe. She'll blame me and have something to say for not getting back with this on time if I don't get a move on.' Daisy grinned. 'Why don't I call for you on Saturday afternoon? I finish at the mill at one, same as you here. We could have a stroll around the shops together, have a look down the new arcade in the centre, and reckon that we are somebody. Mind it will only be a look, I've no brass and I take it you haven't,' Daisy chuckled.

'I'd love to, but I can't. My mam . . . my mam is not good. I don't think she's long for this world.' Meg felt a lump coming in her throat and fought back the tears as she looked at Daisy holding the door ajar ready to

55

go on her way.

'Bloody hell, no wonder you need this job. That's hard on you. Look, I'll have to go, but I'll be in again before Saturday. Perhaps a walk up into Leeds isn't right for you but you could come and see me at home or I'll come to you. It would be nice to get to know one another.' Daisy's smile faded as the mill whistle started to blow. She'd yet to return home with the bread, she was cutting things fine. 'Lord, I'll have to go, I can't get my pay docked again for being late. I'll see you shortly, Meg.' She banged the bakery door to and ran along the streets with her bread in her hands.

Meg watched as she went on her way. She had a feeling that she and Daisy were going to be good friends if given a chance and time to get to know one another.

* * *

The rest of the day went quite quickly and Meg enjoyed the customers coming and going. She already recognized one or two of them who had called in on Saturday. Some were surprised that she was still working there, knowing all too well Ted's way, and others passed the time of day with her if they had the time to do so. She was starting to learn all their needs and quirks, she thought, as she walked back home, weary but satisfied. However, she also knew that a lot more could be done with the shop to make it better. Tomorrow, if her mother would let her, she would take the mop and bucket with her, despite the moans and looks from Ted. At least the shop floor would be clean.

The thought of mice running around the place and

the customers paying for doctored bread lay heavy on her mind. How could Ted treat his customers and neighbours with such indifference? Meg sighed as she opened the kitchen door of her home and shouted 'I'm home!' without even looking up from the step. The house was quiet, the fire had not been lit and it looked as if nobody had touched any of the bread and jam that she had set out for her mother and Sarah. Meg held her breath fearing the worst; she knew her mother would pass away shortly, but not yet Lord, not just yet! Then from above, a voice called.

'I'm still in my bed, Meg, I didn't bother getting up, I was tired and Sarah saw herself to school early on. She said she was going to the market to apologize. Your lecture must not have fallen on deaf ears after all. She's not a bad lass really.'

'All right, Mam, I'll come up in a second. I'll just light the fire and then we can have a brew. Our Sarah could have made sure it was lit before she went.'

Meg looked at the empty fireplace. There was just enough broken wood from the market boxes and coal to last them until evening, and she hoped that Roger Ingram would be true to his word and deliver some broken crates from the market as promised. Once she had seen to her mother, she would go and have a quick walk along the railway bank and hope that no railway worker would catch her while she scoured the banks for any coal that had been lost when shovelled from the tender to the engine. It was a dangerous way of keeping warm, but the coal was free if you weren't caught and it only took her up to ten minutes to get a good bucketful some days if she was lucky.

'Aye, Meg, her head was filled with other things this morning. Don't sound so cross,' Agnes shouted down.

'I'll try not to, Mam, I'm just tired and could do with relying on Sarah for a few simple things, like lighting the fire and backing it up before she goes to school. Never mind as she has saved fuel but I'll see to that shortly.'

Meg looked around her. The small room was cold and miserable, it was still raining outside and now she would have to go back out into the damp miserable day once her mother was fed and watered. Life was not fair. Why had she not been born into a better life, a life with money and graces? She didn't need a lot, just enough for a comfortable life for her and her family. With that she would be satisfied, she thought, as she watched the packing crate splinters start to spit and take hold of the flames that she had lit. At least they would be warm this afternoon and there was enough tea for a drink and some bacon for supper.

Things could be worse. She should be grateful for what she already had instead of moaning, she thought, or do something more about the situation the family was in, but just what, she didn't quite know.

6

'You tell me not to steal and then you are going to steal coal from off the railway banking. You know you nearly got caught last time,' Sarah whispered, not wanting her mother to hear her and Meg's conversation.

'This is different,' Meg replied. 'We have to keep warm and anyway, the coal I get is just going to waste. It's left to go back to the earth, nobody else can be bothered to pick it up, and it keeps us all warm — surely that's not a sin?'

Meg wrapped her shawl around herself and listened at the bottom of the stairs for any sounds of her mother before she grabbed the storm lantern that had belonged to her father and lit it. 'I'll not be long — tell Ma that I'm next door if she asks, there's no need for her to worry about me. I wouldn't be doing this if Roger Ingram had kept his word and had brought us some broken crates, but it's too late now, he'll have been home an hour or two now.'

'I don't want you to go; if the railway police catch you, it will be jail for you. Then what would we do?' Sarah wailed as she watched her sister pick up two buckets for her night's illegal picking in her spare hand.

'They'll not catch me, stop fretting. Now stop blubbing and look after Ma. I'll be back before you know it.'

Meg walked quickly through the streets to where the busy railway track divided the rows of terraced

59

houses. The smell of oil, coal and steam hung in the air and Meg watched as an engine, pulling carriages glowing with gas lights, hissed and trundled above her head as she squeezed through an opening in the fence and headed towards the steep embankment which the train ran upon. She must not be caught by one of the many railway workers who regularly walked the line, especially the railway peelers who would not think twice at locking her up for trespassing and theft from the line, even though the coal was worthless to them.

She swore under her breath as the metal buckets clanked against the wet grassy bank as she climbed up the steep sides of the banking and balanced her storm lantern, which she had turned down low. The best coal was to be found along with the rocky ballast at both sides of the track, lost as the fireman shovelled the coal onto the hungry engines' fire, but it put her at most risk of being seen or being knocked by a train if she did not keep her wits about her.

The lights of Leeds Station could be seen in the distance as she started to search, pouncing on each lump of precious coal here and there but keeping her ears open for any approaching trains or lengthsmen checking the rails. The coal was wet and mucky but that did not matter: it would keep them warm for the next day or two, she thought, as she filled both her buckets up. Feeling relieved, she stood up, carefully carrying her precious loads, then made her way down the banking, balancing them and the lamp, and trying not to spill any of the black nuggets. She was just in time — as soon as she was out of sight, a train made its way along the line on its way to York.

The train's steam wrapped around her like a cloak, and the sparks from its engine lit the sky as she snuck back through the fence. The two heavy buckets pulled on her arms as she walked slowly back home, hoping no one would stop and question her about their contents.

She was relieved when reached the end of Sykes Yard. Her arms ached and she was chilled to the bone — it felt like she'd never been as cold as this. Then she stopped as she noticed a horse and cart outside her home. Instantly she recognized them as Roger Ingram's, the cart painted bright green and his name emblazoned upon it. He'd not let her down after all.

Her heart lifted as she reached her home and saw him and Sarah standing in the doorway. 'Meg, I'm so glad that you are back before Mr Ingram returns home,' Sarah said happily. 'He's brought the biggest load of wood, already split up and ready for the fire. He's piled it up in the backyard — we will not be going cold now.' Sarah beamed up in the candlelight at Roger Ingram.

'I can't thank you enough, Mr Ingram, you don't know how much this means to us,' Meg said, then put her two buckets of coal down next to her feet. She blushed as Roger looked at her and knew instantly that what Sarah had blurted out to him about her sister's whereabouts was true.

'Aye, well I never go back on a promise, and we wouldn't want either of you doing anything you shouldn't. Your mother needs you and besides, she always spent enough money with us market traders when times were better. Now, I'll be back next week with another load for you. All the traders are only too happy to give me their old wooden crates so they just won't be mine. Mixed with a lump or two of coal,

61

they'll keep you warm. Now, behave yourselves and don't do anything that I wouldn't do. I'll see you next week.' Roger felt for his cap on his head and then pulled himself up onto the buckboard before gently urging his horse and cart into motion.

'Thank you!' Meg shouted down the street after him and watched as he raised his hand in acknowledgement before turning his cart around the corner and into the dark night. 'We are lucky to have friends like that on the market, Sarah. I hope you offered him a drink of tea?' Meg said as she picked up the buckets of coal.

'I did, but he wouldn't stop. He just unloaded the wood and said he hoped that he'd see you once you came back from the railway line,' Sarah said and hung her head.

'You didn't tell him what I was doing, did you?' Meg asked as she placed her buckets of coal on the hearth.

'I did, I just didn't think. I was worried that you would get caught,' Sarah mumbled.

'Oh, never mind, he'll know we don't make a habit of it, I hope. He'll think we're a right pair of thieves, but I'm sure he knows we wouldn't do these things if we weren't so desperate. One day, Sarah, when we are rich — although I don't know how we'll become so — we will look back at these days and laugh about them,' Meg smiled at her young sister.

'I don't think those days will ever come,' Sarah said mournfully. 'Nobody on this row of houses has any money. I don't know anybody with any money and never will.' She sighed. 'I'd like to live in one of those big houses out at Headingley and eat and drink until I could eat no more, instead of my stomach always growling because it's empty.'

'You will one day, I promise. We have to take the rough with the smooth but one day our luck will change, it has to,' Meg said and hoped beyond hope that her words would come true but God only knew how.

★ ★ ★

'Mam, I'm going to take the mop, bucket, scrubbing brush and some soda flakes to work with me in the morning, if that's all right with you. There's nothing but a brush at Ted Lund's and the floor hasn't been properly cleaned for years.' Meg sat on her mother's bed edge and watched her finish her supper, taking small bites of the bacon and bread that Meg had put in front of her. She was hardly eating enough to keep a sparrow alive, Meg thought as she watched her leave what she couldn't manage.

'The mucky old devil, he's gone to the dogs since he lost his wife. You can't run a shop if you don't keep it clean but I sent you to help with the baking, not be his cleaner.' Agnes leaned back into her pillow while pulling her covers up around her.

'He's not asked me to clean, but I just think it would look better and he'd happen to get more customers. Besides, I don't like to think that I'm standing on mice droppings all day. Lord knows what his store-room where he keeps the flour is like, I've not been let loose in there yet,' Meg replied.

'You'd better take the mouse traps from out of the privy as well, they will catch a few but not all. I'd never have bought anything off him if I'd known he'd got it in such a state, sawdust in bread and mice running all over the place. He should be ashamed of himself.'

Agnes closed her eyes and thought about the better days when the bakery had been so busy that there was always a queue outside the door.

'I've also made friends with a lass called Daisy Truelove, she lives a few doors down from the bakery. She calls in every morning for her bread before going to work at Hunslet Mill. She asked if I wanted a walk-up in Leeds with her on Saturday afternoon, but I said no. I wondered if I could ask her around here or happen visit her. She's a nice lass, you'd like her.' Meg felt guilty at asking for some time away from her mother with a new friend when she was so ill but she too could do with her spirits lifting and Daisy seemed to be able to do that with her cheerful banter and open ways.

'Daisy Truelove, now was her mother Rosie Holmes?' Agnes mused. 'I think she married a Truelove. Rosie used to work in the corner shop until she got wed and then she soon had a family around her feet, if she's who I think she is. If her lass is anything like her mother, she'll be a good'en. A heart of gold Rosie had, always did you a favour if she could, but she'll not have had it easy bringing up her tribe. I don't think her parents approved when she married who she did, they knew he liked a drink and was only a docker down at the cut.' Agnes opened her eyes and started to think about the Rosie she had known when younger.

'That sounds like her mam; her father still works at the canal and I think there's a few of them from what Daisy says.' Meg smiled as her mother looked at her.

'Happen if you went there, just for an hour. I wouldn't want her coming here and thinking that we had nowt. The house is not at its best, there's nothing that's worth anything in these walls that we haven't already pawned. You go there and see what they live like and then you can ask her back. I'm glad you've made a new friend. You should have a bit of time for yourself instead of looking after this old woman and your sister.' Agnes reached for Meg's hand and squeezed it gently. 'I'd be lost without you. You know that, don't you?'

'I know, Mam, but things will get better. Sarah has behaved herself today and we've got wood and coal for the fire and hopefully, Ted Lund will pay me something at the end of the week so that I can buy some groceries.' Meg leaned forward and kissed her mother on her brow. 'You have a sleep now, I'm going down to Sarah. I've promised to read her another chapter of Mark Twain's *Huckleberry Finn* — at least the books are free from the library and we can borrow them to read.'

'You always were a clever lass, you'll make something of yourself, I know you will. It's Sarah I worry about. She is so headstrong.'

'She will do all right, Mam, I'll always be there for her when she wants me. Now, try and sleep, I'll bring you a drink when we come up to bed but I'll not wake you if you are asleep.'

Meg rose from the side of her mother's bed and looked down at her. She didn't know how she'd cope without her mother by her side for advice and comfort but she knew that the day was looming and she would have to deal with it.

★ ★ ★

65

'I don't know why you feel the need to clean the shop floor and why you've made a show of yourself carrying a mop bucket and such-like through the streets of Leeds to my front door. Anybody would think my bakery was mucky,' Ted Lund grunted as he opened up the bakery door and looked at Meg as she clattered the bucket and its belongings down on the shop's floor that no one had seen the true nature of for many a year.

'I just think it would look better and there's always a lull between the bread being made and the first early customers coming into the shop,' Meg replied. 'You might as well make the most of me and get me to clean the floor; your customers will appreciate it.' Meg hoped that she had not said too much or offended Ted.

'You bloody women are always looking for work, I'd forgotten that. Once it is properly cleaned it will always have to stay that way, it's best left as it is. Black and nondescript, the way I like it.'

Ted looked down at the floor and admitted to himself that he'd forgotten what lay under the years of footprints that had never been cleaned away. Whatever it was would only mean more work and he didn't need it.

'Just let me clean a little bit, then you can see if it's worth our while continuing. If it's all like I found when I was sweeping under the counter, it should be green, white, and yellow tiles with some sort of pattern on it,' Meg said. Looking down at the grot that was on the floor, she'd have her work cut out but it would be worth it, she was sure. She took pride in her home, so there was no reason not to take pride in where she worked. She liked everything clean even if

66

she was poor.

'Bye, your mother didn't tell me when I took you on how feisty you were. Here you are a few days in working for me and you are already telling me how to run my business. I didn't ask for your advice, just your help with baking and serving on in the shop. Think about who's your boss, missy, I'll not take any of your lip. As it is you can clean the floor. I remember now, it's covered with yellow sheaves of corn. My wife had them specially made when we first opened the shop. I couldn't stand the sight of them after her death, so I let them gradually disappear under the footfall.' Ted looked down at his feet then at Meg as she placed her cleaning stuff behind the counter.

'I'm sorry your wife and daughter died, my mother told me what happened to them,' Meg said softly and looked at Ted Lund in the shadows of the newly lit gas lamp.

'Aye, well, I don't talk about it. Now, move your arse else we are going to be late with the morning's bread. I'll see to the ovens, you get on and make the dough. The floor can wait, if you must see what it originally looked like. I will say this: if you are intent on cleaning it, you keep on top of it every day, especially when it rains like it did yesterday,' Ted yelled as he made his way into the bakehouse.

'I will and can I ask: will you let me watch you light the fires under the ovens? Then if you are ever ill or indisposed I can light them and keep the shop open for you,' Meg asked as she watched Ted rake out the ashes and set the wood and coals in place.

'The next thing you will be asking me for is a key for the shop, I suppose?' Ted stood with his hands on his hips and looked at the slip of a lass who in the past few days was starting to be worth whatever he'd decide to pay her at the end of the week.

'Well, it might be an idea!' Meg said quietly.

'Not just yet, in another month or two happen, when I know I can trust you. A day off now and then would be good for me, once I know that you can make bread as I've told you. I think I deserve the odd late morning in bed after baking for the last twenty-five years. I suppose it is no good having a dog and barking yourself all the time.'

Ted grinned; the thought of a long lie-in made him feel light-headed as he watched the flames lap around the kindling in the bottom of his ovens. 'However, now you can get on with making the bread and don't forget the sawdust — like I say, it makes all the difference to if we both eat well or not at all. I'll have to penny-pinch even more now I've you to pay. Did we agree on a fee? You've coddled my brain so much that I've forgotten what I agreed with your mother,' Ted mumbled as he fed the fire and rubbed his hands.

'No, sir, you didn't say how much. You wanted to see if I could bake first,' Meg said and held her breath waiting to hear what she was to earn for her hours with the disagreeable Ted Lund.

'Two shillings is what I'll pay you. That seems fair enough for now. One shilling and nine pence for the weekdays and a threepence for Saturday and you can take a loaf home with you of an evening. That at least will keep you all fed.' Ted grinned as he closed the oven doors to heat them up.

'That's not a lot, Mr Lund, can I ask for two shillings and sixpence and no bread? I'm surely worth that and I make our own bread at home,' Meg said, feeling embarrassed to admit that she would not eat the bread she made for the customers of the shop.

Ted thought for a moment, and Meg wondered if she'd pushed her luck. Finally he said, 'You are a cheeky minx, two shillings and threepence or you can be on your way and I expect some work out of you for that money. No lounging over that shop counter gossiping when you could be helping me and doing some work.' Ted took his usual position in the chair next to the fire to watch Meg making the bread.

'Thank you, sir — can it be subject to a review depending on how the shop sales go? I've got a lot of recipes and ideas that would work if you would let me try them out,' Meg said with bated breath.

'We make bread, and that is all,' Ted said firmly. 'Now, enough of your blether and cheek, get on with your work.'

He watched as Meg reluctantly added the amount of sawdust to the mix. She was a good worker and quick to learn, but she had to know her place. He was in charge, and his bakery would not be changing its ways; leastways, not until he had decided he wanted to.

7

Daisy was the first customer into the shop on Friday morning and Meg welcomed her by giving her the freshly baked bread that she knew she had come in for.

'It makes my day a lot better seeing your face behind the counter instead of old grumpy guts and knowing that I'm not going to be palmed off with yesterday's bread,' Daisy said as she took her bread and smiled at Meg.

'He's not that bad — his bark is worse than his bite once you get to know him,' Meg said, quietly hoping that Ted would not hear their conversation.

Daisy looked down at the now clean and beautifully tiled floor then up at Meg. 'I've never seen the floor looking like this. I take it that you have been busy with a scrubbing brush. I can't see lazybones cleaning it.'

'Yes, I couldn't do with looking at it any longer. It has come up lovely, and the tiles must have cost a fortune when they were first laid. It's been loved has this bakery at some time in its life,' Meg replied.

'He doesn't love anything or anybody, old Ted. Except for money and his bed,' Daisy said. 'I don't know why he doesn't sell this place — his heart isn't in his baking anymore. Not if his bread is anything to go by.' Daisy looked pointedly at the loaves on the counter.

'I'd make it into so much more if I had the chance, but he won't let me. Bread is all we will make, and he's made that perfectly clear.'

'Listen to you, you've only been working for him for a few days and already you are trying to take him over. That will not go down with the old devil.' Daisy gave a quick grin and changed the subject. 'Have you made your mind up about tomorrow afternoon? Do you think you'd like to go for a stroll around the arcade or do you want to come to ours? My mam will make you welcome, our door is always open to anybody. That is if your mam is well enough to leave for a short time. I understand if she isn't. I can always come to yours.' Daisy put her loaf of bread under her arm and prepared to leave.

'I think she might be well enough for me to leave a short time if I can come to yours? I'll ask my younger sister Sarah to stay with her while I'm out — that is if she does as she is told,' Meg scowled.

'Oh, I've two of them as well, my mam soon squares them up though and if that doesn't work, my father takes his belt off to them . . . or rather threatens to. That's all he needs to do when he's in a bad mood,' Daisy smiled. 'I'll see you about two, that'll give you time to go home and check on your mam and then come to us. I'll have the kettle on.'

Daisy gave a cheeky wink as she exited, leaving Meg to think about how she wished her father was still alive to square her young sister up instead of her having the responsibility. Her life was a hard one but that afternoon she was going to make the best of it once she had gone home and checked on her mother. With her hard-earned money, she was going to buy what she could and for once tonight they would eat well — providing Ted paid her like he said he was going to when he opened the shop that morning and had grumbled about it ever since. She'd stock up on flour and lard; some butter; what she could buy cheap from the butcher, perhaps a ham hock and some sausages, and then she'd go up the market for what veg she could get from Mike and Roger Ingram just as they were packing their stalls up and discarding produce that was not good enough for the following day. The good thing about being a baker and cook was that you could make a good meal out of nothing.

She was thankful that she had been given that gift. A frying pan bannock with syrup on it took no making and it filled you up for the day. She'd made plenty of late, mixing just flour and water together, and an egg if she had one, and then frying it like a pancake, serving it warm with syrup on it. The mix had stopped Sarah from moaning about hunger pains most evenings but perhaps if she was frugal with her pay, Sunday breakfast could be one of milky porridge and supper could be sausages. That would put a smile on Sarah's face, she thought, as she turned to serve the next customer.

As the clock struck one, Ted came through to the shop. He'd finished for the day as Meg finished sweeping the newly cleaned floor and made sure all was in place for the following morning.

'I suppose you'll be wanting your brass? Two shillings and threepence seem a lot of money to me for a bit of a lass like you.' Ted looked down at the cleanly swept floor and remembered the time when the tiles had always been kept as spick-and-span along with the rest of the bakery. He put his hand in his pocket and pulled out the money that he owed and looked at it. 'Here, take it then. Mind you don't spend it all at once; I'll not be showing any understanding if you do.'

'Thank you, Mr Lund, this will help my family so

72

much. We can perhaps eat well tonight.' Meg took the money and put it in her pocket. He should be paying her at least a shilling more for all the work she had done in the week, but she'd trusted her luck when bartering for what she had been given.

'Aye, well, it'll put your mother's mind at rest a bit; at least I've kept you out of mischief this week. Now, have you done? I need to lock up, I need to put my feet up for an hour or two. Thank the Lord it's Saturday in the morning, Sunday can't come fast enough in my book. The good Lord knew we needed a day of rest.'

'There'll be no rest for me, I'll have to do some washing and tidy around the house. Mam does what she can, and Sarah runs errands and makes the beds in the morning but I do the rest,' Meg said as she pulled her shawl around her shoulders.

'Aye, well it won't harm you. That's what I tell Mrs Bannister when she's cleaning my meagre home. She moans and complains just like you, even though I pay her well too. The trouble is folk seem to expect a fortune for not doing a lot nowadays.'

Ted followed Meg out of the shop and pulled the door to behind him. 'Don't be late in the morning. I suppose you'll be away spending my hard-earned brass now? It'll be burning a hole in your pocket no doubt.'

'I am but only on things that we need, as I said earlier.' Meg looked at the lazy old miser and wondered if he had always been the way he was. Surely not if his wife had spent money on the tiles that she had uncovered in the shop.

'Be thrifty, don't be flippant with my money,' Ted muttered and then made his way home.

Flippant? Meg thought. There wasn't a chance of being flippant. Every penny was spoken for.

★ ★ ★

'Heavens, Meg, I didn't think your small wage would go this far. You have done us proud.' Agnes looked at the spread of goods that her daughter had brought back with her from her hasty but prudent shop up in the centre of Leeds.

'The vegetables didn't cost me anything — Roger and Mike gave me them for nothing. The apples are a bit bruised and the cabbage is past its best but I can put them to good use. It will be good to see the cupboard filled and I've still got some money to put in the pot for this month's rent.'

'You've done well, lass, I only wish I was more useful to you. I've managed to wash the dirty pots and keep the fire in. I hope you told those two fellas on the market how grateful we are for their help and support. They are helping to keep us all warm and fed out of the goodness of their hearts. They'll have enough on raising their own, I would have thought.'

'I don't think Roger Ingram is married, Mam. I know Mike is, he's got more children than Betsy has next door. His lads sometimes help him on the stall on a Saturday,' Meg said as she put the shopping away and thought of the soups and stews that she could make to keep all three of them full.

'I didn't know Roger Ingram was unmarried! You could perhaps do with getting to know him a bit better. He's happen a bit sweet on you; after all, he seems to be going out of his way to make sure you are fed and warm. He wouldn't be doing that if he didn't think

74

something of you.' Agnes had a knowing smile on her face as she saw Meg look shocked at her proposition.

'Mam, he's old enough to be my father. I couldn't ever think of him in . . . that way. He's just a nice man.' Meg blushed and sat down next to her mother.

'He'd give you security and not ask a lot from you with him being older. It would put my mind at ease knowing that you were to be looked after when I'm gone.' Agnes took her daughter's hand and squeezed it tightly.

'Mam, I couldn't love him, and besides, I've no intention of courting or marrying anyone. I have every intention of being independent of any man,' Meg said and meant every word.

She'd even had enough money for a little indulgence for her young sister. She placed a farthing's worth of sweets on the kitchen table for Sarah. If she could earn a little more, in a month or two she'd make sure that her family was fed and not out on the streets. She needed no man in her life, at least not for now.

★   ★   ★

The hours in the bakery on Saturday morning had soon flown with the thought of having tea at Daisy's house, but now Meg was making sure her mother and Sarah were all right to be left for an hour while she got to know Daisy and her family.

'Perhaps I shouldn't go. I hardly see you now, with work and shopping and Sarah could do with me at home.' Meg paused from washing the dinner pots and looked across at her mam.

'Get away with you, you have earned some time to yourself,' Agnes told Meg as her daughter wiped her hands and fussed around her.

'I'll not be long, but Daisy can talk for England. I might not even get a word in edgeways. Sarah, you will stay about in case Mam wants you, won't you?'

'Yes, I suppose I have to,' Sarah said sulkily. 'It isn't fair though. Harry is waiting for me outside. He said we could play a game of marbles — he's got some new fancy glass ones, his father got them for him.'

'He can wait until I get back,' Meg said firmly. 'Anyway, you know you are best keeping away from him. He's a bad influence on you.'

Meg placed her hat on her head and started to tidy her hair. If she was going to tea she meant to look her best, even if the rose in her straw hat looked as if it had seen better days. She straightened up the brooch that was giving her plain high-necked white blouse a little bit of elegance, even though it was only a cheap alloy.

Sarah stuck her tongue out and pulled a face at her big sister as she walked out onto the street. And then looked shamefaced at her mother as she was chastised.

'Now, stop that, miss. You have a lot to thank your sister for. Right, find something to do while I have forty winks and then we will see about you going out to play with Harry. Only if you're good, mind.'

Sarah said nothing, It was always Meg this and Meg that. Nobody ever cared for her. She'd do as she wanted and nobody was going to stop her.

★ ★ ★

Meg stood outside the terraced house that she knew was Daisy's home. It was just a standard terrace, like so many that were built in Leeds, but she noticed that the doorstep was clean and obviously scrubbed frequently with a donkey-stone like her own home and that the nets at the windows were pristine. Daisy's family obviously kept all spick and span, she thought.

She saw the nets at the downstairs window move as she waited for the door to be answered. Daisy's face beamed at her then disappeared as she opened the front door and welcomed Meg to her home.

'Come in, come in, don't stand out there, it's too parky to stand on ceremony,' Daisy said. 'Mam, Meg's here, I hope that kettle's boiling.'

'Aye, it's boiling, there's tea waiting in the pot and I've got a plate of buttered scones that need eating. Now, let's have a look at this Meg that I've heard so much of lately,' a woman's voice called from the back kitchen.

Daisy ushered Meg along the tiled hallway, which had a giant aspidistra growing in a large earthenware pot on top of a small table next to what was the doorway to the better front room. She led Meg into a homely kitchen with a good blaze in the hearth, a scrubbed pine table in the centre of the room, and a dresser covered with pots and plates all shining in the light of the fire. Daisy's mother, Rosie, turned out to be an older version of Daisy except plumper and with grey hair who smiled at Meg and told her to sit down on one of the chairs around the kitchen table.

'You can go in the front room if you want but we haven't lit the fire in there this morning. We all tend to live in here mainly. It saves coal and we like to keep the front room for best.' She poured Meg a drink in an earthenware mug.

'No really, don't worry, here is wonderful, so nice

and warm.' Meg thought of her home. Seeing Daisy's home first had been a good move. She'd have been ashamed of her clean but sparse house. They had nothing compared to the Trueloves.

'Daisy tells me your mother's ill and your father's dead. That must be hard on you and your sister. I don't know what I'd do if anything happened to my Jake or any of mine — I'd be lost without them. You must find it hard to make ends meet? Food and rent is that dear, although I can't complain — we have everything we need.' Rosie smiled and sat down next to Daisy, and Meg looked at both women thinking how similar they were in looks and mannerisms.

'It's not easy but we manage. Mam says she thinks she remembers you from working in the corner shop,' Meg replied. 'She was Agnes Thatcher before she was married to my father. Her family lived on Brunswick Row, and she used to work for the seamstress next to the shop.' Meg picked up her mug and watched as Rosie tried to recall her mother and Daisy pushed the plate of buttered scones her way.

'Grab one of these while you can,' Daisy told her. 'Our John will be coming back from work anytime now and he will soon eat his way through these!'

Rosie suddenly exclaimed that she knew exactly who Meg's mother was, and that they used to share a conversation with each other most days just like Meg and Daisy did.

'How're things with miserly Ted?' Daisy asked as her mother left the two girls to their conversation with a donkey stone, scrubbing brush and bucket in her hand to scrub the front doorstep.

Meg took a bite of her scone then said, 'He's all right. I get so frustrated though because he could do so much with his bakery, but he doesn't seem to want to do anything.' Meg knew she was moaning yet again about Ted, but Daisy was one of the few people she could talk to.

'Well as long as he pays you, I wouldn't worry. It's his loss. I do what I have to at the mill — nobody would thank me for doing any more. I doubt my boss hardly knows my name unless he thinks I'm not pulling my weight and then he's down on me like a ton of bricks.' Daisy scowled and then reached for a woman's magazine that lay on the dresser. 'What do you think about wearing that? We'd both get a lot done if we trussed up like a goose in that corset! I'd never be able to bend, let alone breathe.' Daisy sat back and let Meg look at the latest fashion in corsetry, each picture showing glamorous women in the tightest of corsets, with waists no larger than the top of Meg's leg and posing with swish hats on their heads as if it was normal to dress in corsets and a hat.

'I wouldn't be much good kneading bread in one of them and look at the price!' Meg exclaimed. 'I couldn't justify spending money on myself like that. I usually dress in hand-me-downs — the rag and bone man usually has something that I can afford if I catch him early enough in the morning or there is a stall on Briggate that I sometimes buy from.' She felt embarrassed once more as Daisy looked with sympathy at her then jumped as she heard a clatter from outside.

'Lord, quick, pass me the magazine quick, our John is back. I'm not letting him look at such, it wouldn't be right.' Daisy took the magazine out of Meg's hands and quickly sat on it and then turned to smile at her brother.

Meg turned to look at the young man who entered

the kitchen. He nodded at her and then threw his cap into the chair next to the fire before acknowledging his sister.

'So, we've got a visitor, have we? You never said, else I'd have been back earlier, our Daisy. Especially if I'd have known she was as bonny as she is.' John grinned and nodded to Daisy to pour him a cup of tea before he sat down in the chair that his cap had fallen into.

Meg blushed but couldn't help but glance at the dark-haired good-looking man with a twinkle in his eye. His clothes belied that he worked in an office and not manual labour as he crossed his legs and waited to be served upon.

'You are full of blarney, John Truelove,' his sister remonstrated. 'Stop embarrassing my guest. This is Miss Meg Fairfax: she works for Ted Lund in the bakery and I've asked her for tea. Now, if you've nothing decent to say, don't bother saying owt.' Daisy passed him his tea and offered him a scone.

'I was only saying the truth. It is a pleasure to meet you, Miss Fairfax. Don't listen to a word that my young sister with no manners tells you. I am not full of blarney, I only say what I see.' John winked, bit into his scone and then warmed his hands around his teacup. 'Old Banks wouldn't hardly light the fire today, so it was freezing in the office. How he thinks we can all concentrate on the plans I don't know.'

'You work in an office, Mr Truelove?' Meg asked, daring to look at the man she found to be quite dashing despite his fun with her.

'He works in the town hall, in the planning department. If you can call drawing lines on paper all day working!' Daisy grinned and joked with her brother.

'You can tease, it's hard work, we've new plans

coming in every day. This town is changing, growing and developing thanks to folk like me and my 'lines on paper'. You know how much you like looking in the windows of the new arcade? Well it was my department that drew that up, Miss Clever Clogs!' John said. He took another sip of his tea and helped himself to another scone. 'So you work for Ted Lund? He, of the chewy bread?' he asked Meg. 'Lord knows what he puts in it. I've heard that many complaints about him I wouldn't know where to begin. I hope your bread-making is better than his!' He smiled at Meg and she felt the blood rush to her cheeks.

'Meg has got all sorts of ideas if she gets her way. She's ten times a better baker than him.' Daisy took Meg's hand and smiled.

'Then I hope he lets you loose in his bakery,' John replied. 'It is needed on these back streets. He's missing good trade if he could only see it and be bothered to get up in a morning. Everybody knows how lazy he is, but perhaps he will mend his ways now that you are there to urge him on.'

He stood up. 'I'll go and change and leave you two to natter. I'm sure you don't want me listening in to your conversation. Besides, Daisy, your magazine is spoiling with your posterior upon it. By the way you need not hide it — I've already glanced through it, I found it most interesting!' He laughed as he left the room. Daisy threw his cap at him then stood with her hands on her hips and shook her head.

'My brother is impossible, I do apologize for him. Now let's have another drink of tea and talk about what we want now we have our privacy and no interfering brother.'

Meg walked home in a lighter mood. It had been a lovely afternoon talking about things that only girls of her age felt important. It was a break from the worries of home and work, and she realized how lucky she was that Daisy had become a friend. She could see them getting closer as time went on.

She also couldn't stop thinking about John, her brother. He was handsome and a charmer. Had he really meant it when he called her a bonny lass or was Daisy right when she said he was full of blarney? Whichever way it was, it had made her feel a bit brighter and she would like to see more of Daisy's brother if she ever got the opportunity.

She walked around the corner into Sykes Yard, where she was met with the sight of Harry and Sarah, sitting on the wall at the top of the yard, both with a grin on their faces, swinging their legs and laughing as they chewed at whatever was going around in their mouths.

Meg looked up at them both and frowned. 'Sarah, I thought I told you to wait for me coming back before you came out to play with Harry?'

'Mam fell asleep, and anyway she said she'd let me out to play after she woke up,' Sarah said and jumped down from the wall and quickly swallowed the toffee that she had been eating, hoping that Meg had not seen her chewing it.

She was out of luck. 'What's that you are both eating? I hope that you've not taken anything out of the cupboard. What's in there has to do us all week.' Meg looked at her sister with suspicion and then looked up at Harry, who jumped down beside Sarah.

'It's only the toffees you promised us, Meg. Sarah and me went up and bought them with the penny you gave her. You don't half get a lot for a penny, I could hardly believe my eyes!' Harry blurted out while Sarah turned around and kicked on the shins to stop him from saying any more.

'What penny? I never gave you a penny. It's more than any of us have ever had to spend on ourselves for months. I gave you a farthing-worth yesterday, have you shared them with Harry?' But then she turned around and saw Harry's siblings also sitting eating sweets as they sat on the steps of their home. 'You haven't, have you? You've not helped yourself from out of the rent jar on top of the fireplace?'

Meg grabbed her young sister by the arm and pulled her up the steps to their home as Sarah swung her arms and protested at being pushed and pulled without a care. 'You little thief, do you know how long it took me to earn that money! It was to help pay the rent, not to be spent on making you look good with that rabble next door.' Meg shook her sister and glared at her as she pushed her towards the fireplace and turned the jar up to count how many coins were in the jar.

Agnes had been asleep but was woken by the commotion and wondered what was going on. It was all too obvious to Meg that a penny was missing from the jar. It had been joyfully spent on toffee from the sweet shop and there was no getting it back now.

'Lord, I don't know what to do with you, I work all hours and then you thieve and think only of yourself!' Meg shouted.

'I hate you, I hate you!' Sarah shouted back, stamping her foot. 'I never have anything and you are always bossing me. Harry is a better brother to me than you are a sister! I'm glad I stole the penny and shared sweets with him!'

'Sarah!' her mother said in a commanding tone that Sarah knew better than to disobey. 'Go up to your bed. I might be ill and not able to look after you like I should, but what you've done today is wrong. Get out of mine and your sister's sight while I talk to Meg. There will be no supper for you tonight my lady, not when you've filled your belly with toffees. Now go before I say something to you I'll regret.'

Agnes coughed heavily then caught her breath and watched as Sarah did as she was told, not without kicking the table leg with temper before she made her way up the stairs.

Meg slumped down in the chair opposite her mother and put her head down and sobbed. 'A full day's work for nothing, Mam. Just for them to eat toffees and for Sarah to look good in Harry's eyes. It was for the rent. I thought just for once we could eat well and not worry, but she's spoilt it. I don't know why I bother.'

'Whisht now, it'll be all right. She shouldn't have stolen your money. I'll go up and speak to her. Your father would have belted her, but I'll tell her there's no going out tomorrow or any time this next month except for school. That will make her think. I rarely lose my temper with her, but she's gone too far this time.

'As for you, don't take on so. Things will take a turn. You'll not always be poor. Things like this will make you stronger. Have faith and something will come along. I only wish I wasn't so ill.' Agnes tried to catch her breath but it was clear to Meg that each day that was getting harder for her mam.

'And I wish I didn't have a sister like Sarah, even though I do love her if she did but know it.' Meg lifted her face to reveal tears running down her cheeks. 'She hates me but at the rate she's going I'm going to hate every bone in her body whether I want to or not. I'm sorry, Mam.'

Agnes shook her head. 'I've spoilt her too much since her father died. I never thought I'd be leaving you so soon and leaving you with all this worry.'

'You don't know that you are that ill, Mam; you'll be with us for some time yet,' Meg sobbed.

'No, I won't lass and you know it. It's time our Sarah grew up, else she's going to live to regret it. Now hold your tears. I'll give her a taste of my tongue, not before time, if it's the last thing I do.'

8

Meg stood on the step of Ted Lund's house and awaited him opening the door. She'd been doing the same for the last two months and she was beginning to think she was a fool for going and wakening him every morning. At least spring was at last with them, and the air along the busy streets was warmer and more welcoming as she stood looking up at the bedroom window. She heard the catch on it being lifted and saw the head of Ted Lund and realized he was still in his bedgown as he shouted down to her.

She looked up at the old man, who was clearly in two minds whether to close the window and go back to bed, and started to yell up to him.

'Do you never give in? Can't a man get a decent night's sleep?' Ted shouted down. 'Go back to your home and put this note on the bakery door before you do.'

Meg watched as a piece of paper flittered down in the slight breeze and landed a few inches away from her feet. She picked it up and tried to read the scrawling handwriting in the morning's light.

CLOSED UNTIL FURTHER NOTICE, DUE TO ILLNESS.

'Are you ill, Mr Lund? Is there anything I can do and what do I do now?' Meg looked up worriedly, knowing that if the bakery was closed that she would not be earning any money.

'You take yourself home and leave me in peace. I need some time away from the bloody place, I'm sick

86

of baking bread and getting up at this unearthly time, woken up every morning with you a-clattering on my door,' Ted growled. 'Now bugger off!'

'But I'll not be earning any money!' Meg protested.

'That's not my concern, now go home!' Ted yelled but Meg persisted and stood her ground.

'You'll not be making any money either. Why don't you let me open the bakery for a while? Just until you've had time to feel more yourself. You know that I can manage everything now.' There was no reply.

Meg sighed as she watched the old man close the window and disappear from view. She felt down-hearted as she started to walk away, wondering what she was going to do now. Even though the pay was not good, it at least had kept the three of them fed, but now they would be back to having to beg or do without. Then to her surprise, she heard the key being turned in the lock of the terraced house door and saw Ted Lund half hidden behind his front door, a bed-side candle still lit in his hand.

'Here, come here. You're right. I can't bear to think of the money I'll be losing if I don't open up, but I can't face the place this morning. I might regret this, especially if you burn the place down. But here, take the key, open up and run the place and then we will see how I feel tomorrow.'

Ted held out the bakery keys and looked at Meg. 'Don't forget to clear out the ashes from the oven and warm it up gently. Don't give folk tick just because I'm not there, and bring me what money you make when you lock up this afternoon. I'll know if you cheat me, I always nearly make the same money every day, so I can tell.' Ted passed Meg the keys while still hiding behind the door.

Meg looked at him and smiled. 'You are sure? You trust me?'

'I don't know about trust, but it would be a shame to lose good money when you are willing and able,' Ted admitted grumpily. 'Now, get gone and leave me to my bed. Not that I'll get back to sleep in a hurry now!'

He slammed the door in her face and left her looking down at the heavy key of the bakery in her hand with a smile on her face. She was in charge of the bakery. A dream had come true. She'd for once bake proper bread, without any sawdust added. Ted wasn't to know and she at long last could rectify a wrong that had been playing on her mind. She had hated cheating her neighbours and customers out of a decent loaf of bread. After all, it was essential to all families, and good bread filled bellies for not a lot of money. Today they would get to know just how good her bread could be.

Meg knew she hadn't time to stand and think about it; there were ovens to light and shop floors to clean. Would she be able to manage it all on her own?

* * *

The ovens were lit and warming up nicely and Meg was smiling as she kneaded the bread. She knew it felt right and would taste a whole lot different than the usual bread that the locals depended upon. She lovingly divided the bread and added her own creative styles to the cottage loaves, revelling in the fact that there was no sour face telling her not to do so. She put the trays of bread to rise then put the kettle on the fire — she'd even time to make herself a drink and have a sit for five minutes before seeing to the shop.

88

She'd known Ted was lazy but hadn't registered just how slowly he worked. There was plenty of time to make other baking, she thought, as she looked around her and had a proper look at the baking tins on the many shelves within the bakery that had not been used for years. The bakery had obviously been a hive of activity, so busy all those years ago, so why should it not be now?

She quietly thought as she sipped her tea. It was as John, Daisy's brother had said when they met: Leeds was growing, and there were more people, more potential customers in the town nowadays, if only they had something to tempt them into the bakery. Not just bread filled out with sawdust.

Ted had let his bakery slip. He'd lost heart and got lazy. Things would be different if it were her bakery, but that was just a dream. She sighed as she placed her empty mug of tea down, looked at the risen bread, and started placing it into the ovens in good time for her first customers.

With the bread baking she went into the shop and looked at the bread she was supposed to sell that had been left over from Saturday. Luckily there were only a few loaves left. She picked them up and felt their weight. They were so much heavier than hers would be, and it couldn't be anything other than a few ounces of fine sawdust in them. She hated having to sell them so took the decision to discard them. She'd not be putting anyone's life in danger while she was running the shop. If her money was down at the end of the day it was down, but at least she'd go home with a clear conscience.

After clearing the counter and pulling up the blinds on the shop's window, she checked the mousetraps that she had placed under the counter and was relieved to find both empty. Previous days had always found them with lifeless bodies caught in the lethal traps but perhaps now she had got on top of the vermin that had taken great delight in making the shop their home.

She stood back and looked at the empty counter. It was clean and now prettily covered with the paper doilies that she had found in the drawers on the wall above her head. This was her chance to quietly make changes at the bakery stuck in time, whether Ted Lund liked it or not. If she had the key for a little longer and with no one to stop her, she'd make a few more, just small ones for now. Perhaps Ted would understand then that the bakery could make him good money, a whole lot more than what he was making now, and surely he could not be against that?

The smell of the baking bread filled the shop and the bakery, and for once Meg felt happy about what she was going to turn out of the tins and sell to her customers. She'd welcome the loss of the feeling of guilt as she passed the bread over the counter. Today it was as it should be and she was glad.

* * *

'Where's Grumpy then? It looks like you are on your own today. He's surely not let you run this place on your own,' Daisy said as she watched Meg wrap up her usual loaf of bread. 'The bread looks and smells different today as well.'

'He didn't want to leave his bed this morning, so he gave me the key to the bakery and shop after I convinced him that I could run it and that he'd be losing money if it wasn't open.' Meg grinned and twisted the ends of the tissue paper that she had wrapped the loaf in tightly. 'This is my bread, made my way . . . although he'd have plenty to say about it if he knew.'

'It looks good and smells good, plus it feels lighter. For the first time, I'm going to enjoy eating bread from here,' Daisy said as she placed the loaf under her arm. 'I hope he decides to stay away a while longer, then we'll all benefit from him not baking.'

'He'd play merry hell with me if he knew what I was up to. I even gave each loaf a quick brush with butter; I always think it looks better and makes the crust not as hard. I hope he stays away for a while, I've enjoyed myself this morning.' Meg smiled and Daisy could see her friend was loving this new freedom.

'Well if he does, I'll tell everyone at the mill to come and buy bread here. It's handy and I think in the past they used to buy it from here when things were better.' Daisy smiled at Meg. 'I don't suppose you have time to come for tea again; our John was asking when we were to see you again. I think it was because he's been dealing with some plans for a new bakery over at Headingley and it made him think of you. I think it was that or perhaps you've taken his eye. You never know with John.' Daisy watched Meg's face light up. 'Perhaps we could come and see you. That would be easier for you, I suspect, with your mam being ill?'

'Oh, you don't want to come and visit me at Sykes Yard. It isn't the best of places.' Meg dropped her head and for the first time in her life, she felt ashamed of where she lived.

'I'm not bothered about where or how you live,' Daisy reassured her. 'You are a friend now, it's you

91

I like, not your home. Think about it and I'll call in again tomorrow, especially if this bread is as good as it feels and looks. How is your mam? Is she any worse?' Daisy asked with concern in her voice.

'She has well days and bad days. It's as if on a good day she spends all her energy, and then the following day, she isn't fit to do anything. At least my sister is behaving herself at the moment. At one time she was leading me a real dance!' Meg sighed and tried not to show her feelings.

'I'm so sorry for you, I don't know what I'd do if any of my family were ill,' Daisy said. 'My father likes a drop of whisky and spends too much money on it sometimes but on the whole, we are all right. My mam holds us all together, as mothers do. Sorry, Meg, I'm going to have to go, but like I say, I'll be back tomorrow. I know I will if this bread tastes as good as it looks.'

'Yes, get yourself away else you are going to be late and if you can tell them at the mill that the bread has changed for the better, I'd be grateful, even if Mr Lund is back tomorrow, which I think he will be,' Meg replied. 'If he knows that the bread is selling I can't see why he shouldn't let me carry on baking it?' Meg smiled. She would prove to Ted Lund that his inferior bread-making and cheap tactics were not worth it in the long run.

* * *

Ted Lund lay in his bed and pulled the covers over himself as the church clock chimed nine o'clock. He'd often dreamt of still being in bed at that time of day and now he was doing it. He didn't feel like facing

92

the world anyway. It was the anniversary of his wife and daughter's deaths, a memory that seemed to get deeper every year — perhaps because he was ageing rapidly and he knew it.

The years had taken their toll on him of late and when he had lost his beloved wife Eleanor and daughter Myra it was as if a light had gone out in his life. The arrival of Meg working in his shop had brought back memories of how happy he had been back then and occasionally he had found himself looking at the lass and nearly calling her Myra when his mind played tricks on him. She was a lot like her but with the drive of Eleanor, he thought, as he remembered Meg scrubbing the floor clean just like his wife did all those years ago.

To make matters worse, Eleanor's sister had written to him to ask him to close the shop for a week or two and to stay with them in Donegal. It had been a long time since he had spent any time with his wife's family, the Murphys, but he had fond memories of the days that he had spent visiting the croft when he had been courting his Eleanor. The long warm summers when they had lain together in the wildflower meadows and had made their way home to find freshly baked bread and newly churned butter with home-cured bacon, and potatoes and vegetables from out of the small garden that fed the Murphy family for most of the year. It was then he had realized what a good cook and baker Eleanor was, and he knew then and there that she had to become his wife and partner in the bakery, even if it meant tearing her away from her home to join him back in the grime and soot of the busy streets of Leeds.

He sighed and closed his eyes as his memories

came flooding back. He should never have asked so much of her. She'd still have been alive today, if he hadn't married her and dragged her away from her parents. She'd have been happy marrying an Irishman and perhaps opening her own bakery or being content with just being his wife. Then she and Myra would not be lying on the deep dark cold bed of the Irish Sea, their bones bleached and picked clean by the creatures of the deep.

Ted curled up in on himself and tried to block the sight out of his mind, turning his attentions to thinking about Meg and if he had done right giving her the key and the run of the bakery. What if she burnt it down? Or even worse told everybody of his scam with sawdust! He would be locked up in Armley Gaol if he wasn't careful.

He'd have to see what she had to say for herself when she returned later in the day but for now, he'd close his eyes upon the outside world and drift back to sleep if the ghosts of yesteryear would let him do so. He closed his eyes and thought of the happy days spent in the arms of his Eleanor. Perhaps a week or two in Ireland would do him good if the lass could manage the bakery without him. He was tired. He was always tired, tired and weary of this life. Although he knew many thought of him as lazy and bad-tempered, it was just that he had given up on life. He wished that it was him that was at the bottom of the sea.

★ ★ ★

Meg walked slowly back home. She'd had a busy day all by herself in the bakery but her mood was buoyant as she thought about what she had achieved in the

94

day and the amount of money that she passed over to Ted Lund. He hadn't shown much interest in what she had to say to him as he counted the money in front of her. She had felt as if she wasn't trusted, that even if there had been a ha'penny less than usual she would have had to explain its loss. As it was he had said nothing, only that he probably wouldn't be in for the rest of the week if she could manage without him, and that she need not bother him again bringing the takings until Saturday afternoon but to make sure that it was safely locked away in the safe.

In all honesty she could have whooped with joy as he had said that. Instantly she started to think of what she could do while he was keeping clear of the shop. Shelves could be cleared, tins tidied and the storehouse that held the bins of flour and other ingredients could at long last be sorted out and cleaned so that she felt happier about the cleanliness of where she was baking. Ted had even given her details of the miller who delivered the flour and other ingredients and told her to just keep ordering the wood and coal that kept the ovens going.

It was as if he wasn't that bothered that he was passing over control for a week. He had even come to the door, looking dishevelled and half asleep. If she didn't know him better, she would have thought that he had been drinking but she had heard him moaning previously about those that drank and put drink before feeding their family, so she knew that was not the case. Perhaps it was that at the bottom of it all; he was just lazy, and now that she had learned the ropes, she was the way to get out of work. Whatever the reason, she was going to make the most of it and keep supplying the customers with proper bread.

Perhaps if they knew the recipe had changed she would get more customers, and more money in Ted's hands would prove that his cutting back on making good bread did not pay. Her upbeat mood changed as she got to her own front door. How would her mother be today and would Sarah have got herself to school? It was not only the bakery she now had the responsibility of but also the care of her family and home, and although she would embrace running the bakery for a week, she knew it was going to be hard work.

'Hello, Mam, I'm back — are you all right today?' Meg put her shawl on the hook on the back of the front door and saw her mother was up dressed and looked to be putting a dish of rice pudding to cook in the side oven.

'Aye, I'm not having a bad day today. Roger came as soon as it was daylight with another load of wood. This time he'd broken up all the crates for us, so it was grand, and he brought half a bag of coal and wouldn't take any payment for it. He's a good man. You know you could do a lot worse, our Meg. Age is a good thing. He will be steady and be able to look after you.' Agnes smiled at her daughter and noticed a flush in her cheeks.

'Mam, no matter how kind Roger is, I could never feel anything for him; besides, I've better things to do than flutter my eyelashes at a middle-aged stall-holder, no matter how kind his heart is. I'll repay him with a loaf of bread on Saturday afternoon and thank him for taking care of us.' Meg sat down and smiled at her mother who did look a bit better today. 'Sarah is at school, behaving herself, I hope?'

'Aye, she went without a murmur this morning. Since that good telling off she's not been that bad. I think I frightened her to death when I said it would be her that was putting me in an early grave and that she'd end up in the workhouse if she wasn't careful. It was time she heard some home truths even if they did frighten her.' Agnes sat down and looked across at her eldest daughter who she knew was carrying the family's worries on her shoulders. 'She's going to be lost when she hears the latest from next door. Betsy has gone and got Harry a job down on the cut. She's lied about his age and he started this morning helping unload cargo, the poor little mite. Although half of what he unloads will be going missing if he can pocket it, I'm just glad that he'll be too busy now to lead Sarah astray.' Agnes's chest heaved as she fought for breath after the effort of making a pudding to fill them up after their supper of bread and dripping.

'And there was me thinking I had it bad! Poor Harry, he is going to come home shattered; it's a man's job unloading cargo down at the canal. He's only six months older than Sarah — he's still a child. If his father worked more and didn't drink it all he'd not have to be working. I'll give Ted Lund his due — he is right when he says it is the drink that ruins folk's lives — although when he came to the door this afternoon he looked as if he was an old soak, but I think he'd only just got out of bed,' Meg told her.

'This afternoon! Has he not been at the bakery with you today?' Agnes caught her breath and looked at Meg.

'No, he was going to close it this morning, pretending that he was ill until I pleaded my case and said that we needed the money and that he could trust me to run it on my own. Anyway, I've had a really good day today on my own; I've realized just how little that

Ted actually does and the best thing is he says he's taking the rest of the week off and leaving me to it. The customers can, at last, have proper bread because I'm not adding his blasted sawdust to the mix. Daisy said she was impressed with the new bread and that if it tasted as good as it looked she would let it be known throughout Hunslet Mill and to expect extra customers in the morning, so we will see. Perhaps I'm making a rod for my back; after all, the profits will all go into Ted's pocket, but I just can't stand back and watch them eat the bread that Ted has been feeding folk with.'

'You be careful, our Meg. Don't be making yourself too much work: remember all the money will go into his pocket at the end of the day. He'll not thank you or help you if you run yourself into the ground.'

'Aye, I know but I love baking, good baking, and now is my chance, if only for a week!' Meg looked jubilant, her mind full of things that she could do with the place. 'Mam, mentioning Daisy, would you mind if she came to visit us here, perhaps on Sunday, now that I'm going to have a busy week?'

A cloud passed over Agnes's face. 'Oh, I don't know, you said their house was quite posh. We have nowt. Just look at us, enough cups for one each and the same with plates; all the best china has been pawned over the years and everything needs a good decorate. I know it's clean but nothing would take any harm from having a good coat of whitewash on it. The bedroom is terrible damp, so she can't go upstairs. Do they know where we live? I'll feel ashamed of living as we do.'

'She's not like that, Mam, she knows where we live and she also knows we've not a lot of money. She's not bothered about that, neither is her brother John. He'll be coming with her, she hopes,' Meg said and looked pleadingly at her mother. 'I know what you are thinking, we do look as if we have nothing but it is as Daisy says: she wouldn't be a true friend if she judged us on wealth.'

'She sounds a wise one, does your friend Daisy. And you say her brother is coming as well. Is he just as open-minded?' Agnes looked at her daughter and saw a spark in her eye.

'I think he is. He's a bit of a tease, there's always banter between him and Daisy,' Meg smiled.

'Well then, perhaps they had better visit. It will bring a bit of new life into the house and perhaps lift my spirits. We'll ask Mrs McEvoy next door if we can borrow her tea service, to keep up appearances. She often rents it out to other folk on the row. She charges a farthing for lending it out, just in case anybody chips any of it. At least they can have a decent drink of tea with us if nothing else.'

Agnes sat back in her chair and looked at the satisfaction on Meg's face. Was it the thought of her having visitors in her home, or was it she was thinking of what to do and bake all week while Ted Lund was lolling in his bed?

9

Meg unlocked the bakery door and lit the lamps and looked around her. Today this was all her domain. She could bake the bread she wanted and tidy up the shelves along with all the other things that she knew needed doing but which she hadn't dared suggest to Ted Lund.

When he came back after his week lolling in bed, she knew he would have words with her but she would take that on the chin. At least she'd know that the bakery was cleaner and more fit for its purpose. She soon set to warming the bakery up by lighting the huge arched ovens and warmed herself up by making her bread, once more without the added ingredient of sawdust.

She was smiling as she started clearing the racks of all the old rusty tins that hadn't been used for years, sorting which could be used and which should have been thrown out to the rag and bone man a long time ago. There was every sort of tin that you ever could want: loaf tins were numerous, small bun tins, even conical metal tins to wrap the pastry around for making cream horns — a real treat that must have been made at some time in the shop.

With every layer of the bakery's history being unwrapped as she tidied and cleared the shelves, she felt sad that the bakery had declined so badly. It must have been a loss to the community; she knew they missed it with the nearest bakery at least three streets away.

Meg quickly moved to put the risen bread into the oven and then prepared herself to get the shop ready for the day's customers. Would word have got around that the bread was of better quality and would she get more customers because of it? She knew that Ted might lose money by her not adding sawdust to the dough mix but she had worked out her costings and the amount of loaves she had to sell was not that great. Her bread tasted much better than his, surely she would sell more?

As she wiped the countertop she hoped that not too many customers would appear before the first batch of her baking had come out of the oven. She'd virtually sold out the previous day and there was the only odd loaf left on its own for the first early morning customer.

The bell above the shop's door went, and Meg looked up at her first customer. She recognized her at once as being the flower-seller that stood at the bottom of the town hall steps nearly every day, no matter what the weather or season. Her flowers varied from holly in Christmas to snowdrops in early spring to the beautiful bright blooms of roses come summer. Her face was tanned and weathered and she had several layers of clothes on as she looked across at Meg.

'I don't usually come this way to my pitch but a young lass bought some flowers from me yesterday and she was telling me that she'd just eaten the best slice of bread she'd had in a long time,' she said. 'So I said to myself Eliza, *it's nowt of your way to call on old Ted Lund so get yourself down there.* So here I am, and I'm hoping I'm not too early. His bread was always the best; folk used to queue up for it halfway down the street, it seems he's back at it.'

Eliza looked at Meg and at the solitary loaf under the counter. 'I'm sorry, my new batch is not yet out of the oven but I've got this loaf left from yesterday,' Meg explained. 'You can have it for half price if you wish? It's still pretty fresh — I wrapped it up in tissue paper last night to keep it so. The batch that's in will be another twenty minutes if you want to wait.' Meg looked at the ageing woman and hoped that she'd say she would come back or if she had to, to take the loaf left from yesterday.

'So is Ted not baking his bread at the moment? It will be a blessing if he isn't! His loaves of late are like lead, they are not fit to eat.' Eliza leaned back against the shop's wall.

'No, I'm baking this week, he's having a bit of time to himself,' Meg said, still unclear which way the flower-seller would decide.

'Aye, that's his problem, he's always having too much time to himself. He's gone lazy and thinks too much about things. He's a miserable old devil, he'll be a bad'en to work for, and set in his ways I bet,' Eliza smirked. 'That newly baked bread smells good. I'll wait if you don't mind. There's nothing like fresh warm bread and I'm early this morning with my barrow of flowers. Violets and daffodils are my flowers that I'm selling today — I walked out into the country lanes and picked some primroses yesterday evening. They smell so sweet, I'm always fond of a primrose myself, they are so delicate.'

Eliza looked around her. 'Well, it's looking a bit cleaner than the last time I was in here. The slovenly old devil. It's men, they need a woman to keep them right. That's why I never bothered with one, I'm better on my own, I have folk to talk to when I sell my

102

flowers and get my entertainment with a drop of gin in me on an odd night of the week.'

The old flower-seller rattled on, talking enough for two or three customers as she waited for her bread. Meg thought of the time she was wasting and the jobs she could be doing while listening to Eliza's life story.

'I'll go and check the bread. It should be done now. Excuse me, I'll have to leave you for a minute or two.' Meg hurriedly went into the bakery and opened the oven doors. Thank heavens the bread looked baked. She quickly pulled it out on the large bread paddle and checked a loaf just like she'd seen Ted do to make sure it sounded hollow on the bottom as she tapped it. Quickly she took a red hot loaf through to the never-quiet flower-seller and wrapped it up quickly in the tissue paper, not wanting to be caught up in her conversation again.

'That smells good, it was worth the wait.' Eliza passed her money over to Meg and tucked the warm loaf under her arm. 'I'll be away now, I haven't time to stop and talk all day even though I know you'd like to. See you in the morning!'

Meg heaved a sigh of relief as Eliza left the shop. She might have gained a customer, but bye, could she gossip. Tomorrow morning, if she could manage it, the fresh bread would be on the shelf for her, rather than Meg have to listen to her talking for twenty minutes non-stop.

The stream of customers started after Eliza had left, eager to try the new bread that they had all sampled the day before. Professor Brown, a quiet man who surrounded himself with books, was her next customer. He asked quietly for his usual cottage loaf and smiled at her for the first time as he took it from her. He'd hardly ever acknowledged her previously, along with the rest of his fellow men, but that morning he looked quite happy as he walked out of the shop thinking about the butter and jam he was about to spread on his newly baked bread.

A group of giggling and chattering young girls came in dressed in pinnies and with clogs on their feet. They'd never been in the bakery before and the one with the most cheek stepped forward. 'Daisy gave us a slice of her bread yesterday and she told us to come here and buy a loaf instead of our usual bakers on North Street. It tasted that good we all decided to come and give you our custom; besides you are cheaper and better quality. My mam will be lucky if she gets any of it taken home tonight. I'll have to tell her about here, although it looks like you only bake bread. Do you not do owt else? I only ask because she's hopeless at baking and I have a sweet tooth. If you made some cake, I'd buy it off you — nothing fancy mind, I haven't the money to be too frivolous.'

The bubbly lass looked hopefully at Meg as she passed her the bread. 'I'd like to make some scones or rock buns or perhaps some currant buns, they are all easy to make; however, I can only bake what the owner lets me bake. If I can convince him that they'd sell, I'd bake them,' Meg smiled.

'We'd all buy them,' the girl quickly replied. 'A bit of sweetness while we work makes life worthwhile. He'd get more of us mill workers in if he had more baking and it was good, not like the stuff his bread has been made of lately. The whole mill knows his bread is not worth eating. Nowt gets past us lot — if something is bad and not worth its money, we soon share and tell folk.' She turned and looked at the next lass in line.

'You'll get all of us every morning then, wouldn't she, lasses?' she said to all of them as she pushed her way through the group for the next to be served. They all replied with a loud aye and waited their turn.

Meg was smiling as she wrapped another loaf of bread and passed it across the counter. If she had all these extra sales on her second day of baking, she was going to have to bake more tomorrow. Which was a good thing, but how was she going to explain the uptake in takings to Ted at the end of the week without telling him what she had been up to? She watched as the giggling mill workers hurried to work. She'd work something out, and anyway, he should be glad that the bakery was making money. Her balancing of ingredients and prices showed she was making good profit and that was without him having to work for it.

Daisy was late as usual when she burst through the shop's door. 'A loaf of your wonderful bread please, Meg.' She put her money down on the counter and looked at her friend. 'One day, I'll not be chasing my tail. The trouble is I'm hopeless at getting up in the morning. My mam plays merry hell with me many a morning because she gets up first for my father and then me and because John works office hours he's always the last down for breakfast but it's always me that has to be shouted at. I'm as lazy as old Ted!' She smiled as Meg passed her the loaf.

'I've had half of Hunslet Mill in this morning because of you,' Meg told her with a grin. 'Not that I'm complaining, but when I've got a quiet spell, I'm going to have to bake another batch. I have got a second lot of dough rising now.'

'Well, that's good. That will teach old Lund a thing or two! He should let you take over more often.

Nobody wants to eat his bread or see his miserable face behind the counter,' Daisy said and pulled her shawl around her. 'Before I forget, what do you want to do about Sunday? John says he'd love to see you, no matter where that is.'

'I've spoken to my mam, you can come to us, and she says the company will do her good. Around two, will that be all right with you both?' Meg said as she watched Daisy grab the shop's door handle in a rush to get to work.

'Yes, grand, we will both see you then, and don't worry, I'm sure your home is lovely. We are looking forward to meeting your mother.' With that, Daisy shot out of the door and ran up the street as the mill's whistle blew. Meg laughed to herself — Daisy would always be late.

Meg went back into the bakery and placed the extra proved batch of bread in the oven. Even as she did so, the shop bell ran again. She'd never had such a busy morning, and it showed no signs of abating.

By the time one o'clock came her shelves were nearly empty yet again, but her till was full. Meg looked at it with pride as she toted up the day's takings. It was a lot more than what was usually taken. Ted was bound to know something was going on, she thought, as she counted it and put the money into a small safe hidden inside one of the cupboards in the bakery. She'd have to think of something to tell him if her success continued.

Although she was tired, she was satisfied with her day's work. It had been nice to hear good things about her baking. She had helped herself to a threepence from out of the money that she had placed in the safe; on the way back home she was going to buy a few ounces of currants from the grocers. She might have to ask Ted if she could start making cakes and the like but there was nothing to stop her from making some currant teacakes. There was nothing nicer than a currant teacake toasted on the fire with butter upon it. They'd sell, she knew they would, and they were easy to make. It would be something else to draw the customers in and if she had any left at the end of the day, they would make a good supper for her mother and Sarah, making her life easier at home.

Ted had wanted to barter a loaf of bread into her wage. Well, today she was taking a loaf for their own use, now she knew it was edible and she'd take some teacakes as well once they were done. At least they weren't going to go hungry this week if nothing else. She'd face the consequences if Ted found out, but he'd nothing to complain about. He was making good money in his absence.

★ ★ ★

Ted looked at the money bag and bakery key that were in Meg's hands as she stood on his doorstep. Saturday afternoon had come around all too quickly for him and the days at home had made him realize just how worn out and tired he was. So much so that he had decided to take the offer of a few days in Ireland with his sister-in-law's family and to close the bakery in his absence. He'd no commitment to the girl who stood in front of him. He'd only taken her on because he felt sorry for old Agnes Fairfax.

'I'm here as you told me to be, Mr Lund. I hope that you are feeling a bit better. I've enjoyed running the bakery this week. It was unfortunate that you weren't in because it has been a good week. We've been busy because they have had a problem with the ovens at the bakers on North Street.'

Meg hoped that she would get away with her white lie and that on the coming Monday she'd have to explain that she had been selling her own recipe of bread. But she'd face the music then and not spoil her weekend. 'Some of the workers from Hunslet Mill have returned to you, so I've had to make more bread than usual — so you've made good money this week.'

Ted looked inside the money bag and felt its weight. 'You must have had a good week, there looks to be twice the money that I usually take. That bakery on North Street was never a patch on ours; no wonder they have come trailing back.' Ted put his hand into the bag and looked at Meg. She had been busy and had made him good money, but he couldn't be too hasty. He mulled his thoughts over before he counted out three shillings in pennies. 'Here, seeing you've run the place and had a good week, I'll pay you a bit more this week.'

Meg looked at the money and her face lit up. 'Thank you. There was no need, I hope you don't mind but I've taken a loaf of bread back with me each day, as I haven't had the time to make it at home.' She felt guilty now for helping herself without his say.

'No, it's all right with me. How's your mother? Is she still as bad?' Ted looked at the young lass who he knew kept everything going at home.

'Mam's all right at the moment, she's holding her own. She's thankful that I'm working here.' Meg lowered her head thinking of her mother at home alone.

'Do you think your new customers will stay with you now they are back with us?' Ted said as he wondered whether or not to change his plans and happen to abandon his trip to Ireland. But his sister-in-law would be expecting him, she'd have received his letter by now.

'Aye, I think the lasses will be here to stay with us, they requested currant teacakes the other day, so I made them some and they've come back for them every day.' Meg drip-fed him her antics and hoped that he wouldn't lose his temper as his face clouded over.

'Well, I'll tell you something, lass, I was going to say that I was going to close the bakery as from today for a week or two because I'm about to travel to Ireland to see my wife's relations. However, if we have new customers and are busy, I happen should abandon my plans and come back to work. Money like this is not to be sniffed at.' Ted couldn't believe the weight of money in his hands; it was like old times.

Meg felt elated but she didn't want to show it. He'd been planning to go to Ireland; perhaps he'd let her run the bakery a little longer if she could convince him to go.

'I've managed well this week, Mr Lund, why don't you let me keep running it while you are away? If you are only going to be a week or two, I'll manage. That's what you pay me for and then you can come back and take charge again. It will do you good to get away for a while — you are looking better already for a decent lie-in of a morning.' Meg knew the old man probably wouldn't take much convincing. She'd brought him more money in one week than he'd taken in a month and he'd not lifted a finger for any of it.

'I don't know, I'd not be here for you to come running to, and the flour needs ordering and other groceries from Dinsdale's need ordering. What if something goes wrong with the ovens? A young skit of a lass wouldn't know what to do.'

But even as he was saying it, Ted looked at her and knew she must have worked hard. It was daft yet again to close the bakery and lose money . . . and he'd set his heart on just relaxing at his sister-in-law's.

'I'll be fine; I've already ordered some flour from the miller because he brought your usual delivery on Friday and we needed more if we are to keep the new customers happy. I hope I did right? As for Dinsdale's, they told me that you had an account with them when I went in to buy some currants for the teacakes from them and was about to pay. They put them down to you anyway, so if you just let them know that I will be working for you for the next few weeks while you are away, I'm sure that they will oblige if I was to order anything.'

Meg held her breath and quietly hoped that he'd be happy and go to Ireland.

Ted shook his head. 'I don't know, I've never hardly had a day away from that bakery. I shouldn't be going, but it might be my last chance. Time is not my best friend at the moment. I'm like your mother and these old bones are weary.'

'It's more reason to go then,' Meg argued. 'I'll be making money for you while you are away. I'll put the takings in your safe in the bakery and you know I'm not likely to do a moonlight flit with them as my mam's too ill to take anywhere and when you come back I hope that I'll still be working for you.'

Meg held her breath and waited as Ted battled with his thoughts.

'You are sure you could manage? I don't want to go

110

to Donegal only to come back the following week to find my bakery burnt down.'

'I can manage and I'll take good care of it,' Meg said, her head held high.

Ted reached his decision. 'Then you keep that key and she's your responsibility until I get back. You make sure you look after the money you make and you don't run my account up at Dinsdale's. I don't mind a handful of currants and the usual but don't think I'll not go through my bill when I get back.

'Right, then on your own head be it, I'll see you in a fortnight, and not a lot can go wrong in a fortnight surely?'

'Not a lot at all, Mr Lund — you'll come back and it will be just like you'd never been away,' Meg said with a huge smile.

Ted watched as she walked away. She was right, it would be like he'd never been away when he returned to the drudge of early mornings and lighting the ovens. He'd feel that way for sure when he came back.

He'd had enough of the bakery on York Street.

10

'They're here, Mam!' Meg gave herself a quick check in the mirror, patting her long dark hair into place and then threw Sarah a quick glance as she sat in the corner of the room after being told to behave for the visitors who stood at the door.

'Well, let them in then. We are as tidy as we will ever be and there's tea in the pot.'

Agnes pulled her shawl around her shoulders and waited for the door to open. It was a rare event to have visitors in the house since she had finished taking in washing and she was all too aware that the house was not at its best. The tea service borrowed from Mrs McEvoy stuck out like a sore thumb, looking decadent and shining, decorated with ivy leaves on the cream porcelain as it sat on the scrubbed pine table. Meg had placed a plate of rock buns and home-made ginger snaps on a plate in the centre of the table and Sarah had looked at them and complained when she was told to wait for her share until the guests had arrived.

Meg opened the door and let her guests in, feeling humbled as she welcomed them into her home.

'Afternoon, Meg, how lovely is this! Afternoon tea with a good friend and look at the lengths that you have gone to to make us welcome.' Daisy kissed her friend on the cheek and looked around at John. 'Don't bother kissing him, he doesn't taste that sweet,' she joked as John followed her into the house, quietly said hello and passed Meg his bowler hat to hang up on the clothes peg behind the door before turning to Meg's mother: 'Afternoon, Mrs Fairfax, thank you so much for having us this afternoon.'

'It will be good for Meg to have someone her own age to tea, she's been working so hard of late. You must be John and you, my dear, must be Daisy. Now I have seen you, I can tell you are the spit of your mother. I remember her from working in the corner shop, she was always cheerful, just like you.' Agnes gave a big smile.

'That's a long time ago, way before either of us two were born, although she often talks about it,' Daisy replied and then turned to look at Sarah, who looked dark and surly sat in her chair watching all the fuss being given to the visitors. 'And you must be Sarah? Let me see in my posy bag, I think I have a treat or two.'

Daisy pulled the strings of her red velvet posy bag open and passed a bag of sweets to Sarah, whose eyes lit up. She smiled as Meg prompted her to say thank you. 'The barley sugar is from me and the liquorice is from John,' Daisy went on, 'but perhaps you had better save them for after your tea. Just look at the lovely china and the baking that I bet your big sister has done. She's such a clever one.'

She couldn't help but notice the cloud come back over Sarah's face at the mention of Meg's skills. The younger girl obviously had a little bit of jealousy eating at her when it came to Meg. It seemed that life had not quite been fair in handing out looks and skills. Meg was by far the bonnier sister and Meg had told Daisy that Sarah found schooling hard. She was also not as open as her sister and sat and scowled at the new company.

'You'll never guess, Daisy, Ted Lund is going on a trip to Ireland!' Meg said excitedly. 'I'm going to be left in charge of the bakery until he gets back. I'm going to take this chance to bake what I want. Surely he can't say anything if I make him money like I did this last week.' Meg poured the tea out and passed the filled teacups to everyone as they pulled a chair up to the table, except her mother who remained in her chair next to the fire.

'He's going to Ireland? I've never known him to go anywhere before. I suppose he's picked a good time of year. Spring is here, and I just commented to John that the daffodils were starting to flower in the park.' Daisy sipped her tea and took a biscuit as Meg offered her one. 'Don't you work yourself into the ground; he'll not appreciate it and he doesn't deserve it, the grumpy old devil,' Daisy commented before licking her lips free of crumbs and smiling at the heat of the ginger within the biscuit.

'I hope that you'll be making these in the shop because I'll be telling Daisy to buy some and bring them home. I could eat them by the dozen.' John helped himself to another biscuit and got his hand slapped by his sister, who knew that the biscuits and rock buns had cost the family dearly as he looked at her but still ate it.

'I don't know if I will. They cook quickly and I'd have to keep my eye on them all the time. Perhaps when I get used to the temperature of the oven I will; you've not much control over it with being fired by wood and coal. The rock buns, I definitely will, and plenty more things once I have tried them out,' Meg said and looked at her baking, the sugar sparkling on the small plain-tasting currant buns that tasted so

114

good when fresh.

'Ah, that's where Frankie Pearson's oven will make a difference to him,' John said. 'He was talking to me when I returned his new shop plans to him. He's fitting his bakery on the Headrow with gas ovens. He says he can control the temperature and so make his baking easier.'

'He'll blow himself up,' Agnes put in. 'I don't like gas. Even if we could afford it, I'd not have gas lighting in this house, it is so volatile and it smells. He'll either gas himself or blow himself up. It's a good job you're not working there, our Meg.' She shook her head.

'It's the way to go, Mam, a lot of the bakeries have it now. It isn't half as mucky. I spend at least three-quarters of an hour just cleaning the ovens and getting them up to heat. Gas would be a godsend. I don't blame him for installing gas ovens into his bakery,' Meg said. 'Is it really posh, John? I bet it is. And is he a good baker? I'm glad that he's on the Headrow, he shouldn't knock my trade.'

'Listen to her! My trade. You'd think Ted's bakery was your own already. He's only gone on holiday and left you in charge,' Daisy grinned.

'Aye, but I can dream. One day I might be able to afford it, perhaps rent it from him if he gives me the chance.' Meg's eyes lit up with the thought of her own business. She'd really work her socks off for that dream.

Sarah had grabbed her bag of sweets and was now wriggling in her chair. She'd sat long enough listening to the conversation about her sister. The sun was shining outside and even though it was Sunday and it should have been a time of peace and contemplation, she could hear Harry and his siblings outside. She hadn't been able to talk to him since he'd started work at the canal. 'Can I be excused please, I'd like to go out and play,' she said and looked all sheepish, knowing that Meg and her mother would not lecture her in front of their visitors.

'I suppose the conversation is boring for someone your age,' her mother replied. 'Go on, but don't leave the yard and don't let that Harry lead you astray, I know it's his voice that you can hear outside.' That made Sarah glare at her as she pushed back her chair and quickly went out of the door, thankful she could escape the conversation around the tea-table.

'She's a wick one is that one, can't sit still for one minute,' Agnes said once her younger daughter was gone. 'She says she wants to go on the stage; now where she gets that idea from I don't know! As if we have that sort of money to spend on such frivolities.' She gave a weary sigh. 'I think if you don't mind, I'll leave you to your conversation and I will have a lie on my bed, I've suddenly come over all tired.'

Agnes unsteadily pulled herself up onto her feet and smiled at the three eager to chat around the table. She'd noticed John looking at her Meg with a twinkle in his eye. She was only going to be in the way of a romance perhaps blossoming between them and that would give her more happiness than Meg would ever know. She would be comforted in the knowledge that Meg had someone to care for her when she was six feet under.

'Are you all right, Mam? You don't have to leave,' Meg said as she watched her mother walk unsteadily to the stairs.

'No stay, Mrs Fairfax, both John and I would like you to if you are up to it,' Daisy said and smiled as

Agnes stopped at the bottom of the stairs to get her breath.

'Nay, I'm away to my bed for a while, you young ones enjoy yourselves. Life is gone all too fast but you don't realize until it's too late.'

Agnes climbed the stairs and lay on her bed listening to the three of them laughing and talking downstairs, and the sound of Sarah, Harry and the rest of the children from the row playing outside in the mild spring weather. She closed her eyes and thought about the look on John's face when he'd been talking to Meg. He was obviously interested in her daughter, else he would not have accompanied his sister to tea at their house. He seemed all right — in fact, he'd be a good catch, with working in the planning offices. However, he'd perhaps be the first of many to court Meg. She hoped he would be, not like her who had married the first man that she had ever known instead of trying the other sweets in the jar.

That was until *he'd* come along and tempted her with his compliments and smooth talk. Bill Sharp his name had been; she could still see his dark brown eyes and his high cheekbones and dark hair with sideburns that were kept immaculate. She could still smell the cologne that he wore, unlike her husband Tom, who when at work smelt of the pit and when freshly washed, carbolic soap.

Bill had been a salesman for the furniture shop across the road on York Street and as soon as their eyes had met, she knew it was the start of something neither could control. She often thought of her hands running down his thick tweed jackets and unbuttoning his trousers as they got lost in one another's arms and a passion that neither could control nor wanted to. So much so, that Agnes had found herself pregnant with Sarah who she knew was Bill's, as she'd hardly let Tom come near her for weeks which he had accepted, not wanting to be responsible for another mouth to feed. Then, she would never forget the afternoon when the peelers knocked on her door, telling her that there had been an accident at Wheeland Pit and her Tom was one of the casualties. Agnes sniffed and wiped a tear away both in memory of seeing her husband's body laid out at the side of the pit and the pain of ending the affair with Bill. She'd thought it was her fault that she was the only one that had lost her husband that day. That God had looked down and taken vengeance on her as she enjoyed making love in another man's arms while her husband hacked away in the earth's bowels and her daughter was turned outside to play on the streets while she satisfied her carnal needs.

But how she had loved Bill. She'd loved him so much and still did. Sometimes she could see in Sarah her true father, his dark looks and his selfishness; he too had been married with children. She had a lot of his traits, completely different to Meg. Meg was her father's daughter and Agnes only hoped that she would never learn that Sarah was only her half-sister. She aimed to take that secret with her to the grave. There was no need for either sister to know any other than that they were true sisters even though she knew that sometimes she was too lenient with Sarah because of guilt over her secret lover.

Her thoughts came back to the present as she heard more laughter coming from downstairs. It was good that Meg had made friends with someone her own age and that Daisy had a brother. Perhaps love would bloom between them and hopefully her heart would not be broken, she thought.

She closed her eyes and reached for the laudanum which Meg had bought for her with the extra money given to her by Ted Lund to help the pain. She was a good'en just like her father, she thought, as she closed her eyes and drifted off into a drug-enhanced sleep and into Bill's arms.

★ ★ ★

'Don't flirt with Meg too much, John, you know you shouldn't,' Daisy lectured her brother as they walked home together arm in arm in the mild spring weather.

'Why not? She enjoys the attention and she's such a bonny lass, I can't help myself,' John grinned. 'She's got her head screwed on when it comes to business. Old Lund is going to come back to a ready-made empire if she isn't careful.'

'Yes, she knows baking and is good at it but perhaps she's not as experienced with men, so behave yourself,' Daisy said. 'I feel sorry for her. Her mother's that ill, and her sister is full of mischief — did you see her pulling her tongue out at us as we left the yard? She was with that lad that looked like a waif and stray.' 'Aye, I saw her. She needs some lessons in manners given her; she wouldn't have said thank you for the sweets if she hadn't have been prompted. They've not got a penny to their names, have they? I hope that Meg makes money at the bakery and that Ted Lund rewards her. They could do with some money and luck by the looks of it.'

John started whistling as they rounded the bend into their street.

'Stop it,' Daisy said firmly. 'You only whistle when

119

you are up to something. Whatever you are thinking, don't do it. I know you, and it will only end in tears.' She tugged on her brother's arm.

'Ah, but you don't know what I'm thinking and I'm not going to tell you, sister dear. It's my secret!'

★ ★ ★

Meg cleared the kitchen table and carefully washed Mrs McEvoy's best china in readiness for its return. Upstairs her mother lay asleep and through the window she could see Sarah sitting on the wall top with Harry.

All was done for the day, she thought, as she sat in front of the fire and recalled her visitors. Daisy was always full of life, a right chatterbox, and John was polite, although a tease. He was handsome and she was sure he kept looking at her with interest. He'd talked a lot about Frankie Pearson's new bakery but she knew there had been more to interest him in her. She realized she was smiling, thinking of John and knew that she found him attractive. Although she had told her mother that she had no time for men in her life, she wouldn't mind walking out with him on her arm. However, it was only a fancy — he probably had a sweetheart although he'd never mentioned one and neither had Daisy.

Meg sighed and closed her eyes. She'd enough change in her life with running the bakery. The last thing she needed was a man in her life to complicate it. Still, he was handsome, she thought, as she opened her eyes and looked into the fire. Perhaps if he asked her to walk with him she would.

There would be no harm in doing that, surely?

11

At least the weather is improving, Meg thought as she stretched and prepared herself for the day in the bakery. Another few weeks and it would be light as she walked to work and that would feel a whole lot better.

Neither Sarah nor her mother stirred as she made her way down to the living room, making sure the fire was still alight and glancing around to make sure everything was in place for the other two before she left home. Her heart was lighter this morning; she knew that she was in charge of the bakery and she could do whatever she wanted.

She already had plans and recipes swimming around in her brain. Today she would bake the bread as usual, but in a larger quantity and she'd also bake the currant teacakes. They had been appreciated by the customers who had bought them on Saturday. There was so much she could make, she thought, as she yelled her usual greeting to the knocker-upper and turned the key in the bakery door. Her dream had come true . . . if only for a week or two or until Ted decided to return home, which she hoped would not be too soon.

The bakery was soon filled with the smell of baking bread and the whole of the bakery and shop warmed nicely as Meg gazed out of the shop's window, her hands around a warm cup of tea. It was early yet, but the bread was baking and the teacakes were waiting to be put put into the oven. Tomorrow she would bake her usual rock buns, they were easy, and by the time the oven had reached heat it would just be right. There was not much difference in the mixture for scones so she would also make a batch of those.

She wondered whether she dare risk making some Victoria Sandwich Cake They were a luxury at her home, but she could surely get away with making them at the bakery. Victoria Sandwich was everybody's favourite cake, named after the Queen herself after her chef had made it for her knowing that she had a passion for a small light cake at tea time. Did she dare order a jar of raspberry jam from Dinsdale's?

A familiar face looked at her from the opposite side of the glass. It was John and he waved at her wildly as she smiled at him before opening the shop's door, the bell of the door jingling as loudly as Meg's heart as she looked at him over the counter.

'I know I'm early, but I thought I might save Daisy a job as I woke up and couldn't get back to sleep. I thought I'd pick up the bread and spend a minute or two with you. It would make a good start to the day.' John smiled at Meg over the counter and lifted his head to take in the smell of the baking bread. 'It smells good, Miss Fairfax . . . Meg.'

'Yes, it's still baking. You're just a little bit too early. Are you usually awake at this unearthly hour? I thought it was only the likes of me that did that, and that you would work more civilised hours at the town hall?'

Meg looked at him and felt her heart flutter as he watched her every move.

'I do, Meg, but I found myself tossing and turning in my bed, unable to sleep, and do you know why and who is to blame?' John looked at her with a serious look on his face.

122

'I do not, John. Is work giving you worries?' Meg asked. 'No, it's nothing so simple. I'm afraid that it's because of you. I keep thinking of your sweet face and I'm afraid if I'm being forward with you please say so, but I would be most honoured if you would take a stroll with me. Perhaps this evening? The day looks as if it promises to be good.' John smiled at the shock on Meg's face.

Meg blushed. 'I don't know what to say, you've left me speechless.'

'And breathless, I hope, if you feel anything like me,' John said with a pleased look on his face.

'I don't know. I've never been asked to walk out with a man before, but I don't know if I can. My mother . . . ' Meg trailed off. She wanted to say yes and stroll with him there and then but she knew that her commitments at home restricted her from giving a firm answer.

'Of course, how selfish of me. Please ask your mother's permission, providing that she is well enough to do so, and then we can arrange another evening. How about Wednesday? I'll call for you at the end of your yard and then we could perhaps take a stroll down Briggate or perhaps a stroll along the Calls if you feel like it?' John was persistent.

'Yes, perhaps Wednesday, it would give me time to ask my mam and to see if she will be all right with Sarah.' Meg couldn't quite believe that she was agreeing to walk out with Daisy's brother. The invitation had come out of the blue. 'I'll call by your home if it is any different or tell Daisy.'

'Don't be telling Daisy; she will only want to come with us and she would feel like a gooseberry. If you are not at the end of your yard at six then I know that

123

you have not been able to leave your mother. However, I do hope that you are there — I'll be counting the hours.'

John reached for the door handle and left Meg smiling to herself and thinking about the way John had looked at her. Had he really asked her to walk out with him? She hardly knew him . . . and why should she not tell Daisy? She thought and then she decided he was right. Daisy would only take over the conversation; she would not say a word when she came in that morning.

Life was certainly changing in her favour, she thought, as she went back into the bakery and slid the baked loaves onto the table. She placed the fruit teacakes into the oven before she started to mix the ingredients for her rock buns, having to think about the quantities and doubling the amount she usually made. She never weighed anything — her eye was good enough when it came to quantities. Flour, baking powder and salt were added first to the bowl, then Meg stirred in currants, mixed peel and sugar, rubbed in some butter, then bound the mixture together with eggs and milk before placing it in rough heaps on a baking tray and finally sprinkling each with sugar. She then made the same amount of plain scones, putting flour, baking powder and salt into the bowl. Then she rubbed in butter again and added enough milk to make the gentle mixture soft but firm before patting it out upon the table until it was half an inch thick. She then cut this into circles and placed these on another baking tray and brushed with an egg.

Meg stood back and looked at her work, which had taken no time at all. If Ted Lund had not sat and stared into the fire each morning and stopped feeling sorry for himself, he could have done just the same as her, she thought, feeling jubilant. Not only had she managed to make the scones in such a short time but she had John wanting to court her. If only her mother would improve, then everything would be perfect, she thought, as she took the teacakes out of the oven. Then she stoked the fires up beneath a little, and crossed her fingers as she placed her scones and rock buns into the oven before going into the shop with the morning's bread.

It seemed as if the shop bell never stopped. Old customers of Ted's commented on how the bread had improved in his absence and there were new customers to the shop, faces Meg had never seen before. Word was spreading that things were changing in the old bakery, that it was cheaper and of better quality, that the young lass that Ted had let run with his dead-on-its-legs bakery was reviving it, and if he gave her enough time there she'd turn it around in no time.

'Lord, you are busy this morning,' Daisy said when she came in. 'I hope that you've kept me a loaf. I'm a bit put out — I'm usually one of your first customers and it looks as if half of your bread has gone already.' She passed over her penny ha'penny for the usual loaf. 'Look at you: scones and rock cakes today as well. I bet they sell well.' Daisy was glad that her friend was doing well in the absence of Ted.

Meg smiled and passed her the loaf. She didn't know what John had done with his loaf of bread but he had obviously not taken it home. 'Yes, I've been run off my feet, but I'm not complaining. Do you think a Victoria Sandwich would sell, or do you think it's a bit upmarket for around here?' Meg asked, still toying with the idea of making a proper cake, an easy one at first and then perhaps more complicated if time and Ted allowed her to do so.

'I don't see why not. People like a treat and if it's good enough for the Queen then it's good enough for the rest of us,' Daisy laughed. 'You don't half like making work for yourself — you wouldn't find me working this hard for my bosses. Old Dodgson and Hargreaves never look the side I'm on anyway, so why should I be bothered if they make money or not? I just go to my weaving bench and get on with my lot. The clatter of the machines drives me almost mad some days. If it wasn't for having good friends in the mill I wouldn't have lasted this long: the job's dangerous and all the frames go back and forward. I've to be nimble with my fingers or lose them within the machines,' Daisy moaned.

'I've never been inside a mill,' Meg admitted. 'I've heard all the noise from within but never been in one. I used to walk past Marshall Mill just to look at the fabulous designs on the building and wonder what they were about.' Meg passed Daisy the bread.

'You just keep doing what you are doing,' Daisy said firmly. 'Mills are soulless places, though they're not as bad as they used to be. John Marshall, the owner of the main mill and the Temple Mill next to it, used to be a horrible man. He once strapped a nine-year-old to a pillar in front of all the workers and whipped him until he fainted; Lord knows what he'd done to deserve that. He thought highly of his fancy mill, with its fancy Egyptian pillars and carvings, while behind the exterior was the largest flax factory in Leeds if not the world, where he ruled with a rod of iron. I tell you: keep your job here and don't venture into the mills, no matter how low you get.'

126

Daisy made for the door. Meg wanted to say, 'Your brother asked me to walk out with him this morning,' but she stopped herself. She didn't like keeping a secret from her good friend as she left the shop. Surely Daisy would not have minded — in fact, if the shoe had been on the other foot she would have been glad if Daisy was to walk out with her brother, if she had one.

The rest of the morning flew by. All her new items proved to be popular, with customers commenting how good it was to see new blood baking there, and how it was like the good old days when Ted's wife had hold of the reins.

Meg cleaned and tidied away the remnants of the day's trading and ensured the embers were nearly out in the ovens then she locked the door and made her way down the street to Dinsdale's, the grocery store where Ted had an account. She'd made her mind up about preparing the Victoria Sandwich Cake. She was going to make it in the morning, so she needed raspberry jam, margarine, some more eggs and sugar, and would see if they sold desiccated coconut. The talk of Temple Mill and its Egyptian exterior had reminded her of a simple recipe for coconut pyramids that took no making at all but were lovely and luscious to eat. Her mother had shown it to her when she had helped Agnes to bake when times were better and when she was just old enough to follow her instructions. They only took five minutes in a coolish oven so they could be the first things to go in of a morning while she was waiting for the bread to rise. If she planned her baking out, all sorts could be made, she thought, as she walked into the shop that she remembered visiting when younger, but not so frequently as money had got tighter. Dinsdale's smelt of spices and freshly ground coffee and was an Aladdin's cave of everything that was needed for baking and cooking. Shelves were stacked high with glass jars, cans and tins all labelled and filled with goods from all around the world. She walked across the wooden floor and waited her turn at the counter.

'Yes, miss, can I help you?' The shop lad smiled and waited to hear what she required.

Meg told him what she needed and added a measure of glace cherries to her list to place on the top of her coconut pyramids once baked. She asked it to be put on Ted Lund's monthly bill as he was wrapping the butter in baking parchment and noting down everything she had ordered along with the price.

Seeing this, Joe Dinsdale, the owner of the store, walked over to check. 'Mr Lund doesn't usually get all these,' he said. 'Are you sure you need these?'

'Yes, I hope he's told you that I'm looking after his bakery while he's in Ireland and that I can use his account. I'm just trying a new recipe or two in his absence,' Meg said and looked at the number of ingredients she had bought and realized it did look a lot but knew it would keep her going for at least that week.

'Aye, well that's all right by me,' Joe replied. 'He did say you'd be coming in, as long as you or him will be paying for them. I just thought I'd better have a word. Do you want them delivered? There's a lot for you to carry in that basket of yours?'

'I need some of them for tomorrow.' Meg considered. 'If I take the coconut and cherries now, can you deliver the rest in the morning as soon as you can?'

'Aye, George here will have it with you by six, if

128

you've closed for today. It can be his first job of the day,' Joe Dinsdale said and watched as his assistant tried not to let his feelings show at the earliness of his delivery.

'Thank you, that would be really appreciated,' Meg said and placed the coconut and cherries in her basket. 'Good afternoon.'

The two men watched her leave.

'I don't know what old Ted's going to say when he comes home,' Dinsdale said finally. 'His bill is going to be twice the price he usually has, although I can see why. A customer told me this morning that it was the first time she had seen a queue of folk at his door in a long time. Besides, it's nowt to do with me. As long as she or him pays the tab at the end of the month.'

Joe Dinsdale shook his head and went back to his books. Ted Lund was going to be in for a shock on his return but perhaps it would do him good.

★ ★ ★

Meg waited for her moment when she was alone with her mother to ask her what had been on her mind all day since she had spoken to John.

'Mam, I had John visit the shop today, he called in right early,' Meg began tentatively.

'It seems you've had nearly everybody in that bakery since you started making more baking and got rid of Ted's rubbish bread. But go on, I can see you've something else to tell me when it comes to John.' Agnes waited for what she already had a good idea was coming.

'He asked if I'd go a walk with him, just a quick stroll down Briggate and happen as far as the Calls. I

129

won't be long; he says he'll meet me at six tomorrow night at the end of our yard but I don't want to leave you. I know Sarah will be home but it's not the same.'

'My lass, stop worrying about me. I'm not thinking of kicking my clogs this next day or two,' Agnes replied. 'Nothing would give me greater pleasure than for you to walk out with that young man. He's got a good job and is well spoken. I know his father works on the cut and likes a drink, so he must take after his mother.' Agnes smiled. 'If I knew what I know now when I was your age, I'd make the most of every minute and walk out with as many good-looking young men that I could. Just remember to keep your legs closed and don't encourage them too much,' Agnes added and watched Meg blush.

'Mam, you should know me better,' Meg said, her head down.

'Aye, I know, but these men like to have their way, and sometimes in the heat of the moment it's easier to say yes to their demands. Just think on, my lass. Other than that you go and enjoy your walk with him and you have my blessing. Sarah and I will do a little bit more of the sampler that she's working upon. She's good at sewing, I'll give her her due.'

Agnes picked up the sampler from by her side that Sarah had been working on and inspected the stitches that her daughter had made showing her age and name and a sample of the many stitches that Agnes had shown her how to do. 'She's got a real eye for detail. Everybody is blessed with some skills; it is just finding them and putting them to use.'

Her girls were growing up, and she was sure they could look after themselves if the worst came to the worst.

Wednesday evening soon came around and Meg found her legs feeling like jelly as she looked at herself in the mirror. Why had John even bothered looking at her? Her hair was a mess, she was dressed badly in hand-me-downs. She was a true second-hand rose; nothing that she was wearing had been bought from new. He could do so much better for himself, she thought, as she turned and looked at her mother and Sarah sitting close together enjoying one another's company as Agnes taught Sarah how to embroider French knots into her sampler.

'Go on, get yourself gone, he'll be waiting for you,' Agnes urged. 'Although why he can't knock on the door I don't know. He came to tea after all.'

Agnes raised her head and looked at her eldest. She looked bonny, her long black hair hung over her shoulders, loose for once and she'd put on one of her prettier dresses bought from the rag and bone man on his early morning rounds.

'You don't mind our Meg going out with that snotty John, but you don't like me playing out with Harry,' said Sarah as she lifted her head up from her work.

'That's different. Harry's a bad lot, he's a devil and besides, you are only young. Your sister's old enough to walk out with a man — she's got to that age. Now concentrate: wrap your silk tight around the needle,' Agnes chided and winked at Meg as she opened the door and stepped out into the yard.

Meg felt her heart beating fast and her stomach churning as she walked out of the yard. Betsy's children were playing out in the dirt, no shoes on their feet and their faces filthy and unwashed. With Harry working down at the cut, the next oldest was now in charge of her siblings, and Bridie, who was only seven herself, was comforting her younger sister on her knee as Meg passed them by. Harry no longer bothered with his younger sister and brothers, even though he was still as thick as thieves with Sarah.

She saw John standing at the end of the yard and quickened her step, feeling a little insecure as she looked at him still dressed in his office suit and knowing that she was dressed as an ordinary lass from the back streets.

'Hello, I thought for a moment that you were not going to show, but I was early, I came straight from my work.' John smiled as Meg looked up at him.

'Sorry I kept you waiting, time just flies at the moment. I could do with double the number of hours in the day,' Meg replied. John offered her his arm to link with hers as they made their way up the street.

'I thought that you may like a change to our plans. I've heard that Frankie Pearson has got ahead of himself and has already started altering the shop that he's moving into, even though his plans were only given the go-ahead last week. I just thought I'd be nosy and see that he is adhering to what was agreed on during our walk,' John said as they turned in the direction of the Headrow.

The name sounded familiar to Meg, but she couldn't place it. 'Frankie Pearson? Who's he and what shop is he opening?' she asked with interest.

'He's the man I told you about who's opening the new bakery when I was visiting at your mother's. He's putting a lot of money into his business. It will be for the better-off classes in Leeds, not some grubby little back street bakers which is stuck in time,' John said without thinking.

Meg went quiet. Was that what John thought of Ted Lund's bakery? Perhaps he had been right a few weeks ago but since then she had spent hours cleaning and making things better. She was growing to be quite proud of the grubby backstreet bakery that she was enjoying running.

She quietly walked by his side as they walked up the wide street of the Headrow, which was still busy. Hackney and hansom carriages filled with people returning from work passed them by. The horses looked tired and weary as they had already done a hard day's work before taking the businessmen who had started to move out to the better-class suburbs of Roundhay and its newly built homes. A Coates bus drawn by three horses passed by them, filled to the open roof with folk returning home. The advertisement board on the sides promoted NEAVE'S FOOD in garish lettering and the bus driver swore as the new tram bus fought for the same space on the road making him swerve to get out of its way.

'It's a bit busy along here and all these folk needs feeding,' John said. 'Frankie Pearson has got the best position in Leeds — he's going to be run off his feet once he's opened.'

John let loose of Meg's arm as they crossed the busy street and stood outside the Horse and Trumpet Inn that had been a favourite drinking place of the Leeds-based Yorkshire Fusiliers and was always busy. Next door to it stood the new bakery of Frankie Pearson, the shop window shining, with a newly painted sign in red and gold advertising FRANK PEARSON'S PATISSERIE AND BAKERY.

John cupped his hands together and stared in

through the clean window. There were newly placed wooden counters with spacious walkways for both Frankie's staff and customers. Glass shelves had been already added to the shop and they sparkled in the late spring light. Although the bakery was currently void of baking and goods, both John and Meg knew it was going to be a success.

Meg placed her face alongside John's and looked with awe at the new shop.

'You can't see the ovens but they should be in and safely placed at the back. I hope that he's made sure all is in place for the tea rooms that he says he wishes to open on the upstairs floors. It really is going to be the baker to visit if you're shopping in the centre of our now growing city,' John said as he admired the new business.

'City? When did Leeds become a city?' Meg asked.

'It is to change from a town to city status this year because it's growing and expanding so fast,' John explained. 'Have you not heard? I'm surprised if you haven't!'

'No, I'd not heard and can I ask what patisserie means? I've never heard of the word before.' Meg looked up at the lettering and felt a little inferior as John laughed at her.

'It means pastry maker, in French. You really don't know a lot, do you?' John smirked and left Meg feeling as if she was ignorant compared to him as he coupled her arm in his once more and patted her hand pretentiously as they walked a little further and turned the corner down into Briggate.

Meg said nothing but she was beginning to dislike the man who was on her arm. Just because he had a good job and was well dressed, he seemed to think

134

everyone else should be like him. She said nothing but kept thinking that his mother had only been a shopgirl and according to her mother, his father was too fond of the drink and only worked down in the warehouses along the canal. So he did not need to think any more of himself than anyone else.

Briggate was busy, the stallholders beginning to pack up their goods, and horses and carts waited patiently for goods to be loaded on the back of the carts and stalls folded away for the next day.

'Hey up, Meg, are you taking a stroll out with a young man?' Mike on the veg shouted and made everybody turn and look at the young couple as they packed their goods away. 'Hello, Mike, this is John, yes, he just asked me to take a short walk with him around the centre.' Meg stopped John in his tracks and smiled at the fruit stallholder as he grinned up at her from one of his crates of fruit.

'You take care of our Meg, mate, else you'll have half the market to answer to. She's a grand lass, only deserves the best,' Mike said and winked at Meg as she took John's arm.

John didn't say anything. He just looked at the stallholder with disdain.

Behind Mike, Meg saw Roger Ingram looking at them both. She put her hand up to wave at him, but he put his head down and continued packing his cart to go home, ignoring the young couple.

'For heaven's sake, Meg, do you associate yourself with these sort of people?' John asked, as they walked away. 'You could do so much better. You are attractive and are obviously talented. You'll never get yourself out of the gutter if you are not careful who you associate with.'

They reached the bottom of Briggate and started to walk along the roadway called the Calls that followed the River Aire where they stood for a while watching the trade along the busy river banks. After a few minutes, John commented about some slum dwellings that were being pulled down across the river to make way for new housing, making the homeless poor that once lived within them sound nothing better than animals.

'I'm sorry,' Meg said sharply. 'I don't think walking out with you was perhaps a good thing. I don't think we have much in common. I am happy knowing where I come from. I'm not ashamed of my upbringing. My friends are my friends no matter what or who they are.'

'What are you talking about?' John replied, clearly put out. 'I thought that you were like me, that you were hungry to shake off your past and perhaps become someone. I aim to become one of the main planners for this new city and you seem to be dragging that useless bakery out of the dirt. That's why I showed you Frankie Pearson's bakery to show you just what you could do with your life.' John shook his head in disbelief.

'People are people, John. Just because they work hard for their living and still haven't got a lot in their lives, they deserve respect. I do want to better myself, but unlike you, I would never belittle people. I don't think myself better than them.

'I should have known what you were like when you didn't come and knock on my door this evening to pick me up. Is Sykes Yard too much of a slum for you? I'm surprised that you could be seen walking out with me!'

John's face was like thunder. 'I'll not be talked to like that. There was me thinking that I knew you and thought I'd offer some help. However, now I really see you for what you are: a chancer dressed in a washed-out dress who will never better herself because she knows no different.

'I wish you a good evening and you can be assured that I will not be asking you to stroll out with me again.'

John glared and started to walk away from Meg and then turned for a second. 'You were only going to be my bit of fun for when I was bored; I am betrothed to be married to a much prettier and richer woman than you. I have no need of you, Meg Fairfax, even though my sister seemingly does.' Meg watched as John walked down the riverside. She was glad to see the back of him. If all men were like him she was better off without them, she decided as she wandered back home to the love and safety within its four walls. She might be poor but she knew who she was and had no intention of ever changing, even if she did make it in life.

12

The rest of the week seemed to pass at speed and although the work was hard and the hours were long, Meg enjoyed every minute. She filled the shelves and by the time she came to lock up on the stroke of one, they were just about bare. If her mother had not been alone, she would have worked a fuller day, knowing that she could still sell her baking in the afternoon and evening if she had the chance. However, at the end of the day it was only for Ted Lund's benefit, she thought, as she looked at the bags of money piling up in the safe, waiting for his return and took the change she needed for the shop that Friday morning. The shop bell rang with the first customer of the day and she made her way through the sweet-smelling bakery with her spotless white apron wrapped around her to serve and smile and chat to whoever was waiting at the other side of the counter.

'Morning, Mrs, I've not seen you all week,' Daisy said cheerfully. 'I've come a little earlier and then I can catch up with the gossip. It's just nice to get away from the atmosphere in the house this morning, I don't know what's wrong with John but he's been like a bear with a sore head since Wednesday. Something has upset him.' Daisy leaned on the counter and looked at Meg, and as far as her friend could see, Daisy was clearly innocent of the knowledge that it had been Meg that had upset him.

'Oh, so he's not his usual jolly self then?' Meg asked, quizzing to see how much Daisy knew.

'No, not at all, but it will be his own fault. He thinks himself as God's gift and keeps walking out with young women just to make himself feel good. He's an ignorant pompous idiot sometimes. You know he's engaged to be married? I hope some young lass has given him a piece of her mind and I only hope that he's behaved himself and hasn't got himself or her in any bother.'

Daisy did have her suspicions that it had been Meg that had caused John to act like he was and was glad that her friend had seen through her shallow brother. 'You know what I mean.'

'I know what you mean. Who is he engaged to? Will I know her?' Meg asked.

'She's the head councillor's daughter, Amelia. She's a nice lass but he's only courting her because he thinks it will get him further up the ladder when it comes to working. I know that he's been as sweet as pie when he's been around you, but he can be a real ignoramus when he wants to be. He forgets we are only ordinary working folk and if one of us doesn't work then we could well end up on the streets. After all, my father is all too fond of a drink, he doesn't contribute a lot, so our John needn't walk about as if he's got a bad smell under his nose, the bloody snob.' Daisy looked at Meg and noticed a very small smirk on her friend's face. 'He's not walked out with you, has he? You're not the one who's made him sulk this last day or two?'

Meg considered for a moment before finally saying, 'Yes, we walked out together. He took me to look at the new bakery up on the Headrow, but we had a row. I wasn't impressed that he thought himself better than us hard-working folk and that he forgets that folk struggle to put bread on the table every day. I don't think he'll be visiting me again or will be about if I'm ever invited back to your home. I feel sorry for this poor Amelia — does she know what she's about to marry?'

Daisy was grinning. 'He met his match with you then. I'm glad. He can be such an idiot. Don't worry about Amelia, she's just as bad as him, a right spoilt bit of stuff — although as I say she's always been all right with me. They will be ideal for one another: she's spoilt, and he'll find it hard once he's married to her to toe the line.

'And don't be silly, of course you'll be invited back to our house. It'll do him good to hear the truth for once, and he shouldn't cheat the one he supposedly loves. It will all end in tears.'

'Brothers and sisters, they lead us both a fair dance,' Meg said dourly.

'Why, is your Sarah still not behaving herself?'

'No, at the moment she seems to have settled down. She's getting herself up in the morning and going to school and my mam is learning her embroidery stitches which seems to give them both enjoyment. So I can't complain really,' Meg said as Daisy made for the door.

'Then don't complain, it'll not last forever. Bye, I'll see you when I see you. Your bread is fantastic, I hope Ted Lund never comes back! Happen he'll enjoy Ireland so much that he will stay there and you can rent the shop off him,' Daisy joked and then left in a hurry to go to her work.

* * *

140

Back home, Meg watched her mam and Sarah sitting and talking together as she cleared the supper table. She was tired and her legs ached from standing on them all day. It was not easy running the bakery, but then again a lot of it was her own fault, thinking that she could bake and make all sorts of things when she was on her own. She was also worried about how she was going to explain to Ted Lund the number of different products that she was now selling without his permission and the bill at the end of the month with Dinsdale's. The miller was no problem: she paid him with every delivery so nothing was outstanding but Dinsdale's was different. Joe Dinsdale had actually asked her again if Ted would be happy that his account was considerably more than in usual months and she had lied through her teeth when answering yes to him. She only hoped that Ted would look at the money she had made and be content that paying the bill at Dinsdale's was of little consequence to the amount that he could place in his bank, even after Meg had taken her wage from it.

Her worries were interrupted with a knock on the door and Sarah jumped from the side of her mother and pulled the lace curtains back from the window to peer outside into the oncoming darkness.

'It's only Roger Ingram. He's got his horse and cart outside full of wood and rubbish again; I suppose he'll want help unloading it,' Sarah moaned and looked around at Meg and her mother.

'He's a good man, he turns up every week with a full load for us and he will never take a penny for it,' Agnes replied. 'Mixed with a little bit of coal it has kept us warm all this winter. Open the door, Sarah, and let him in.'

Sarah opened the door slightly then quickly made for the stairs.

'Hey young lady, get yourself down here and lend a hand!' Agnes yelled but got no reply.

'Leave her be, Mam, I'll help Roger, it won't take us long,' Meg said then went to the door and greeted Roger. 'Sorry, Roger, our Sarah has no manners sometimes. I'll walk with you and your horse and cart down the back alley and help you unload. We are so grateful that you keep bringing us the broken crates. Mam had just said that without you it would have been a cold winter.'

Meg pulled her shawl over her shoulders as she walked out of the house and joined Roger and his horse. It plodded steadily over the cobbled back alley, the cart behind it rumbling as Roger held the bridle and guided the animal to stop outside the backyard of number 10.

'Aye, well as I say, it's nowt out of my way and it's an easy way for all us stallholders to keep our pitches tidy without having to worry who's sniffing around them for whatever they can scrounge,' Roger said as he lifted the first pile of discarded wood off his cart and threw it over the backyard wall.

'You mean like I used to do?' Meg said and took as much as she could carry and threw it onto the heap into the yard ready for her to sort through the following day.

'Aye, but nobody minded you doing that. We knew that nothing else would be going missing, unlike some of the scavengers who hang around the stalls. Besides, we knew it was keeping your mother and family warm. That's why I'm here now.'

Roger leaned against his cart and watched as Meg

threw another load over the wall of the yard and reached for another load. 'Did I see you walking out with a young man the other evening? Have you got yourself a beau?' he asked.

'Yes, I walked down Briggate on John Truelove's arm,' Meg told him. 'He asked me to take a stroll with him, but I won't be doing it again. We had words!' She leaned back on the edge of the cart next to Roger.

'Oh, was he that bad? He didn't try anything on with you, did he?' Roger asked with concern.

'No, it was just a difference of opinion. I had to remind him where his roots lay and he didn't like it.'

'Perhaps got too big for his boots, eh?'

'Yes, you could say that,' Meg replied, taking another armful of broken boxes and splintered wood.

Roger hesitated for a moment and then reached out for Meg's arm as she returned to the cart. 'I don't suppose you'd take a walk with me one evening?' he asked quietly. 'When I saw you strolling with him, I suddenly realized that you were now a young woman, not the child that I had seen these past years around the market.'

Meg was taken aback. She'd never expected that from Roger. He was nearly old enough to be her father and although he had shown her every kindness, she had never thought he felt that way about her, despite her mother's flippant suggestion. 'I'm very honoured, Roger . . . But after walking out with John, I found that I don't want a man in my life just yet. I haven't the time, my mother needs me and I'm busy at the bakery,' Meg said equally quietly.

'I understand, I'm too old for you. It's just I felt so jealous when I saw you with him. I'm old enough to be your father. I can't help but feel slightly protective

143

of you and you have grown into such a bonny woman. Mike often tells me that I'm an old fool and that I give my heart to everyone too easily.'

'It's not your age at all,' Meg said. 'I'm just not ready for courting anybody, no matter what their age. I would rather be an independent woman. I'm enjoying my work at the bakery. I know it won't last forever but it has made me see what I can do under my own steam. Let's keep it as friends, which would be better all around.'

She watched Roger gather the last remnants from off the back of the cart before he turned to her with a rueful smile and said, 'Aye, and I'll stop being an old fool. It's as they say: there's no fool like an old fool. That fits me well and I should have known better.'

★ ★ ★

'Aye Meg, I can understand you standing your ground with John Truelove; he thinks himself something that he isn't,' Agnes said a little later. 'But to knock Roger back, that's just foolish. He would have given you a good lifestyle. You would have wanted for nothing, he'll be worth a good bob or two.' Agnes had listened to Meg's tales of her two admirers as she sat near the fire before making herself ready for her bed.

'I'm not ready for any of that, Mam. I'm enjoying life at the moment and besides, I'd rather be at home with you and our Sarah,' Meg replied.

Agnes shook her head. 'Just because I'm a little stronger at the moment and you have your hands full with the bakery doesn't mean both will last forever,' she told her daughter. 'You need to look to your future and not bother about anybody or anything else.

144

Security is what you need, my lass, not a headful of dreams.

'I don't know what I've done to deserve all this! I've one daughter so headstrong she's her own worst enemy, and the other is a dreamer. A woman will never be independent. This is a man's world and you had better get used to it.'

Once Meg had gone back downstairs, Agnes put her head in her hands. All she wanted was for her daughters to be secure and happy but sometimes she despaired of the pair of them.

13

Meg sat at the kitchen table and looked at the letter that had been waiting for her when she had returned home from the bakery. It had an Irish stamp on it and Meg knew straight away that it was a letter from Ted Lund.

'Go on then, get it opened,' her mother said. 'You'll not know what's in it if you don't open it.' She could see the worried look on her daughter's face. 'Anyway, whatever he says, you have nothing to worry about. He's had more customers and made more money than he's ever done in these last few years. He should sing your praises and hopefully pay you better for all the work that you've put into that place.'

Meg felt her stomach churn as she opened the letter and read the scrawling handwriting, her face brightening with every word that she read.

'He's not coming back for another month. He says he's enjoying being with his sister-in-law and hopes that I am managing the shop on my own.' Meg read further. 'I've to pay the monthly bills, especially the one at Dinsdale's, and to make sure that the coal and woodman are not diddling me while he's away. He was good enough to let me see what they usually charge him, thank heavens. Other than that he's not said anything else.'

Meg folded the letter, relieved that she had not got to explain herself for at least another month until his return.

'You know, I can tell by the look on your face that

you were worried about what he was going to say on his return,' Agnes chided. 'Do you not think you should happen to calm the amount of baking you are doing for the shop? After all, he's just been selling his uneatable bread for years. He will have a fit when he sees what you have been up to and the bills that you have run up, even if you will have paid them before his return.'

'You don't know how much money is in his safe awaiting his return,' Meg retorted. 'He'll not complain, I hope, when he sees just how much money I've made him, or he shouldn't. I am worrying that I didn't ask his permission to take it so far, but every day I think of a new cake or scone or something that I know the folk of Leeds will enjoy. It is so good to see the enjoyment on their faces and hear their comments after they have loved eating it. I also don't charge ridiculous prices. As long as the costs are covered and Ted has made a bit, that's enough for me because I know it gets folk into the bakery, and the more folk in the shop the better.'

She fell silent but Agnes could see there was more. At the quizzical look on her mother's face, Meg continued, 'I just worry that he won't keep me on after his return.'

'He'll keep you on if he's any sense, but Ted Lund is a funny old stick. It doesn't take much to upset him,' Agnes said as she eased herself out of the chair. 'I know one thing: we have all benefitted from you working for him and him being in Ireland. The odd piece of baking that you have brought back with you has kept us well fed but he'll not appreciate finding that out. I hope for your sake he doesn't ever find out where the last scone or sponge cake goes to at the end

147

of the day, else he will be taking it out of your pay on his first week back. Ted Lund is as tight as a duck's arse, always has been. He might have made a hundred pounds but if he's lost sixpence, it will be that sixpence he frets about. So just you be careful, Meg.'

Agnes made her way to bed, leaving Meg to worry about the position that she had put herself in.

* * *

Meg sat in her chair and looked into the dwindling fire. She couldn't help but feel her stomach churning with anguish. Had she done right? She'd built the bakery up in Ted's absence but she had also made sure that her family had benefitted from her work.

Her mother was right: Ted was an awkward old stick; he could cut up funny about the things that she had been up to. She breathed in and calmed herself. It would be all right, she said to herself, he had made good money in his absence and all was accounted for. He couldn't say anything about the bit of food she'd been bringing home because he'd never know, and besides, she deserved it after all the time and hours she had put into his bakery. She had, after all, just taken her agreed-to wage out of the takings and he could see she had on the accounts that she had been making in her own notebook. Tomorrow she would go and settle the monthly account at Dinsdale's and then whatever money was left in the safe was Ted's.

He should be impressed, she thought, and just hoped that she would be right.

* * *

'I know that I'm perhaps a day or two early in requesting the bill for Ted Lund's bakery, but I'd like to know how much I owe for the month and settle the bill tomorrow after I close for the day,' Meg said and saw a look of relief upon Joe Dinsdale's face at the thought of her settling the account that he had been worrying about.

'It's a tidy amount, I've never known Ted owe me as much — that is; not since his wife died. Do you want those currants and sugar adding to it for the month?' Joe looked at the goods she had already been served with and then reached for his accounts book from under the counter.

'Yes, please. Don't worry, the account will be paid tomorrow. I've been busy at the bakery, plenty of customers have been through the doors.' Meg stood and felt her stomach churning as Joe Dinsdale totted up the account and she waited for the exact amount. However much it was, she knew that she had never owed that much in her life and she felt sick as Joe pulled the top sheet of the invoice out of the book and passed her it.

'I've kept hearing that the bakery was busy, but this will make a good dent in your profits. Not that I'm complaining as long as you pay me. You are more than welcome back in this shop if you are to spend that much with me every month.' Joe watched her face as Meg assessed what she had spent and checked for any discrepancies that were obvious to her.

'Thank you, I will be back in tomorrow to settle it as I say.'

Meg tried not to show her true feelings as she placed the currants and sugar on top of the invoice in the safety of her basket and walked out with her head held high, even though she was secretly feeling weak at the knees. Two pounds two shillings and sixpence was a lot of money. No wonder Joe Dinsdale had looked relieved when she said she was about to pay it. Thank the Lord she knew she had enough in the safe to pay it. After the day's takings, she had counted the money in there and she had near enough five pounds of clear profit, even after paying the grocery bill. Ted Lund should not complain about that, she thought, as she walked home and calmed herself down.

The following day the bakery was just as busy, the currants had been made into a sly cake which seemed to be going down really well along with some courting cake, or kiss-me-cake as Sarah called it: a shortbread mixture with raspberry jam sandwiching it together. It was the normal everyday recipes that Meg baked that were making her popular. She only wished that she could make some pastry products, pies and pasties, but pastry took time and on her own she hadn't the time to faff about with it. She also hadn't been blessed with cool hands, which always came as a blessing when handling pastry.

Her mother was also right. Perhaps she should keep her feet on the ground and stop her obsession with baking and making people feel fulfilled with a bit of goodness in their bellies. After all, Ted Lund would complain and she knew it. She was only trying to kid herself into thinking he wouldn't say anything. He would have to, to show his authority; at the end of the day, it was his bakery and his money.

When the last customer had left, she pulled the window blind down then tidied the counter, swept the floor and went to make sure all was tidy in the bakery and that the fires had gone out. She sat down at the

150

large wooden table where she kneaded the bread and did all the baking every day. She was tired. She'd been a fool to do so much baking and now there was no getting out of doing it without losing face; she'd have to continue. Once Ted returned, if he ever returned, he would either see that the place was profitable while making what she had been doing or he'd put his foot down and stop her from doing so much baking.

Meg took her notebook out of her pocket and counted the day's takings and wrote it down into the Money In a column and then looked at the invoice from Dinsdale's and wrote the two pounds two shillings and sixpence in the Money Out column before counting the money out for payment from the day's money and the money within the safe. She looked at the healthy balance that was left written down in her notebook and wished it was hers. She wouldn't then have minded the long days and how tired she felt if the shop was hers; in fact, she would look at baking more. Sarah could join her and serve on in the shop, she thought. Another few months and she would be old enough to leave school and do just that, if only she owned the bakery. That was just pie in the sky, she thought, as she sighed and placed the money and invoice for Joe Dinsdale in her basket ready for payment as she made her way back home.

Dinsdale's shop was busy when she arrived there. There was a queue in the shop and Meg waited in turn. Ben, the young lad, was run off his feet as he climbed up ladders for goods and wrapped cheeses and butter and smiled at each customer. She smiled back at him as she got nearer the counter and she noticed him blush as he knew she had caught him looking at her.

'Miss Fairfax, what can I do for you today? Have you come to settle the bakery's bill?' Joe Dinsdale said with a look of apprehension on his face.

'I have indeed, Mr Dinsdale. I said I would and I never go back on my word.' Meg looked up at the ruddy-faced grocer with his handlebar moustache waxed and groomed with care.

'I'm glad to hear it, Miss Fairfax. I must admit, the bill was worrying me slightly. As I've said, Ted Lund never spends that much with us. I thought that you might be unable to pay for it. I should have known different, from what I've overheard from our customers saying. It sounds as if you are good at your craft; Ted should think himself lucky.' Joe Dinsdale took the envelope out of Meg's hand, counted the money and signed her receipt, then marked it down as paid in his invoice book before putting the money in the till.

Meg watched him and smiled. 'I enjoy baking — I always have.'

He handed her the receipt of payment back to her and thanked her.

'If it wouldn't hit your own trade, I'd say I would sell some of your baking here, but your bakery is too near. By the time we had negotiated a price that I'd be willing to buy it from you, I'd probably have you out of pocket. I've got to make a living too.' Joe looked at Meg and watched her wondering if it would be worth her while to supply Dinsdale's with some of her baking.

'It's a kind offer, Mr Dinsdale, but as you say, I don't think it would be worth my while. Seeing that you don't sell bread and baking, let us keep it at that. Each man to his own.'

Meg put the receipt safely away in her basket, to

add to her notebook and other receipts that she had kept as a record of her dealings. 'Thank you. I'll be back with my needs for the bakery so we are both benefitting from that. Perhaps you could give me some discount . . . after all, I am buying quite a bit from you?' she asked with a smile on her face.

'Now, don't be too hasty, Miss Fairfax. Perhaps I'll discuss it with Ted on his return. After all, it his is business.' Joe Dinsdale looked at the young woman. She might be dressed poorly but she had brains.

'Ted is to return at the end of the coming month; perhaps you could talk to him then. Good day, Mr Dinsdale.'

Joe Dinsdale watched as Meg left his store. She obviously was a worker. Ted would be a fool if he did not keep her on at the bakery upon his return, no matter how much she had spent in his store.

14

Frankie Pearson stood outside his new bakery on the Headrow and looked up with pride at the lettering up on the board above the window. PEARSON'S PATISSERIES. Now that was posh and swanky, and so it should be, because this was not going to be just any ordinary baker's, he thought as he smiled to himself. His years in Paris with his father and mother both working as artists had given him a love of top-class patisserie and he was about to introduce the good people of Leeds to a finer side of life.

Choux pastry, light, and fluffy sponges, and delightful meringues would soon be displayed in the window and his two hand-chosen pretty girls, along with the older stickler, Brenda Jones, who would keep them both in line, would serve the masses of customers that he envisaged entering through his doors. He meanwhile would make creations that ordinary folk could only dream of, his early years working as a pastry chef in one of the leading hotels upon the Champs-Élysées teaching him all the tricks of the trade.

Six months earlier he had left Paris, a disillusioned chef deciding to make his own way in the world and to set up in business in the town of his mother's birth. He'd been fortunate enough to be left a substantial legacy by his father with which he'd bought the dilapidated property on the Headrow. Now he stood with a huge smile upon his face on the day before opening the doors of his business to the first customer. It had cost him dear but every penny was worth it. He could bake and cook what he wanted and just to see his own name over the door was worth every moment that he had washed dishes, scraped leftovers into bins, and been screamed and shouted at while learning his trade.

He walked inside to his bakery and shop and looked around him. The clear glass shelves of the counter were waiting to be filled with the delicacies that were about to be made in the bakery and the mirrors behind the shelves reflected brightness and light into the bakery's shop. On the top of the counter already, there were bakery-made brandy snaps and packets of tightly sealed almond-flavoured biscuits, dipped in chocolate. On the shelves behind where the customers would stand were boxes of chocolates from Terry's of York, decorated with bows and kittens upon them, and tins of toffees and eclairs for the person who was looking for a gift for a loved one. At the side were three wooden sealed boxes from Carr's of Carlisle holding scrumptious biscuits to be sold and weighed out at the shopper's request.

The shop already looked wonderful, he thought, as he walked past the stairs which in time he hoped would lead to two floors of café space if his bakery and shop proved to be a success. He stopped and smiled again as he looked at the heart of his empire, his bakery. The two newly built gas ovens had already been tested and found to be more than adequate. He could control the temperature at a turn of a dial and there was enough room in both ovens to bake three or four products at once.

The surfaces to work on were spotless and smooth, one being marble to keep chocolate cool upon as he or his second in command moulded and poured it into shape. The walls were covered with shelves

155

holding any ingredient that could be found in the finest of bakeries, along with mixing bowls, whisks, jugs and weighing scales. His bakery wanted for nothing, he thought, as he leaned against the doorway and felt a deep feeling of satisfaction. Now, he'd just to bake and prove his worth to the folk of Leeds — the upper end, he hoped, the ones with money. After all, there were plenty of backstreet bakers who supplied the basics but this one was going to be for the connoisseur. This would be the one to be seen shopping in. Well-dressed ladies and distinguished gentlemen buying that sweet treat for their wives or mistresses — that's who he envisaged as he sighed and pulled and locked the door behind him.

It was time to make the final preparations before the big opening.

★ ★ ★

The next morning, Brenda Jones was casting an eye up and down the two girls who served behind the counter and scowled. 'Now, Marie and Norah, remember the customer is always right. Remember your manners, keep a smile on your face and for heaven's sake, Norah, put your cap straight on your head. Smart is what this shop is and don't you forget it. Now, I hope that you have learned the pronunciations. It's not a 'stick of bread', Norah, it is a 'baguette' and it is not 'Slippers a la cream', it is 'Slippers a la Crème' when it comes to the pastry fancy on the first shelf. I expect you girls to improve your French accents with every day's work in this shop. Mr Pearson wants this shop to succeed and it is up to us to make sure it does. Now are we ready, girls?'

156

'Yes, Mrs Jones,' both girls said together as Frankie came out, carrying out his latest concoction of a tray of vanilla slices to be placed under the counter before the first customers came into the shop.

'Are you ready, girls? My, you look so beautiful, just like my delicacies, how can people resist?' Frankie said, and grinned as he saw Mrs Jones grimace at his flirting with his girls. 'You too, Mrs Jones, very professional, just what the shop needs for it to be kept in order.

'Well, that's my last batch for this morning — let the doors be open. Mrs Jones, you do the honour: open our doors wide and let the customers come streaming in,' Frankie said as he placed the last vanilla slice onto its shelf and looked at the laden shelves of baking that he'd been making since before early light. Slippers a la Crème, St Honoré Cake, Florentines, cheesecakes, gateaux and meringues were waiting to be sold, along with the fresh crusty baguettes which Norah kept calling sticks of bread to the displeasure of Mrs Jones.

'Here goes, Mr Pearson, we all wish you well.' Mrs Jones said as she unbolted the door and stood back as the first customer entered the shop. She nodded at the girls to see to their needs.

'Can we help you?' Norah said politely to the elderly woman who was looking at the things under the counter and shaking her head.

'Have you got an ordinary loaf of bread? Them sticks wouldn't feed my Arthur, he'd say they were all crust,' she replied.

'I'm afraid it is all we have baked today, but it is extremely fresh and tastes wonderful,' Norah said and smiled.

'Nay, I'll not bother taking one of them. And your

cakes look all sickly and rich — have you nothing plain? These are all too sweet,' the old woman complained then saw the sultana biscuits made by Carr's in the boxes by her side. She decided she'd better buy something from out of the newly opened bakery. 'Give me a few of them. Not so many, though — by the looks of the price they must be made with pure gold!' She opened her purse and found the correct money for her treat and put them into her basket.

'Well, I hope that they aren't all like that,' Marie said once the woman had left. 'You did well not to get rattled, Norah.' 'We learn from everyone who comes in,' Frankie said, trying to look cheerful. 'There will be a few like that until folk understand what we sell. The right sort of person will soon be giving us trade, don't worry, my girls.'

He could have done without someone like that for his first customer but he was sure the rest of the customers would be more grateful for the new delights within his shop. Or so he hoped.

★ ★ ★

Jenny Pratt, with all her aches and pains and an ailment for every member of her family, had become a regular since Meg had been in charge of the bakery. She spent quite a few minutes discussing the news from the streets and giving Meg the latest gossip, in between moaning about her ailments.

'That new bakery on the Headrow has opened up,' she prattled on. 'It looked right posh when I walked past it, so I thought that I'd have a nosy. It's not like here, Meg. The lasses that were serving on looked down their noses at me and I didn't know half the

158

things that they were selling, it all looked foreign to me. I'll not be going back anyway, and don't worry I bought nowt because there was nowt I could afford in the shop.'

Jenny folded her arms and waited until she got her loaf of bread handed over to her. 'He's not going to be a threat to you anyway, it's far too posh. Working folk will not be giving him any trade whether his family is originally from Leeds or not.'

Meg didn't know whether to take the fact that his shop was not going to be a threat to her as a compliment or not. 'So, his family is from Leeds, are they?' she asked with interest.

'So I heard. His grandmother used to live out near Kirkstall near the iron forge and from what I understand, his mother ran away with an artist to Paris, of all the places, after leaving his father. That's why his baking is all foreign rubbish and that's why he's here living in his father's old house in Headingley. His father died two years ago and from what I've heard he left him a fortune.' Jenny folded her arms even tighter under her bust and breathed in. 'It always comes to those who don't need it. It'll never come to the likes of me and you, lass.'

'You hear a lot, Jenny, I don't know where you get all your news from. And unfortunately, you are right. I've nobody about to leave me a small fortune, else I wouldn't mind buying this place of Ted Lund.'

Jenny tucked her bread under her arm. 'If he's any sense he'd rent it to you,' she said. 'He'd make as much money with the rent as he did with his baking and wouldn't have the work. Let's face it, he's not keen on working. I've never known this bakery open as early as it has been of late and your baking is beyond beat.

Think about it, Meg; renting off him could be the answer to both your worries and it would be nice to still to come in and have these natters.

'Now, I must get back, I left my Jim with a mustard plaster on his chest. His breathing's been really laboured of late but not enough to stop him from cursing me if I don't get back. Ta-ra, see you in the morning.' With that, Jenny scuttled off down the street back to Jim and his bad chest.

Meg watched her go. Perhaps she was right — maybe she should ask Ted Lund if he would rent her the shop. After all, she had proved to herself that the shop was profitable, but asking him to rent it and him agreeing would be another thing, but it would be worth trying. After all, if you didn't ask in this world you didn't get.

Then reality hit her: he'd not rent it to her and besides, she hadn't got the money to rent it and never would have. She put a brave smile on her face as the next customer came in to be served. She was busy again and that was a good thing, it would stop her from daydreaming.

After closing at one, Meg decided to just take five minutes out of her day and quickly have a look at the new bakery on the Headrow. Curiosity was the main reason for her visit. Not one of her customers had said a good word about it, but she wanted to see for herself what it was like.

She stood across the other side of the street and watched people going in and out of the shop. They weren't her sort of customers — they were far more refined and better to-do. Ladies so well dressed that she swore she had never seen anything like them before, with spectacular hats and gloves to match, were visiting the shop and coming out with little white boxes tied with a string containing whatever had caught their eye. No wonder her customers had reacted like they had: this was for the well-to-do and more refined tastes. The confectionery, as it was called, was what Meg had only dreamed about making as she crossed the road and looked through the shop window.

She found herself pressing her nose closer and closer to the glass to see what was under the counter as well as what was on the shop's counter, not able to believe her eyes at the fancy pastries and overindulgent cakes. Her eyes rested on the St Honoré Cake, amazed at the pastry base with cherries glistening like jewels upon it, and then choux buns topped by white fluffy spoonfuls of meringue. They looked good enough for the queen herself to eat and was a million miles away from her baking. How she would love for someone to teach her the art of such baking, she thought, as she gazed into the shop window.

'You like what you see, my dear?' Frankie Pearson asked quietly as he stood on the steps of his shop trying to get a minute away from the heat of the bakery.

'I do. I'm fascinated, everything looks so decadent, I don't know hardly any of these cakes and they all look delicious,' Meg said and turned to look at the man standing next to her. He had blond hair and a kind face with blue eyes that were sparkling as he talked with a hint of a French accent. It was then she realized that he must be the owner of the shop and the baker as he was dressed in an apron and had the accent that some of her customers had commented upon.

'They are nothing really. I have made these many

161

times, but you have to make them with passion for your love to show within your baking.' Frankie smiled at the young woman fixated on his cakes.

'Yes, I know what you mean — if you are not in the mood for baking, it always goes wrong. You have to love what you are doing else it is better not starting anything.' Meg moved her gaze from the cake to the man who obviously thought the same way as her.

'Would you like to come in and see what else we have to tempt you?'

Meg shook her head. 'No, I'm afraid I have no money on me and even if I did I couldn't spare it on such delicacies. Although it is beautiful and I would if I could,' she said sadly and turned to walk away.

'No, don't go, wait there just a second.' Frankie disappeared into the bakery and she watched as one of the serving girls reached down into the shop window and took the St Honoré Cake from out of the window to cut a slice for a customer.

'Perhaps I can convince you to come back when you have some money in your pocket?' Frankie said and passed Meg her own little white box tied with string and smiled. 'I wish my baking to be for everyone to enjoy, not just the wealthy of Leeds. I aim to expand when the time is right and have a wider range of patisserie that will be attractive for everyone's pocket. Please take it and enjoy.'

'Oh, I couldn't, I should pay you!'

Meg blushed but couldn't resist taking the box from his hand.

'Your smile is enough and to know that if you had the money, you would be a customer. Now enjoy,' Frankie said and smiled at the girl with the bonny face. Even though she was dressed in rags, she was the most beautiful woman he had seen all day and he would have given her the whole cake if she had asked for it.

★ ★ ★

'And he gave it to you?' Agnes looked at the delicious cake that Meg had brought home with her.

'Yes, he wouldn't take a penny, which was good because I hadn't a penny on me,' Meg replied. 'You should see the shop, Mam, it is so beautiful with all sorts of cakes and fancies in the window. He's got three staff as well, all dressed in natty uniforms and their hair just so. It makes Ted's bakery look like something from out of the dark ages.' Meg passed her mother a spoon and smiled. 'Come on, we will share, there isn't enough for three, so what Sarah doesn't know about she won't miss.' Meg put her spoon into the cake and took the first mouthful, not even bothering to take it out of the card box. 'Oh Lord, it's heavenly. If only I could bake like this. I know nothing compared to this man.'

'You stop putting yourself down,' Agnes told her firmly. 'That bakery of Ted's has never been as busy, and that's a recognition of your skills. This is a different style of baking.' She closed her eyes while she tasted the meringue and choux pastry. 'Heavens, lass, you are right, it is heaven in a spoonful, but at a price, if what you tell me is right. He might have given you this slice but normal folk will never be able to buy it. You keep to the simple things — folk will always want them. He's no competition to you. You are as different as chalk and cheese but both as good at serving your sort of people. You are both needed in Leeds.'

'You might be right, but that doesn't stop me from being jealous,' Meg said. 'Now, quickly let's eat up and put the box on the fire before Sarah returns from school, else she won't half moan when she finds out that we didn't leave her any.'

'She's spoilt enough. I know you buy her the odd thing here and there. She should be thankful for having such a good sister. It'll not hurt her to miss out for once. She's growing up fast, thank heavens. Another few years and she'll be nearly a woman. I only hope that I'm here to see it.' Agnes looked across at her oldest with fondness.

'You will be, Mam, you are not going anywhere just yet.' But both Agnes and Meg knew that her words were hollow. Agnes was extremely ill, despite her good days, and her time was nearly at an end despite all the care and love that Meg lavished on her.

15

'What sort of day have you had at school, Sarah? You look tired out.'

Meg looked across the table at her younger sister while they were eating their supper of vegetable broth with one of Meg's crusty loaves.

'It was all right, just the usual,' Sarah said, not bothering to raise her head.

'I went and had a look at the new bakers on the Headrow this afternoon,' Meg told her, trying to engage Sarah in conversation. 'It's right posh, not for the likes of us. I don't know half the things Frankie Pearson makes but I'd like to try to make them.'

'It'll only be baking. That's all you think about, and it's all we ever hear about,' Sarah said and looked at her mother. 'Can I go up into town on my own on Saturday morning? Madiah Surith is visiting the music hall and I'd like to catch a glimpse of her as she arrives.' Sarah knew what the answer would be, but it was worth a try.

'You know I don't like you hanging around there,' Agnes said immediately. 'Swan Yard is not the place for a young woman your age. That music hall attracts all sorts of rum folk, folk you shouldn't be seen with.'

Seeing Sarah's face fall at the response, no matter how much she expected it, Agnes felt guilty. Her youngest hadn't been given much freedom of late.

'If you can wait until the afternoon, I'll go with you after I've closed the bakery and I'll walk down the market and leave you at the stage door for a while,'

Meg offered. 'Mam will be all right for an hour on her own, won't you, Mam?' It meant she could look into the patisserie again on their way down to Briggate and the market.

'Yes, both of you go, it will do you good to spend some time together,' Agnes said, glad that her two daughters were getting along better.

'I suppose I could make it the afternoon, but you would leave me there wouldn't you? You wouldn't stay?' Sarah asked sheepishly.

'No, your big sister will not embarrass you. I've never heard of this Madiah Surith, whoever she is, so I'll not be stopping hoping for a glance. I'd rather get the shopping for the week.'

'She dances with a six-feet-long python wrapped around her.' Sarah smiled, knowing that Meg hated snakes. 'She's really famous!'

'Then I will definitely be leaving you,' Meg replied. 'I don't want to see her or her snake. I'll leave you to it. I'll close as early as I can and then pick you up from home.'

The two girls sat quietly for the rest of the meal. Meg was thinking about her chance to look into the bakery window again and hopefully see the dashing Frankie while Sarah thought about her favourite place, outside the doors of the music hall.

* * *

Saturday came all too quickly for Meg. It was getting nearer and nearer the time that Ted Lund would be thinking about returning, which Meg was dreading. As promised, she closed the bakery on time and made her way back home to pick up Sarah to take her into

166

the centre of Leeds. She smiled; she'd had a profitable week again, and while she might not sell many fancy foods, what she did sell folk enjoyed.

'Are you ready, our Sarah? Let's get gone!' Meg shouted up the stairs as she emptied her basket of the weekend's bread onto the table and looked at her mother. 'Are you sure you will be all right for an hour? I'll not be long. How are you today?'

'I'll be all right, get yourselves gone.' Agnes looked up at the jar with the rent money in it as Meg placed her hard-earned wages within. 'Hold a bit back, Meg, we can just about afford it. On your way back, go into your fancy bakery and choose three fancies for us all. It can be a treat. We never have one and I feel guilty — we enjoyed that cake and Sarah didn't get a chance to share.'

'Are you sure, Mam? Isn't it a bit wasteful, especially when we struggle some days to make ends meet?' Meg felt she had to make the point.

'As they say, a bit of what you fancy does you good,' her mother said. 'Now go on, bring us all something back to enjoy. It will cheer us all up.'

Agnes smiled as she saw Meg's face light up. It wasn't just the cake that had caught her daughter's eye, she thought, as she watched Meg and Sarah walk out of the house together.

★　★　★

'You'll be all right if I leave you here?' Meg asked Sarah as she watched her looking at the poster that had been freshly pasted onto the billboard outside the music hall. On the poster, Madiah Surith was standing provocatively dressed in a scanty covering made with

167

jewels, a python in her hand and around her body. Its headline read A DARK AND PASSIONATE TASTE OF THE EXOTIC.

'Yes, I'll be all right, stop worrying. Doesn't she look marvellous — just look at all the jewels upon her, and the snake!' Sarah said as she admired the poster. 'I only hope that she appears while I'm waiting here.'

'She'll not look like that, you know. She couldn't really walk around Leeds with her belly button showing and just dressed in a skirt and top of jewels. She'd catch her death if nothing else,' Meg grinned.

'I know, I'm not that daft.' Sarah sat herself down on a wooden box outside the stage doors, ready to wait until somebody of notoriety came out of the music hall.

'Hey up, Sarah. Are you back again?' a lad in a flat cap said as he passed Sarah but she ignored him and hoped that Meg had not heard him as she walked away. She had been skipping school too often of late just to watch people come and go to the theatre. She knew it was only going to be a matter of time before her sins found her out. And then there would be hell to pay. But she hated school and she missed Harry's presence there.

Meg made her way around the market, buying the cheapest pieces of meat — some mutton, tripe and pigs liver — then made her way to the fruit stall where she bought apples from Mike, who asked her if she was all right, before visiting Roger Ingram on the vegetable stall. Roger had not delivered any more wood cast-offs since his proposal to her and she knew that he may have felt rejected by her answer to him.

'Afternoon, Roger, it's not a bad day. At least the sun is shining for you.' Roger tried to look busy, but didn't offer her his usual banter or smile. 'Aye, it's made for a busy day. Trade has been good. What can I get for you, Meg?'

'A pound of potatoes, a cabbage, a pound of onions and that's it for today,' Meg said and watched as he placed what she'd asked for in her basket and waited for his payment.

There was no offer of a few extra vegetables or asking if she wanted some wood delivering. It seemed obvious that Roger had washed his hands of her and her family as she passed him his payment. She felt sad as she walked away from the stall. She'd thought that they'd had a good friendship and now it would seem it was at an end.

Sarah had a wide beam on her face as Meg walked down the bustling Swan Yard.

'I've seen her, Meg, she looked so beautiful, but she was dressed just like me and you, and she didn't have her snake with her,' Sarah bubbled. 'You were right. But she did walk daintily, I'd love to see her dance.' Sarah glanced back at the poster as she kept up with her big sister.

'Well, I'd take you to see her but we haven't the money to spend on the music hall. As it is, our Mam has given me some extra money and she says we have to treat ourselves from the new bakery, so you will have to tell me what takes your eye. I've no doubt I'll regret buying anything from it when I find us short for the rent man knocking on the door on Friday. We only just can pay him as it is.'

'I'd rather you bought me a ticket than a fancy cake. One bite and it will be gone but I'll always have the memory of the music hall,' Sarah moaned as she followed her sister along the Headrow where they both

stopped and looked at that day's display in the patisserie window.

'Come on, there's more inside,' Meg said, then
warned her sister, 'Watch your manners, though, they
are snobby in here.'

She looked at her reflection in the shop window
and wished that she wasn't holding a basket of meat
and vegetables as a woman dressed in the latest fashion came out of the shop all grand and smelling of
perfume.

Sarah stood and looked at the cakes through the
glass of the counter and could feel her mouth drib-
bling as she looked at the various confectionery, the
likes of which she had never seen before.

'Well, what do you fancy? I think I'll take Mam
and me a vanilla slice each,' Meg decided. 'They look
lovely. That just leaves you, Sarah, still making your
mind up.'

Meg smiled at Norah behind the counter as she
lifted the stand with the slices out of the display to put
them in the usual white box.

'I'll have one of them, whatever they are,' Sarah
said, pointing to a long finger of pastry filled with
cream and covered with chocolate. 'They look lovely!
Why don't you bake things like this?'

'Because this baking is special and besides I don't
know the recipe for that pastry but I'd like to find
out how to make it,' Meg told her as Norah boxed
the éclair up along with the vanilla slices. They were
going to be a real treat, she thought, as she found the
money to pay for them and felt quite guilty at spending the amount of money on three cakes that would
be eaten in a matter of seconds.

'Ah, I thought I recognized the voice,' came a man's

170

voice from behind her. 'It's the lady who was admiring my cakes the other day. I told you that you would be back. My creation was good? Did you enjoy every last morsel?'

Meg turned and looked at Frankie, the man that she admired just as much as his baking. 'Yes, it was delightful. My mother shared it with me and asked us to return today so that my young sister could also try your baking.'

'Ah, so this is your sister,' Frankie said, smiling at Sarah. 'She is going to enjoy the chocolate éclair, that I can tell.'

'Our Meg would like to know how you make the pastry,' Sarah spouted up, much to Meg's surprise. 'She doesn't know and if she did, she would make things just as good in her bakery.'

'Sarah, hush, you shouldn't ask that and I can't bake half as well as Mr Pearson. He's a professional chef, you can tell,' Meg said sternly to her sister.

'You have a bakery?' Frankie asked Meg and looked at her with a different kind of interest from before.

'It's not mine,' Meg explained. 'I'm just minding it until Ted Lund, my boss, returns from his trip to Ireland. I just bake the simple things that everyday folk like, it's not special like yours.'

'Where are you in Leeds? Nearby?' Frankie asked.

'The bakery is on York Street,' Meg said. 'It's not half as grand as yours, and in fact, it is a little run-down, if I'm honest.' She looked down, feeling embarrassed.

'That does not matter if your heart is in your baking just as mine is,' Frankie told her. 'It's the love that makes the difference, my dear.' Frankie smiled. 'Enjoy your éclair and vanilla slices, it has been nice to see

171

you yet again.'

Frankie watched the two sisters leave. He hadn't wanted to be asked for his recipe for eclairs now he knew the girl who made his heart beat that little bit faster was a rival.

* * *

'When did you and my mam have one of his cakes? You never got me one then,' Sarah moaned as Meg walked quickly homeward.

'It was only half a slice of a fancy cake from out of the window that he gave me and I shared it with our Mam,' Meg told her. 'There wasn't enough for three. Anyway, you've got your own now, so stop whinging.'

Meg could have sworn at her young sister for telling Frankie Pearson she was also a baker. She would never ever class herself as within the same trade as him. In fact, she wished her heart didn't miss a beat every time she looked at his face. Both he and his baking were far out of her reach. In future, she'd try to keep away from the patisserie, away from temptations of the sweet kind.

172

16

'Who on earth is that knocking on the door at this time of day?' Agnes complained. 'It's when decent folk sit down and eat of an evening and there they are banging on the door loud enough to break it.' Mother and daughters had just sat down for their Monday evening's supper.

'I'll get it, Mam, you stay still,' Meg said. 'Whoever it is, they won't want much.'

Meg left Sarah and Agnes eating their supper and opened the door out onto the front yard.

'Oh, Meg, it's you, I need to talk to your mother. It is quite important and I will not be brushed off with you saying that she's not in.' Miss Pringle, Sarah's headmistress, was standing on the doorstep, looking angry and determined. She was a sharp-faced lady, clad in a sharp tight-cut skirt and spotless blouse, her spectacles perched on her nose.

'Miss Pringle, I wasn't about to say she was not in. Please, whatever is wrong or if there is something we can do for you, come in and tell us within our home, not on the step for all our neighbours to hear.' Meg opened the door wide and let the stern headmistress into their family home.

'I'm sorry, I appear to have arrived at an inconvenient moment, but this cannot wait another day or week longer,' Miss Pringle said, realizing she'd interrupted the meal. 'It has been going on for the last two months and I at least deserve more respect than you seem to be giving me, not to mention the lack of

173

Sarah's education.'

All eyes turned to look at Sarah, but nobody said anything. She hung her head, knowing already what was going to be said by the headmistress.

'I'm afraid because you have ignored the letters that I have sent home with Sarah and because her attendance has not improved, I have decided that I have no other alternative but to say that she is no longer welcome at our school. I'm sorry but I've no alternative. Before she started her non-attendance, her behaviour was disturbing the rest of the class. She really does try my patience.' Miss Pringle spat her words out as if she had been building them up for weeks as she looked at Sarah. Wisely, Sarah said nothing.

Meg looked at her mother and didn't know whether to reply on her behalf or not. She felt partly responsible, but Sarah was her mother's responsibility.

Agnes folded her arms and sighed. At the moment the lass was pushing her to her limits.

'Sarah, go up to your bedroom, I'll talk to you later,' she said, not even looking at her daughter, who pushed her still-full dinner plate to one side and climbed the stairs to the shared bedroom, fully aware of what was about to be said and her mother's reaction.

'Now, Miss Pringle, let us start this conversation again please,' Agnes said calmly. 'Would you like a cup of tea, while you tell me what my youngest has been up to because I've never received a letter or notice of any kind from you?'

Meg offered the teacher a chair and placed a cup in front of her but she gestured with her hand that a cup of tea was not wanted.

'Sarah has not attended school for the last two weeks. She did bother turning up for the odd day or two a few weeks before. That is when I sent a letter to inform you of her lack of attendance and her disruptive behaviour in class. She will not listen or partake in any of the lessons and just causes the rest of the class to misbehave when she does appear.' Miss Pringle sighed. 'By the look on the both of your faces, I take it she never gave you the letters, am I right?'

'No, she certainly did not,' Agnes told her. 'Else she would have had a right good squaring up. This lass is going to be the death of me, the way she carries on. As you can see, Miss Pringle, I'm not a well woman. Perhaps that is influencing her behaviour, and she already has lost her father, as you know. However, that's no reason for me to be lenient with her. She's going to have the sharp edge of my tongue — but before that, may I ask that you reconsider your decision. She will be attending school from now on.' Agnes caught her breath and looked at Meg before continuing. 'After all, another four months and she will be eleven. She can leave then if she is still determined to join the hard world of work. If she can find employment, she will realize then that school days are the best years of her life. Unlike some, I was hardly schooled and I have lived to regret it all my life.'

Meg looked at the teacher. 'I think this has started because my mother has got worse of late and she is no longer able to work, so I am working at the bakery, leaving early in the morning. Sarah is left to see herself to school, which we thought she was doing. Plus she is missing Harry from next door, they used to go to school together.'

'Now that was a pairing that tested me,' Miss Pringle admitted. 'I was glad, although I shouldn't say it, when Harry's mother took him out of school. I even overlooked that he was too young to do so.' Miss Pringle sat quietly for a moment, pondering. Then she looked at Agnes and Meg. 'Now, because I know that you didn't realize she was not at school, I'm willing to reconsider and take her back. But, the first sign of her not attending then I don't want her back — and I want a better attitude from her. Other children have just the same problems. At least Sarah is loved and cared for. Some of my children are treated nothing better than animals and are hardly dressed and fed. School for them is a refuge and they are willing to learn.' Miss Pringle pushed back her chair and looked around the sparsely furnished room. 'Make sure she's at school tomorrow and this will be the last of it until she leaves.'

'I thank you, Miss Pringle. She's not a bad girl really, just a little selfish, like all children can be.' Agnes sat back in her chair feeling weary with life and silently fuming over her disobedient daughter.

'I'm sorry I brought bad news to your door and have given you more worry,' Miss Pringle said, then smiled at Meg. 'I've heard that you're making Ted Lund's bakery a success while he is away. You were always a bright girl. It's a shame your sister doesn't take after you.'

'She's bright in other ways,' Meg said, feeling the need to defend her sister. 'She likes needlework and dancing but she's not good with schoolwork. Everybody has a skill within them somewhere.' She guided the teacher to the door.

'Indeed, let us hope that it's not too late for Sarah to realize that you need a basic education to get you through life and that she's lucky that she was born when she was. A few years ago at her age she would

176

have been working in one of the mills risking her life cleaning under the spinning machines. Now, I'll wish you a good evening and I hope to see Sarah at school tomorrow.'

Meg closed the door behind the teacher and leaned back against the door and looked at her mother. 'Why can't she just behave, Mam? I wish I was back at school, instead of working all these unearthly hours . . . and what has she been doing if she's not been at school?'

'I don't know, Meg, but we are about to find out,' Agnes said quietly then yelled out as loud as her voice would let her. 'Sarah, get your arse down here, else by God for the first time in my life I will come up with the belt that hangs behind the kitchen door and put it across your backside. And don't think I'm not strong enough because at this moment I want to do just that if it's the last thing I ever do.'

Sarah walked down the stairs, tears running down her cheeks but her face defiant. She sat back down at the table and sobbed.

'Well, I know you heard every word! What have you got to say for yourself? Is she right in what she says?' Agnes glared at her daughter. She felt too ill to have to deal with this, but she had to if she was to keep Sarah in school.

'I hate school, Mam. I just hate it and that old bag just picks on me. I want to leave. I'm not learning any-thing there, and I might as well be making us some money.' Sarah sobbed and sniffed.

'You might not like school, but I'm not breaking the law by bringing you out of it. You've to stay until you are eleven. That's just a few months away and then you'll be leaving soon enough. It's no fun in this grown-up world, Sarah; you work until you drop so

177

don't be so quick to want to join it. Now, where have you been going, that's what I want to know!'

Agnes folded her arms and waited for the answer. Sarah's sobbing died down. She knew she would have to answer.

'Some days, I've just sat outside the music hall in Swan Yard, watching the performers coming in and out, and some days I go down to the Cut and share my sandwiches with Harry,' she said and dared to look up at her mother and Meg to see what they say.

'Lord above, I would have had a fit!' her mother said. 'Anybody could have picked you up — you could have been taken to join the local circus for all I'd have known. And I should have known that bloody Harry would have something to do with it!' Agnes threw her hands up into the air. 'When are you going to learn to keep away from that lad? Every time he gets you into bother and yet you defy me by trailing about with him. He had to leave school, his father's a drunk and his mother is no better than those that raise their skirts down at the Cut. I suppose it could be worse — you could be one of them, but thank the Lord you are not quite that age yet.'

Agnes put her hand on her chest and gasped for breath.

'Mam, calm down, she's all right, nowt has happened to her,' Meg put in. 'She's here, not hurt and in one piece. She's just been bunking off school, and now we both know, we can do something about it.' Meg scowled at Sarah. 'You know I trusted you; I get up at three every morning to work in that bakery just to bring home money for us all to live on. All you've got to do is make sure Mam is all right in the morning and then go to school. Even your sandwich in your bait box is ready for you to take to school each morning. You are spoilt, Sarah, that's the top and bottom of it.'

'I'm not spoilt!' Sarah wailed. 'We have nothing. I wear your hand-me-downs and my shoes leak, how can I be spoilt!'

'You go to school tomorrow, even if I have to drag you there myself, madam!' Agnes told her. 'But for now, get yourself to bed before I say something I might regret.'

Sarah looked at her uneaten supper but Agnes's heart had hardened for now against her clearly unrepentant daughter. 'You can leave that and all. Happen if you go to bed hungry you will realize just how hard it is for your sister to earn the money to keep you fed. You can finish it for your supper tomorrow night.'

Sarah dropped her spoon in her supper and pulled a face as she pushed her chair back. 'I hate you both, I hate school and I hate living in this house. I wish someone had pinched me for the circus!' she yelled as she stomped up the stairs to her bed.

'Oh Meg, I don't know what to do with that lass. You were never this bother.' Agnes lowered her head, feeling tired and worn out with the conflict that Sarah had brought. 'It will be all right, Mam, she'll have calmed down by the morning. She's just angry that she's been found out. Perhaps the sooner she can leave school the better, then she can earn her own way in the world,' Meg said and hugged her mother. 'She'll only spend it all on herself when she does, like she did the rent money, selfish little minx,' Agnes maintained. 'She just doesn't understand the hardships we are going through. She would be better working but she needs an education; I'll not have her leaving school with nothing in her head.

'I'll go up to my bed and make sure that she's all right. I can hear her sobbing, and she is right — she's not got much in her life really.'

As she climbed the stairs, Agnes felt as if she had let both of her girls down. Neither had good prospects in their lives, nothing to look forward to except hunger and poverty. That was a bad inheritance, she thought.

She sat herself down on the bed next to her youngest. 'You know, Sarah, both Meg and I love you so much. All we do is for the love of you.' She stroked Sarah's hair as she sobbed curled up in a ball with her back to her. 'You'll promise me that you'll go to school tomorrow and that you'll stay there until your birthday. It's not far away now, you haven't long to wait, and then we will have to find you somewhere to work. Don't be in a rush to grow up. Harry has had to and it will make him a hard man.

'Now promise me school in the morning!' Agnes hugged her daughter.

'I promise, Mam, I'm sorry. I bunked off for a day or two and then I couldn't stop myself from taking other days off,' Sarah said, without daring to look at her mother's face.

'We'll leave it at that then, but don't let me down again. I'm an ill woman and I could do without this worry. I only send you to school because I want you to be strong after my day is done. You and Meg will have to be there for one another when I'm not around,' Agnes said gently. 'Now, go to sleep, and tomorrow morning we'll start afresh.'

Agnes kissed her on her brow and pulled the covers over her. But she knew her words would only be heeded for so long and then Sarah would slip back into her selfish ways, just like her true father.

From under the covers Sarah asked. 'What did you mean that Harry's mother is always lifting her skirts like the women down at the Cut?' She'd been pondering about it since her mother had said it and wondered why her mother was so against it.

'It means she goes with men down there, Sarah. She's no morals. That's what happens to lasses who don't get an education: they've to rely on their men and not all men are worth much,' Agnes said quietly.

'Oh, I just wondered,' Sarah said and wondered even more about what was so wrong about going with men as her mother left the bedroom.

17

Frankie Pearson stood next to Brenda Jones listening to her give an account of the first few weeks of trading and how his staff had coped. He knew from his takings that things could be better and, unbeknown to Brenda, he was already thinking that the shop could run without her being there and save him money.

'You know, Mr Pearson, if you don't mind me saying, a lot of the customers, ordinary everyday folk are coming in and just not buying anything. Your pastries are too fancy for them and they just can't afford the price.' Brenda then noticed the look upon Frankie's face and quickly added, 'They are worth every penny but perhaps the folk of Leeds are not quite ready for them.'

'I thank you for your comments, Mrs Jones, I too have heard a voice or two saying that my creations are a little too expensive for the common man's pocket,' Frankie replied. 'However, there are plenty of other everyday bakeries that they can go to for a less specialised fare. If they have any taste buds at all they will shop here before wasting their hard-earned money on tasteless bread and days-old scones.' Frankie knew he sounded defensive but the patisserie was his new baby and he knew with time it would grow with popularity.

'You know, I've heard the bakery on York Street mentioned a lot as customers have gone out of the door,' Brenda pointed out. 'All the ones who don't buy anything seem to plan to visit there after coming to us. I don't know what it is like, I don't tend to walk the backstreets of Leeds. I come here to work and then return by train to Harrogate. Leeds' backstreets are not for the faint-hearted, I have heard.' Brenda Jones looked down her nose and her facial expression made her views of the less salubrious streets of Leeds obvious to her employer even if her words hadn't.

'York Street . . . ' mused Frankie. 'Now, that pretty slip of a girl who came in with her sister runs a bakery in York Street if I remember rightly. Her young sister told me when they came to buy a cake. In fact, she wanted to know how I made the choux pastry but I ignored the question and told her that I had work to return to. It's perhaps as well as I did; her sister could have been serious opposition then. Like a fool, I felt sorry for her when she was looking through the window and gave her a free slice of St. Honoré cake and then she returned and bought what she did.'

'Well, she, it seems, is your opposition,' Brenda replied. 'Even Norah and Marie have heard about her baking skills. I heard them talking about her the other day. Their mothers both buy from off her — you'd think that they would support you, Mr Pearson. They spend plenty of time giggling and carrying on when you brush past them with the baking,' she added with a sardonic note in her voice.

Frankie was quiet for a moment, then said, 'I think now I've finished the main baking, I'll pay this bakery on York Street a visit. Just to see what opposition she really is.'

Brenda's face showed her disgust at the thought of her employer walking in streets she considered filled with vermin of all kinds, human and otherwise. 'Very well, Mr Pearson, if you think that's wise,' she replied. 'I'm sure that she can never give you any problem.

Your patisserie is far superior to any other bakery that I know.'

'Perhaps that's the problem,' Frankie said thoughtfully. 'Maybe we are a little too posh for a lot of people. Anyway, we will see. I'll be back in about an hour. I am sure you will manage without me.'

Frankie stepped out onto the busy high street and made for York Street. He didn't know exactly what he was going to do when he got to the bakery that he'd heard was booming. Perhaps he'd just watch and see what custom she really did have for a while, then perhaps enter the shop and ask to see the girl who had taken his fancy long before he knew that she could bake. He felt conflicted: he was excited at seeing the girl who he had found attractive on both their meetings, but at the same time he was worried that her business was affecting his.

There was a queue of four people outside Ted Lund's bakery as Frankie leaned against a terraced house wall across from the shop. He watched people come and go, and all seemed to be happy as they left, after buying what they wanted and passing the time of the day with whoever was serving on behind the shop's counter. Her clientele was definitely not as well-to-do as his, Frankie thought, just as he had expected. He saw women in shawls and clogs on their feet leave the shop, some with children at their sides, others sending their young children to shop for them. What this lass lacked in wealth she had in numbers, he thought, as he listened to the banter between neighbours and customers.

'Are you waiting to go in? Or are you just thinking about it?' asked an elderly woman who had just come out of the shop. Her basket was full of bread and other

184

baking that had taken her fancy. 'It is the best bakery for miles around at the moment. Everyone is hoping that Ted Lund never returns, else it will go back to his rubbish. Meg is such a grand lass, she works so hard. He'll hardly be paying her anything for all the hours she's putting in and he'll not know what he's got in her.'

'I'm going to pay her a visit when the queue has died down,' Frankie replied. 'Do you say her name is Meg?'

'Aye, Meg Fairfax — she's a local lass. I'd get going; look there's only Mrs Birbeck in the queue now and she'll not want a lot. Go while she's quiet,' the old woman prompted, leaving him to disappear into one of the terraces that lined both sides of the street.

Frankie saw Meg tidying the shelves within the shop as her last shopper left. He took a deep breath, not knowing what he was exactly going to say to her now he knew just how popular she was.

He raised his hat as he entered the shop. 'Good morning, my dear. I thought I would visit you for a change. I keep hearing about this bakery and I took it upon myself to look at it with my own eyes.' He smiled as she turned from tidying her batch of newly baked bread and caught her breath.

Meg felt the colour rise to her cheeks both at the sight of Frankie standing on the other side of the counter and at the thought of him visiting her scruffy bakery in the backstreets.

She looked bashfully at Frankie. 'Good morning, thank you for coming,' she said finally. 'I'm afraid, as I said, it is not a patch on your bakery. For a start we still have the original coal and wood ovens, not like your gas ones. And as you can see, the bakery's setting is not exactly salubrious.'

'You know that I have gas ovens, how so?' Frankie asked as he looked around at the shelves stacked with scones, teacakes, sponges and bread.

'I'm friends with Daisy Truelove,' Meg explained. 'Her brother John works in the planning office and he told me — only because he knew I had started to work here and it just came up in conversation.'

'Ah, that John, yes he was impressed but I think he is impressed with anything that he thinks is progress,' Frankie replied wryly. 'Sometimes progress is not a good thing; sometimes the old ways are the best. For instance, just look at the baking you have done here — it looks truly delicious.

'I think perhaps it is time I introduced myself. My name is Pearson, Frankie Pearson, and I am just as much in awe of your bakery as you are of mine. Do you do all this on your own?'

Meg felt her heart miss a beat as she replied. 'I'm Meg, Meg Fairfax, and yes I bake all this and run the shop, just until the owner Ted Lund returns . . . and then I will have to see what he wants to do.' Her eyes looked straight into his and she felt her stomach churn.

'Everyone tells me good things about the bakery on York Street, so I thought that it was time to come and see what exactly you did. I did not put two and two together originally that it was you but when I realized, that made me all the more determined to give you a visit. I'm glad that I did now. The bakery is beautiful, the smell is wonderful, and just look at your bread — you put mine to shame.'

'Oh no, really mine is just simple baking, yours is an art. Your pastries are delicious. If only I was half as good, I'd be happy!'

'Well, Meg, may I take four of your scones, they look delicious,' Frankie said. 'I will treat my staff for their lunch, it will make a change for them.' He saw the worry on Meg's face as she chose the best four scones from the shelf for him to take back with him. 'They all look wonderful, *ma cherie*,' he said as she placed them in a paper bag and passed them across to him. 'How much do I owe you?'

'You gave me a slice of your cake so I should not charge you at all for them,' Meg said, 'but this is not my bakery, so I will have to ask for tuppence if you don't mind.'

'Honest as well as a good baker. I hope this Ted Lund knows just what he has got in you. Here take my money and don't worry about it, my dear.'

Meg took the money and smiled and said, 'Can I ask why you called me Ma Sherry especially now you know my name is Meg?'

Frankie gave a little laugh. 'It is a French expression. It is part of my French upbringing, as well as my slight accent. I just automatically say it when I see a beautiful woman. It means 'my dear', and is a term of endearment — but if you do not wish for me to call you it, I won't. From now on I'll call you Meg, now I know your true name.'

Meg could feel her cheeks ablaze as she looked at Frankie. Had he just called her beautiful? 'No, no, it is fine, I was just curious. I'm afraid I don't know French, my education was limited,' Meg said feeling stupid.

'Not when it comes to baking though, with that I can tell you excel,' Frankie said hastily, not wanting in any way to offend her. 'I wonder — and please say no, if you prefer not to — would you like to visit my bakery? I can show you the new ovens and the rooms that I hope to soon be turning into tea rooms. I could also show you how to make the choux pastry that you showed an interest in, if you wish.'

Meg was silent and he hastily added, 'I promise I'll behave if that is what you are worrying about.'

He hunched his shoulders and waited for a reply. He knew now that his bakery and that of Ted Lund's were like chalk and cheese with completely different cuisine. Giving Meg his recipe for choux buns would not hurt his business. Choux pastries would not sell in these backstreets. But he also knew that he could make use of Meg Fairfax if she ever left Ted Lund and besides she was a beautiful young woman that he recognized he was slightly smitten with.

'Oh, I don't know, your shop is always that busy,' Meg said eventually. 'What would your staff think?' She tried not to let it show how much she really wanted to go, not so much to see the ovens but to see how choux pastry was made.

'They can think what they like,' Frankie said. 'If it's them you are worried about, why don't you visit one evening when the shop is closed? Perhaps that would work better for both of us?'

'Yes, that would be better. I nurse my mother when I am at home, she's rather ill at the moment, but my sister will be with her of an evening.'

'The outspoken one! Although she stuck up for you like a sister should.' Frankie laughed again but became serious. 'I'm sorry that your mother is ill — nothing too serious I hope?'

He saw the sadness come into Meg's eyes.

'I'm afraid it is. It's the wasting sickness. I don't

think we will have her for much longer,' Meg replied and had to take a deep breath to maintain her composure.

'Oh, I'm sorry. Then it will do you good to come and forget your worries for an evening. How about Saturday evening? All my staff go home early and it will be Sunday the following morning, a day for us both to relax.' As he waited for her reply, Frankie thought how beautiful Meg was despite her worn-out clothes and the tatty surroundings of the unloved bakery.

Meg looked bashful. 'I don't know, we would be alone . . . but I would like to.'

'I promise I will be the perfect gentleman. I will leave the door open so you may leave at any time,' he said reassuringly. 'Besides, it would not do my reputation any good at all if I were to do anything. You could soon ruin my business if word got round that I behaved like that. Do come, I want to share my dreams with someone who understands the love of baking.'

It was that which made up Meg's mind. 'Then I'll come. What time?' Meg asked as he turned to the door. Customers were waiting outside to be served but no one had wanted to interrupt Meg and this fancy-looking gentleman.

'Six o'clock, Meg, I'll be waiting,' Frankie said as he walked out of the door.

Meg's next customer had a grin on her face as she entered. 'Oh Meg, have you gone and got yourself a fella? He sounds foreign to me. You can't trust foreigners, you know, I'd be careful.'

'I think I can trust this one, Mrs Bailey, he seems a good man,' Meg said, unable to contain her excitement about her meeting on Saturday evening.

'Aye well, they all seem to be good men, until you marry 'em and then you find out what they are really like,' Mrs Bailey said dourly, but Meg just smiled and passed her the bread she always asked for.

18

'You need to be careful, our Meg. Going into a closed shop with a man on your own and a foreigner to boot. He might be a good baker but you know nowt else about him.'

Agnes looked at her daughter but knew no matter what she said, she would not deter her daughter from her meeting with Frankie Pearson. She'd not even asked her if she would be all right left with just Sarah, her daughter was that determined upon her meeting.

'He's not a foreigner, he's as English as me and you, his name tells you that. It's only his accent that's foreign with him being brought up in France. And he's promised he'll leave the door open.' Meg looked at herself in the mirror and thought how plain she looked compared to some of the fine ladies that she had seen coming in and out of his bakery.

'Well, I'll not rest until you are back. You take care,' Agnes said as she watched Meg leave the house and noticed the smell of rose water on her and how excited she seemed at the prospect of meeting Frankie Pearson. Perhaps it was her imagination but perhaps there was more to it than just a visit to see his bakery.

★ ★ ★

Meg walked with a purpose to Frankie's bakery. Leeds was busy with people returning home after a hard day's work, and the horse trams were filled to the rafters with workers and shoppers. She bustled her way along the street and held her breath as she stood in the doorway of the patisserie. The window was empty, all the cakes had been put away for the following day. She was a little early, she thought, as the church clock struck six and she looked at her reflection.

'Well good evening, Mr Pearson. I'll be with you bright and early on Monday morning. The girls have left everything tidy — after being prompted may I add,' Brenda Jones noted as she stepped down onto the street and suddenly turned to see Meg standing in front of her. 'I think you'll find the bakery is closed for the day,' she said, looking Meg up and down with an air of superiority.

'Thank you, but I have come to see Mr Pearson,' Meg said and looked up to see Frankie standing in the doorway.

'Really . . . ? On business I suppose!' Brenda Jones looked up at Frankie and in a terse voice said 'Good evening' and then left with her head held high on her walk down to the main station.

'I don't think she thinks you should be seeing me,' Meg said as Frankie held the door open for her to walk inside the bakery.

'She can think what she likes. I sometimes wonder why I ever employed her. She is nothing but an old dragon but she came recommended to me and I was in a hurry to find good staff.

'I'm glad that you have made it and that is all that matters, Meg. You see I've even used your name this evening to put you at ease,' Frankie grinned.

Meg smiled back at him, although secretly, now she knew what ma cherie meant, she would have preferred that.

'Now, before I take you into the bakery, let me show

you the rooms upstairs,' Frankie continued. 'You already have seen the shop, but just wait until you see the space upstairs. I think that it would make the most wonderful tea rooms: the windows overlook the Head-row and people would be entertained for hours just looking at the business carried out along the street as they drink tea and eat cake.' Frankie walked past the counter and started to climb the stairs and noticed that Meg was hanging back. 'Don't worry, my intentions are honourable. It's not a bedroom up here! It's just an empty room in need of some attention before I put my plans into action. I am just excited with what I could do once I am properly established, just as you are now with running the bakery while Ted Lund is away.' He smiled and let Meg follow him up the stairs in her own time.

'I think this used to be a coaching inn and belonged to the Horse and Trumpet next door. It will have seen some comings and goings over time,' Frankie said as he reached the top of the stairs and walked across the bare-boarded room. 'My vision is to have tables with chequered tablecloths on them just like in Paris, and pot plants and perhaps a nice William Morris wallpaper on the walls. The smell from the bakery downstairs would fill the room and my customers could order whatever pastries that they fancied from a glass counter over on that side of the room.'

Meg relaxed as she saw Frankie's eyes light up as he thought of his plans coming to life.

'Yes, I can see it all now. You are right, people would love to sit in this window and gaze out at others going about their business without seeming to be nosy. It would be delightful. I could even see my own baking selling well in here, the classier end, of course.' Meg stood with her back against the window and looked around her, seeing Frankie's vision unfold in front of her own eyes. 'I wish the bakery I work in was my own, I too could do so much more with it if given a chance.'

'Ah, well, stranger things have happened,' Frankie replied. 'Perhaps Ted Lund could be persuaded to sell you it on his return? You never know!'

'Even if he did, I couldn't afford to buy it,' Meg admitted. 'We can hardly clothe and feed ourselves, let alone go into business.'

Frankie's eyes were now full of sympathy. 'One day, things will change, I'm sure. I can tell that you will not always be poor. You have too much spirit and fight in you. I can tell you will succeed in life.

'But as for now, let me show you how to make choux pastry . . . just as long as you don't start selling it in your shop, or even worse, sell it and undercut me with the price! My customers think that it is a special French recipe and is exotic. I want them to keep on thinking that.'

Frankie laughed as he walked back down the stairs and went into the back of the shop to the bakery, Meg following him.

'Oh no, I'd never do that,' Meg promised. 'My customers probably wouldn't appreciate it anyway — they like plain things to eat.'

Frankie opened his arms out wide as Meg looked around the bakery they'd entered. 'These, my dear, are my beautiful new ovens and my clean tiled bakery. It has cost me a great deal of money but it's worth every penny.'

Meg looked around her in disbelief at the well-stocked kitchen. It was everything she had ever dreamt of. The new ovens looked spotless compared to the old red brick ones at Ted Lund's. They were shiny black and made of wrought iron. There was no fire under the large ovens, just gas pipes, where the burner had to be lit every day. They were clean and gleamed just like the rest of the kitchen.

'How lovely, no need to stoke a fire up each morning,' Meg exclaimed. 'Oh, it must make life so much easier. And look at all your walls and shelves. I'm so jealous of that long table that you have to work with . . . and is that what you cook on? Is it one of those fancy cookers that I've heard of ?' 'It is.' Frankie reached into his pocket and brought out a large box of lucifers. 'Watch, I've just to turn the gas on like so, light a match and the flame is ignited so that I can put on a pan or a kettle whenever I want to. There is a small oven below that I will be using to cook what I make tonight. The only thing is you have to be quick, else the gas soon escapes, and if you didn't light it, there would be an explosion. It smells as well — no doubt you can smell it in the air now — but it soon goes.'

'My mam said you'd blow yourself up with it,' Meg told him. 'She doesn't like the use of gas, mainly because she remembers the riots it caused in Leeds when I was still small. The gas stokers ran riot along York Street after their meeting in the hall. I can still remember the noise of the fighting between them and the soldiers that were brought in to calm things. My mam always says it was a stand for the little man when the gas stokers won their grievances over the hours that they worked, but she's always been suspicious of gas since then.'

'Well, I've no complaints as of yet. I'll see how it

works out for me in the future; it is early days yet and I've not blown myself or anyone else up. Now, have I to show you how to make choux pastry and make some plain eclairs for you?'

'Yes, I'd be ever so grateful. I promise not to bake it for my shop but I would like to know how you make it. I've never eaten anything like it before.'

Meg noticed bowls with ingredients already inside them. Frankie had obviously been confident that she was going to keep to their arrangement.

'Look, it's as easy as this. You place a quarter of a pint of water and two ounces of butter in a pan and melt together gently at first and then bring to boil.' Frankie lit one of the burners on the top of the stove and Meg noticed the flame beneath the pan glow white and yellow and smelt the pungency of the gasses in the air. 'Once it is boiling, take it off the heat and stir in four ounces of flour and stir quickly until it forms a ball.' Frankie showed Meg the yellow blob of half-made pastry in the bottom of the bowl and then put it to one side to cool for a while. 'Do you want to whip some cream for the middle? I have some in a bowl here waiting for you. We have to wait for the mixture to cool before I add the eggs.' He passed Meg a bowl full of cream and a whisk.

Meg smiled. She was enjoying her time with Frankie — it was good to be with someone with a passion for baking just like her. She whisked until her arm ached and the white cream had formed soft peaks within the bowl.

'That will be perfect, Meg.' He took the cooled pan and contents, adding three lightly beaten eggs into the mixture a little at a time. 'This is the hard bit — you have to beat it until it is smooth and if the water hasn't previously boiled, your pastry will be too thin.' Frankie tipped the pan on its side and beat with all his might until the pastry was perfectly formed. 'There, it's as easy as that. Now all we do is put it into a piping bag and make eclairs or profiteroles. Tonight we will make eclairs and fill them with the cream then cover them with the chocolate I am about to melt upon the stove- top and then you can take them home to your mama and that sister of yours to enjoy.'

'I would never have thought that you made it that way; I really appreciate you showing me how,' Meg said. 'But really I can't take all these home — you'll lose your profits for the week.' She watched as the filled piping bag left perfect shapes of eclairs on an already greased baking tray and Frankie placed them into the oven to bake.

'Nonsense, they are my treat, Meg, I've enjoyed your company. They don't take long in the oven — about twenty minutes — and then we will have to wait for them to cool before we add the cream and chocolate coating.

'Now tell me a bit about yourself while we are waiting. All I know of you is that you have a love of baking, a cheeky sister and an ill mother. There must be more to you than that?' Frankie looked at Meg with a twinkle in his eye. He couldn't help but feel besotted by her looks and ways.

'No, that's about my life, apart from my work for Ted Lund, which I don't think I will have on his return,' Meg told him. 'He will not be that happy that I have introduced some new recipes to his bakery since he went on his visit. So I'm not expecting for him to keep me on.'

'But you have made him money, which I can tell

because I know that you have more visitors than any other bakery along those backstreets,' Frankie countered. 'My staff and I hear your bakery mentioned nearly every day at our shop. I will be honest, I came partly as a spy the other day — I needed to know what you were baking and if you were a threat to me.' Frankie smiled at the startled look on Meg's face.

'I'm no threat to you, my baking is so much simpler,' Meg replied.

'But it is still delicious. Perhaps I should be following your example, especially if I was to open upstairs up as a tea room,' Frankie said and watched Meg's reaction.

'Then you would be stealing my trade . . . although in another week or two if I'm no longer working there, I won't be bothered. I say that, but I really can't afford to lose my job with Ted Lund so I hope that I will be worried about what you get up to and that he keeps me on.'

She determined to change the subject. 'What about you?' she asked. 'Where do you come from? My mother didn't like the idea of me being alone with you this evening — she had heard that you were foreign.' Frankie grinned at her. His smile was so beguiling, she thought.

'I'm no more foreign than you are,' he told her. 'My mother and father were both from Leeds, both artists who followed and lived their passions. My mother left my father to follow her heart and went to Paris to follow her latest love and her ideals and took me with her. My father lived in Headingley until his death and it was then that I decided to return to my true home, so I am as local as you are. Now that may disappoint or might be to my advantage in your eyes. I've never been married, never had the time, and I have never met the right girl as of yet! And you — do you have a beau and would he be angry if he knew you were here with me this evening?' He hoped that her answer would be no. Even though he hardly knew the lass next to him, he felt something within him that he'd never felt before.

'No, I've nobody special in my life,' Meg said, somewhat to Frankie's relief. 'I'd rather keep myself to myself. My mam keeps trying to marry me off to who she thinks are reliable men. She's frightened I'll be on my own after she's left this life but she shouldn't worry. I'll cope without a man. Especially a man who I didn't love.' Meg blushed as she saw the interest on Frankie's face. She felt her heart beating faster. Frankie's good looks and ways had her heart captivated if he did but know it.

'We are both married to our baking then? Until that someone special comes along?' Frankie looked into Meg's eyes and the baker's girl couldn't help but feel a rush of warmth from him.

'It would seem so,' she said quietly.

They both looked into the bowl of melting chocolate upon the stove-top. Their heads close together, their cheeks almost touched as they turned to look at one another.

'May I kiss you, Meg?' Frankie asked in a soft voice.

Meg nodded. She could hardly speak. She'd never been kissed before by a man and had never wanted to be . . . until this moment.

Frankie stepped forward and held her in his arms and kissed her gently on the lips before stepping back. 'I've wanted to do that since I first saw you but I didn't know if I dared,' he admitted. 'I don't want to lose my heart to anybody just yet, my bakery is everything to me and it wouldn't be fair for me to ask anyone to share my passion along with themselves.'

Meg looked up at him with kindness. 'It seems we are both the same. We both have the same passion, so that wouldn't be unfair.'

Those were the words Frankie had hoped to hear. He held her again and kissed her, this time with more passion. Meg broke off the kiss. 'Hey — watch the chocolate. It will be getting too grainy if you don't remove it from the heat.'

'Just for once, I don't care,' Frankie said, then he kissed her again.

'Just one more kiss and then we behave,' Meg said, feeling her heart beating fast as he held her in his arms.

'Whatever you say, *ma cherie*,' Frankie said quietly and held her tightly as she returned his kiss more openly this time and put her arms around him tightly as they embraced. Just for once, there was something more important to them both than baking.

★　★　★

Meg walked along the dark streets back to Sykes Yard. In her hands was a biscuit tin filled with the chocolate eclairs made with passion in the bakery. She kept smiling to herself about the kisses that she and Frankie had shared. Nothing more — he had been a perfect gentleman as he looked at her and whispered sweet nothings. Her heart felt like bursting as she remembered the hour or two that they had spent together, talking and getting to know one another.

The only sadness had come when she had to say

good-night to Frankie and he'd asked to walk her home. She couldn't let him know the poverty that she lived in. He was far too fine to be ever seen with a girl from such a poor area, she thought, as she reached the turning into Sykes Yard and was hit by the smell of the midden. How she wished that she had been born to a more wealthy family and was not a girl from the backstreets with no money and dressed like a pauper.

It hadn't worried her until now, but when she had looked around her at the wealth on display in Frankie's kitchen, she knew that she was not good enough for the likes of him, no matter how he had kissed her. She only wished that he had not stolen a piece of her heart with each kiss given.

As she entered her humble home she felt as if her mother and sister both knew what had happened in the bakery and were both looking at the eclairs that had been made with love.

'Did he give you them? Did he not charge you?' Agnes noticed the glow in her daughter's cheeks.

'No, he was really kind,' Meg said, trying not to make eye contact with her mother. 'I've to return the tin though.' 'Well, that's good of him. Perhaps he was after something else in payment!' Agnes said suspiciously, determined to pry into how the evening had gone between her daughter and the Frenchman.

'No, he was the perfect gentleman. We have a lot in common, as we both love baking. He's no threat to Ted Lund's and I'm no threat to his bakery. We are completely different bakers. I just wish I had a bakery like his, it's so new and clean.'

'You can go back anytime, our Meg,' Sarah said as she ate her way through one of the eclairs, 'as long as you keep bringing these back with you for nothing.'

'Aye, they are good,' Agnes said, 'but be sure he doesn't expect something in the way of payment for them, that's all I'm saying.'

Agnes licked the cream from her mouth. She hadn't really felt like eating of late but these looked and tasted so good she had to make the effort to enjoy them.

'No, Mam, I keep telling you he's not that sort.'

Meg smiled, remembering the touches and kisses shared. She would return the tin and hope that there would be more sweetness awaiting her return.

19

It was Saturday afternoon and Meg was tidying the shop shelves and dampening down the ovens in the bakery. She looked at the cake tin belonging to Frankie and felt her heart fluttering with the thought of returning it later that after-noon. She was stupid, she thought to herself as she swept the shop floor and walked to turn the shop sign to Closed. How could a man make her feel like this? No other man had had this effect on her, so why should he?

'Aye, hold on Meg, don't close just yet,' came a familiar voice. 'Have you a loaf left? We've visitors tomorrow and my mam's making sandwiches, so we need an extra loaf.' Daisy stopped the door being closed in her face just in time.

'You are lucky, I've just the one. Take it, I'll not charge. It just would have been used by us at home, probably in a bread and butter pudding, if I had got around to making it.' Meg smiled as Daisy caught her breath and leaned against the counter.

'I'll not be taking it if it's of use to you and your family. It's only our John's in-laws-to-be that's coming round. They can make do with some of my mother's biscuits although they'll break their teeth on them.' Daisy laughed then looked at Meg and noticed that for a Saturday morning she was looking very glamorous. 'You are looking a bit swish for a Saturday afternoon. Is that rouge I see on your cheeks? Are we going somewhere nice this afternoon or are we trying to impress somebody?'

'No, I'm just warm,' Meg replied. 'It's a lovely day. Just look at the blue sky. It's a pity all the smoke from the chimneys blocks the sun out on good days — there's something to be said for living in the country. I've always dreamed of a little cottage out in the countryside with roses around the door.' She leaned on her brush thinking about her ideal home and realized that it included Frankie waiting for her at the door.

Daisy looked at her friend. Something had definitely changed about Meg this last day or two. 'I thought that you were just dreaming of your own bakery, not a life of rural domestic bliss. You wouldn't last five minutes out in the country; you're a town lass. Have you heard from Ted Lund? He should be on his way back shortly, shouldn't he?'

'No, I haven't heard a thing. I'm hoping that he'll never come back but that's too much to hope, I suppose. I'd love for this bakery to be mine but I know all too well that it never will be.'

'Now, that sounds more like you. I thought for a minute there might be a man involved somewhere along the line with you having pictures of domestic bliss in your mind.' Daisy laughed and made for the door, leaving the loaf of bread for Meg, knowing that she would need it more than her family.

'No, there's no man, just me dreaming. I can dream, can't I? Sometimes I get fed up with these backstreets and would like to breathe clean fresh air,' Meg said defensively.

Daisy saw right through her. 'Ohh, I think I may be right, there is a man. Come on then, tell me, who is he and how did you meet him? I want to know everything.' She leaned back on the counter, waiting for Meg to tell her everything. 'There isn't really, we are only friends,' Meg said coyly, wishing Daisy didn't know her so well and that she didn't show her feelings so openly.

'Go on then, get on and tell me!'

'I've got to know Frankie Pearson. He's the owner and baker at the new patisserie on the Headrow. It's only through our baking — nothing else,' Meg protested.

'Oh, posh. That's one up on our John, I'll have to tell him,' Daisy joked. 'It will be love amongst the jam tarts, is it? He'll be a bit passionate, I bet — after all, isn't he French?' Daisy teased and looked at Meg react as she always did to teasing, with a bright blush.

'He's not French, you know he isn't. His parents are from Leeds and just left for Paris to follow their passion for painting. He's good company and a good baker.'

'I thought of asking you to go shopping with me next Saturday afternoon if you have time between baking and lover boy? I need one or two things for our John's wedding. He's set the date now: it's the end of summer, the thirtieth of August. That's what her parents are coming over to discuss tomorrow. Do you fancy? You could introduce me to your Frankie then. It's a pity he doesn't have a café. We could have had a cup of tea and I could have watched him and told you if I thought he was suitable for you.' Daisy laughed at the thought.

'It's not that serious,' Meg protested again. 'Stop it, we have just got things in common. However, I will go shopping with you, but I can't stay long. I don't like leaving Mam on a Saturday and Sarah always wants some time to herself and waits for me to return home.'

'Right you are then. I'll let you go to your lover boy. I'll be in sometime through the week, chasing my tail as usual before work. If it's any different, then you can always tell me.'

With that, Daisy headed out down the street. Meg watched her go, wishing that she had never said anything to her, but she had been wanting to tell somebody about her new love and how she felt about it. She was finding it hard to hide her feelings at home. Her mother had even commented on the songs she had started to sing as she did her work around the house. She had better control her feelings before she made a fool of herself, she thought, as she hung up her apron, pinched her cheeks and picked up the cake tin covered with bluebirds. She felt like she was flying like the bluebirds on the tin to her love and she couldn't wait another minute.

* * *

Brenda Jones looked at the girl who had just come into the shop and recognized her straight away from the previous Saturday when she had been lurking outside the bakery.

'I'll serve this customer, girls,' she said tartly to Norah and Marie as they stepped forward to see what Meg needed. 'Yes, may I help you?' she said, looking down her nose at Meg.

'I'm here to see Mr Pearson, I have his tin to return,' Meg said with a huge smile on her face. 'Is he busy in the bakery?'

'He is far too busy to speak to any visitors,' Brenda said haughtily. 'Let me take the tin, and then we don't disturb him. I'm sure he'd prefer it that way.' She held her hands out to take the tin.

'But I'd like to speak to him if possible?' Meg said politely and held onto the tin, watching Marie go into the bakery behind Brenda Jones's back.

'As I say, he's busy. Perhaps you could call back later, or is there anything we can serve you with today? Or perhaps our fancies are a little too expensive for you, we don't usually sell many to people like you.' She folded her arms, looking as if she had won a victory for the upper classes as she stared down at Meg, whose face was burning bright with embarrassment. Before Meg could reply, a familiar voice came from the bakery door. 'Meg, I didn't hear you arrive. Please, please come this way. In fact, come upstairs where it is quieter. I've actually had some tables and chairs delivered this week so we can have a sit together for a while.'

Frankie gave Brenda Jones a dark glance as he put his hand into the small of Meg's back and urged her up the stairs out of the earshot of the pompous woman and his two serving girls. 'I'm so glad that you are here, I've been thinking of you all week. I haven't the time through the day to visit you and I don't know where you live, else I'd have been knocking on your door,' Frankie said all in a rush as he sat both himself and Meg down on the cane-backed chairs with tables to match that now crowded the first floor of the bakery.

Meg ignored his subtle attempt to learn her address. She already felt out of place with the snooty Brenda Jones and didn't want Frankie to know how right his manager actually was about her life.

'I know, I'm the same,' she told him. 'I don't know your home address either and I haven't the time through the day to visit . . . and besides you are too busy to see me really.'

Frankie reached for her hand and cupped it in his. 'Take no notice of the dragon downstairs. Marie came and told me that you were asking for me. I never heard you, else I would have come out of the bakery straight away. I was busy sieving some flour for tomorrow's use.' Frankie held her hand tight and smiled. 'I didn't know whether you would return or not, but I knew that you would have to return my tin so I was praying that I had not deterred you by showing my feelings to you.'

Meg looked at the man who had captivated her heart. 'No, although I don't understand what you see in me. There must be hundreds of beautiful wealthy ladies that come into this shop, a lot more educated, wealthy and beautiful than me, so why do I attract you so?'

'It isn't about wealth. And you are as beautiful as any of the women that enter the shop. Some of them have so much paint on you can't see the true woman, but with you, I know that you are both beautiful on the inside and the outside and to me, that is all that matters. And also you share my one passion in life.' Frankie smiled and leaned forward and kissed her on the lips tenderly. 'Now where we go from here, I don't know; neither of us has much time on our hands with one thing and another.' Frankie looked at Meg and spoke quietly. 'I will meet you outside the Victoria Parade next Saturday after you have finished work, we can stroll around the shops and perhaps have tea together if you wish?'

'Yes, I'd like that. Oh . . . but I promised my friend Daisy I'd help her do some shopping on the same day.

I don't want to let either of you down.'

'Then you must keep your promise to Daisy. I realize you ladies like to shop and gossip between yourselves; how can I, a mere man, come between you? One evening next week, how about Wednesday evening? Down by the Corn Exchange, we can walk by the riverbank, now that the nights are lighter?' Frankie tightened his grip on Meg's hand, waiting for her answer. 'Unless you would like me to visit you at home? I could meet your mother then and put her mind at rest that I am a decent man. I hope once she sees me and gets to know me?' Frankie asked but saw a worried frown on Meg's face.

'No, I'll meet you outside the Corn Exchange. Sometimes my mother is not that well and she wouldn't want you to see her at her worst. Wednesday night will be ideal. Or perhaps I should come to your home?' Meg suggested, keen to avoid any idea of Frankie coming to the yard.

'I live right down at Headingley. It would mean you getting a horse and cab or a very long walk, so no, we will meet at the Corn Exchange as planned. I'll be counting the hours. At least then we will be out of prying ears and eyes.'

'Yes, I will too. I'll really look forward to our meeting and walk. I can't believe that you would look twice at me.' Meg looked into the kind loving eyes of the man sat next to her.

'Meg, you are beautiful, it will be with pride I walk out with you. Now, you return to your mother and I will return to my bakery. The dragon downstairs will be pacing the floor, wondering what we are up to. I think I probably made a bad decision when I employed her. She doesn't know it but I think we will be parting company before long.'

'Really, I must say, I'm not keen on the woman. She looks at me as if I'm not fit to walk upon this earth,' Meg said quietly. 'All the more reason for her to go. Now, my dearest Meg, I must go about my work.' Frankie bent and kissed Meg tenderly and smiled. 'Thank you for returning the tin and I'll see you Wednesday evening.'

'Yes, I'll be there.'

Meg caught her breath and smiled at the man she was starting to have feelings for. He was everything she had ever dreamed of. Gone was the idea of her never wanting to walk out with a man or a life without a man by her side.

★ ★ ★

'Mam, are you all right?' Meg stood by the side of her mother's bed and looked down at her in the dim light of the early morning.

'Nay, I'm not so good. I've had a bad night, I've got a lot of pain. I just don't know where to put myself.' Agnes fought for breath and winced as she turned in her bed.

'Have you taken the laudanum that I bought you?' Meg looked at the bedside for the bottle of liquid that had been easing the pains of her mother and noticed that it was empty. It had only been bought with Friday's money that she had taken for her wage for the week but now it was gone and her mother was in pain. She could barely afford another bottle but anything was better than seeing her mother in such a state, she thought, as she looked down on the drawn face of the woman she loved.

'It's all gone, lass. I rely on it more and more these days. It feels like my body is just being eaten alive with this disease and there's nowt I can do to stop it.' Agnes bit back a sob of pain. 'You get yourself to work. Folk will be wanting their bread. You can't do owt for me; I've got Sarah with me until she goes to school so don't worry. Once the pain eases I'll sleep,' she said through gritted teeth and looked at her daughter with tears in her eyes.

'I can't leave you like this. I'll stay at home today,' Meg said and felt downhearted. It was Wednesday and she had been looking forward to her meeting with Frankie, but her mother came first, never mind the bakery.

'No, you go and make your bread,' Agnes insisted. 'Serve the folk that comes early and need it for their work, and then if we can afford it, get me some laudanum from the apothecary's on your way home. I'll be all right on my own for an hour or two.' Agnes tried to smile at her daughter, failing to keep the grimace from her features.

'I'll do that, Mam, I'll be back as soon as I can. I'll only make bread today, serve my early morning customers, and then I'll put a note on the door telling other folks that I'm closed for the rest of the day. Don't worry, I'll take some money out of the safe. I can always go without it on Friday when I give myself my wage. Ted will never know that I've taken a sub.' Meg kissed her mother and looked across at Sarah who was sitting half-asleep on the edge of her bed but in tears as she listened to her mother in agony.

'Don't leave me, Meg, I don't know what to do. What if Mam dies?' she sobbed.

'She's not about to. Now you sit here by her side

and talk to her until school time, and then I'll be back home as soon as you've gone. I can't get any laudanum until the apothecary opens at eight and I have to go to the bakery for some money anyway. Stay strong, Sarah.' Meg hugged her little sister and then bent down to talk to her mother. 'Mam, I'll be back just after nine. Sarah will be with you until then.'

Sarah wiped her eyes and pulled the rickety chair from the side of her bed and took her mother's hand as she sat down and looked with pleading eyes at Meg as she left the room. 'We'll be all right, Mam, I'll wait until our Meg is back from the bakery. If Miss Pringle is mad with me she's mad with me, I don't care, I'll soon be leaving school anyway.' She closed her eyes and squeezed her mother's hand as she moaned in pain and she prayed that her mother would not die on her watch.

Meg made her bread and wrote a note apologising that she was only making bread that day and that the bakery would be closed after nine that morning due to family illness. She placed it on the door and wished for nine to come as quickly as it could. She shouldn't have left Sarah with her mother. She should have stayed herself, she thought, as she helped herself out of the full to brimming safe of enough money to buy laudanum for the next few days for her mother. She didn't put her withdrawal in her accounting book as she would take a cut in her agreed wage for the week so that Ted Lund need never know. It was out of desperation anyway; surely he would have understood, she told herself as she put the money in her pocket and waited for her customers who relied on her each morning to appear, watching the clock and praying that her mother would be all right until her return.

However, the pang of guilt would not subside. Taking money that was not hers was wrong, even though it was to give relief to her mother and she would eventually repay it. She still felt uneasy as the first customer entered through the doors and she smiled, trying not to show her personal worries and that she felt like a thief.

★ ★ ★

Meg raced up the stairs with the bottle of laudanum in her hand. 'Sarah, you are still here, you should have gone to school.'

'I couldn't, I couldn't leave Mam, although she says she's feeling a little better.' Sarah turned and looked at her mother, whose pillow was wet with sweat.

'That's right love, it must be your soothing ways. But now you must go to school. Meg's back, she'll keep me right now,' Agnes said quietly and watched as Meg spooned her some laudanum. She lifted her head to sip it eagerly, knowing that it would bring her the relief and sleep that she was craving.

'There, Mam, that should make things better for you. You'll happen to get some sleep now,' Meg said. She hoped the dose that she had given her mother had not been too much but she watched her mother's face relax and sleep at long last came to her as she muttered, 'Bless you both, I'm lucky to have such good daughters.'

'Now she'll sleep most of the morning, Sarah, and I'll stay with her, so let's get you to school. I'll write a note to Miss Pringle and explain why you're late and then you won't be in bother.'

Meg knew that the drug would free her mother of

pain for just enough time for her to have a sleep. The trouble was she was starting to become more and more reliant upon the drug and they just couldn't afford it.

'I hate school and I hate batty Pringle, she can say what she likes!' Sarah said as Meg wrote a note to her teacher.

'You've not long to go now, don't let her think the worst of you. Now, go to school, they are supposed to be the best years of your life. Lord knows, work is not to be wished for. Mam will still be here when you return.' Meg gave her young sister a quick hug, gave her the note and sent her on her way with her feet dragging. One day she would return from school to some bad news but hopefully it would not be today!

★ ★ ★

It was showing five to six on the mantel clock and Meg felt her heart aching and a feeling of resentment that her mother was too ill for her to leave. She had been quietly counting the days and minutes to seeing Frankie again and now he would be standing outside the domed shape of the Corn Exchange wondering where she was and had she stood him up? She couldn't help but feel a little sorry for herself as a tear trickled down her cheek as she let her feelings out.

'It's all right love, there's no need to cry. I'm feeling a little stronger now the laudanum has eased the pain.' Her mother reached for her hand and smiled. 'I'm sorry, I'll be back on my feet tomorrow. You and Sarah are my reason for living, you know that, don't you, my darling? I'll hang on for as long as I can. I'm not meeting my maker yet,' Agnes said in a drug-hazed voice.

214

'I know, Mam, and we are here for you, we always will be. Now sleep, I'm here and I'm not going anywhere,' Meg said. She thought of Frankie's kisses and sweet words and held her tears back.

★ ★ ★

It was Friday morning and Agnes had now fought back the pain with the help of laudanum as she whispered to Meg to keep the bakery open as long as she needed and that she would stay in her bed until her return. Although weak, Agnes didn't look as grey and she had managed to drink some broth the previous evening.

'I'll close at twelve then, Mam, I'll be no later than half past. Sarah promises she'll go to school on time as well, now you are a little better. You're sure that you'll be all right?' Meg said as she pulled her skirts over her hips.

'I'll be grand. What can I get up to if I stay in my bed and drug myself up with this stuff? You are sure we can afford it? I feel so guilty, but it's the only way I get through the days.' Agnes put her head back down on the pillow.

'Don't worry, Mam, we'll manage, whatever keeps you going. Now, I'll be away. See you at dinner time.'

Meg bent down and kissed her mother on her brow and noticed that the laudanum bottle was nearly empty. She would have to buy some more on her way home if her mother was to remain pain-free. That would eat into even more of their money for the week and they could ill afford to do so, but there was nothing else she could do if she was to keep her mother for a little longer on the Earth.

Once at the bakery and she had completed all the regular tasks, Meg looked at her accounts book. She realized she had never accounted for the money that she had taken for her mother's laudanum and now, as she sat and wrote down her weekly wages into the pages, she thought twice about putting a deduction in wages. Ted Lund would never know and she'd worked bloody hard for him, harder than her piddling two shillings and threepence that she paid herself every week. He was making money hand over fist yet she was not gaining from it. In fact, she would help herself to another sixpence for her mother's medicines and not bother putting that down either.

She also looked at the month's invoice from Dinsdale's that had just been delivered to her by George. She'd pay that at the end of next week before Ted arrived back from Ireland and then all would be straight in the world to his eyes.

As she put an extra sixpence in her pocket she felt a pang of guilt. She'd never stolen in her life and it felt wrong. She tried to convince herself that she wasn't stealing, that she had earned it ten times over and that God only helped them that helped themselves. She folded her accounts book and put it into the safe as she heard the shop bell ring and tried to forget her guilt as she greeted Daisy with her usual smile.

'Are you still all right for Saturday?' Daisy asked. 'I noticed the other day you were closed early — are things all right at home?' She looked at her closest friend and could see the worry on her face.

'Oh Daisy, my mam is getting worse. She's trying her best but this last day or two she's been in a lot of pain. I'm keeping her going on laudanum, it is the only thing that stops the pain.' Meg sighed. 'I'd

216

forgotten all about Saturday. Would you mind if I don't come with you? I can't leave her alone and I already ask so much of Sarah. She's not quite eleven yet and she's having to grow up so fast.'

'Of course I don't mind. We can make it the following Saturday if you want. It fits in better for me anyway. I thought that I might help my mam with the sewing of her dress for the wedding because she's getting herself into such a tizzy with it.'

'Thank you, it's just I don't want to leave her when I don't have to. Work and school are different — both Sarah and I have to do those — but shopping that I can ill afford can wait.'

Daisy looked at Meg and said carefully, hoping that she was not going to dent her friend's pride, 'You are all right for money, aren't you? Laudanum is an expensive habit but if it keeps your mother free from the pain she needs it.'

'We are managing, thank you,' Meg said defensively.

Daisy knew something was wrong but didn't want to pry. 'Talking about Sarah, I heard on the grapevine that Hunslet Mill is going to be advertising for some burlers and menders. I thought of her straight away when I heard. It's an ideal first job for a young lass, especially with her being so good with needlework and having a sharp eye for detail. She wouldn't be near machinery either. As soon as I know more I'll let you know if you want. I know one of the managers there so I could always put in a good word for her.'

'Yes, that would suit her,' Meg agreed. 'She hates school and if anything did happen to my mam, I couldn't make sure she would attend all the time. Besides she's nearly done her schooling. It's time she was earning some money and her keep.'

'Right, well, if I hear any more I'll let you know, and don't worry about this Saturday, we'll put it off until the following one. Would that be all right with you?' Daisy asked and looked at Meg, who she thought looked near to tears.

'Yes, providing my mam is all right, there shouldn't be a problem. Thanks, Daisy, sorry I sound an ungrateful soul but I'm so tired and worried about one thing or another.'

'It's all right, my love, I understand, you don't have to explain to me. Just look after yourself and try to do what is right for your mam, that's all that can be expected when someone's so ill.'

Unusually, Daisy left without buying anything, leaving Meg mulling over her words. 'Try and do what is right for your mam.' That's what she was doing. She'd pay Ted Lund back when she could, and besides, a shilling was not a lot to help save her mam from pain. Especially when she had made him good money while he was away.

20

The chemist looked at Meg as he passed over the bottle of laudanum.

'That's the second bottle I've administered to you this week. What are you doing with it?' he asked and looked stern.

'It's for my mother, she's dying from cancer. She gets worse with each day and it's the only thing that helps her with the pain,' Meg said and passed him payment.

'It's costing you a pretty penny. It is to be hoped that the good Lord takes her soon else she'll need more and more to fight the pain. She'll get addicted and then nothing will help her,' the chemist said, not unkindly, looking at the young lass who looked as if she hadn't a penny to her name.

'It doesn't matter. As long as it helps her for now, we take each day as it comes,' Meg said and turned to leave, pushing past the next customer without looking at them in a bid to get out of the shop.

'Poor lass, her mother is dying and she's working every hour she can for old Ted Lund at the bakery,' Mrs Thomas, one of Meg's regulars, told the chemist once she'd gone. 'She's a blinking good baker, but Ted will not be paying her that well, they'll be struggling. There but for the grace of God go I.'

'He must be paying her something decent. She's spent a good deal on laudanum for her mother — she can't carry on doing that forever.'

The chemist shook his head. How she was paying

for them was none of his business but he thought he might just mention it when Ted returned and came in for his usual gout pills.

★ ★ ★

Meg rushed through the streets. She had one more place to visit before returning to her mother, one that she had not been able to get off her mind no matter how bad things had been at home.

She stood outside Frankie's patisserie and looked through the window. Marie and Norah were busy serving their top-class customers and Brenda Jones was watching them as they smiled and made sure the customers got what they were asking for. Meg looked at her reflection in the shop's window and could see just how scruffy she looked in her cast-off clothes, that she smelt of her morning's work and there was a stain down the front of her dress where she had accidentally cracked an egg and it had spilt down the front of her. Compared to the shoppers in the bakery, she looked a mess and she decided to wait until the shop was empty before going in.

Once it was, she decided to enter the shop but found her way barred by Brenda Jones.

'Sorry, may I enter please, I need to talk to Mr Pearson?' Meg said.

Brenda looked down at her and sneered. 'He's not in today, he's got business with his accountant. Besides, why would he want to see a street waif like you? Look at you, you are filthy and look as if you have just crawled out of the gutter.'

'I'm sorry, I think you will find that me and Frankie ... Mr Pearson are friends and that he

220

doesn't think that of me at all. Now if he is in there I need to see him.' Meg tried to push past the woman who blocked her way.

'You stupid girl!' Brenda said venomously, refusing to move out of the way. 'He's only friends with you because you are his opposition. He's been leading you on, finding out what he can about that filthy backstreet bakery that you work in. He means to buy it and close you down once the owner returns. Don't you see, you silly child? You have been used. How could you actually think that a man that had the choice of any woman he wanted in Paris would think twice about looking at a backstreet girl like you? He's with his accountant planning the takeover now. You'll soon be without work and will have to crawl back to your squalor.'

'You are wrong, we are friends because we have the same passion for baking, and we both have the same dreams. Frankie would not do that to me.'

Meg felt tears starting to sting her eyes and started to question the time and conversations that she had shared with Frankie.

'Go home and don't waste any more of your time swooning over a man who is way far beyond you,' the older woman said waspishly. 'I'm only saying this to you to save you from a broken heart. Men will always use us women, and you should learn this lesson now.'

Meg fought with her feelings and eventually decided that if Frankie was not there, it was a waste of her time standing arguing with Brenda.

'Can you tell him that I called and that I'm sorry?' she said after a time. 'That's all you need to tell him, nothing more.' She felt a fool. Of course Brenda Jones was right. Why would somebody like Frankie Pearson show an interest in her? She had been blinded by his flattery and good looks, not to mention his baking skills. She had been an idiot. He could never love a girl like her a girl from off the backstreets who hadn't a penny to her name.

Tears ran down her cheeks as she walked home briskly, trying not to look at the people she passed. She didn't want her broken heart to be seen by one and all. She wanted to get home and weep in the privacy of her own surroundings. She'd never go near the fancy posh patisserie on the Headrow ever again and she tried to clear Frankie Pearson and his foreign baking out of her head. She only hoped that he would not buy the bakery from Ted Lund on his return because she never wanted to see the man again.

* * *

'Meg, is that you?' Agnes called down the stairs and heaved herself up into a sitting position in her bed.

'Yes, Mam, I'm back now. I'll bring you a cuppa up and can you manage some dinner?' Meg shouted back up the stairs then wiped her nose and her eyes on the apron that she put around her waist on entering the kitchen. The fire was nearly out and she tried to bring it to life with what sticks and coal that there were in the hearth.

She shook her head. Here was another man who had only been after what he could, she thought, as she stoked the fire into life and hoped that there was still some coal and sticks in the backyard left from Roger Ingram's visits. She stood up, watching the fire's flames lick around the newly added sticks and put the kettle on the hook above the fire.

'No dinner, love, but I'd die for a cuppa. I'm feeling a lot better though today,' Agnes shouted down and Meg smiled. At least her mother sounded a bit brighter this morning and there were no groans of pain from the bedroom above her.

Frankie Pearson could go and boil his head if he'd been leading her on, she thought, as she gazed out of the window and into the yard that had always been her home. She should have known she wasn't good enough for him. How stupid she had been. She'd look after her mam and Sarah, and run the bakery until Ted returned, and then she would see what became of the mighty Frankie Pearson and his offer, if it ever happened! She could live without a man in her life. She had her family and true friends like Daisy. That was all that mattered.

'Daisy told me today that some jobs are going at Hunslet Mill,' she said to Sarah, who was seated at the table, working on some embroidery. 'She knows one of the floor managers and he's told her that they will be looking for some burlers and menders. It sounds like a good job, no mucky and dangerous machinery, you just check and mend the cloth for any defects or anything that's left in the material like burrs or straw left from weaving the flax. She said it needs a good eye — that's why she thought of you.'

'It's no good telling me that, I haven't left school yet,' Sarah said pointedly. 'I thought that I had to stay there whether I liked it or not. You told me more times than I care to remember.'

'I know, but our mam is getting worse. I might not always be able to work at the bakery — besides, Ted will be back shortly and he might not want to keep me on. We'll need some money coming in from somewhere to keep all going.' Meg knew that she was going back on what she had been drumming into her sister for weeks, but that was when she was confident that Ted would keep her on. Now she wondered different, especially after what Brenda Jones had said. 'You mean, I can leave and take a job and you and Mam would be all right with it?' Sarah looked in disbelief and sat back in her chair.

'Yes, I'll ask Daisy for more information next time I see her and then if you manage to secure yourself a job at the mill, I'll go and see Miss Pringle and make it right with her. She knows you hate school and after all, you only have a few more weeks then you can legally leave. She knows our circumstances; as long as you have a job to leave to, she'll be right with us.'

Meg hated having to say what she did. She'd always vowed Sarah would be left in school as long as they could afford it, but she was preparing for the worst. Besides, burling and mending was a good job and ideal for Sarah. If she didn't grab it now there might be nothing for her when she did leave school.

'Oh, that has made my day,' Sarah said. 'I hate school, I hate Miss Pringle, and I'll do anything to leave that place. I can't believe you've said that. Tell Daisy if I'm sweeping floors and getting paid for it I don't care, as long as I can get out of that prison of a place.' She gave a huge grin.

'You'll have to prove your worth to them. You just don't walk into a job. It's different from school: if you don't do as you are told, you'll not get paid, and all mill owners talk to one another. If one gives you a black mark they all know about it, so you'll have to behave yourself.' Meg looked across at Sarah — it was clear nothing would wipe that happiness from her face.

'I'd do anything to leave school and earn some money. You promise you'll tell Daisy that I want the job and that you'll see Miss Pringle?' Sarah said excitedly.

'I promise, but it will be up to you to secure the job and keep it,' Meg warned her.

'Can I go and tell Harry? I can't wait until Sunday and I know he'll be at home now. I can't wait to see his face,' Sarah said and hoped that she wasn't about to get a lecture about the boy next door.

'Go on then, but you haven't got the job yet. No job, you stay at school!' Meg shouted as Sarah made for the back door to climb the wall to tell Harry her news. However, she was soon back with a sullen look on her face. Harry was still hard at work, making every penny he could for his family.

Meg wandered up the stairs to her mother. She was weary with life, and things were not going her way. The more she thought about her time with Frankie Pearson, the more Brenda Jones' words rang true. She had better keep her feet on the ground and know what she was and who she was. She'd never be anything other than a working-class lass who worked in a bakery and not perhaps long doing that if Ted Lund found out that she had stolen a shilling off him. Although she hadn't meant to steal it, just borrow, where she would get a shilling to repay him she didn't know. She couldn't just take a shilling less — they needed her whole wage, and more. It seemed that the more she tried to mend her lot, the deeper she got herself into trouble, she thought, as she tried to smile at her mother then sat down by her side.

'Did I hear you saying to Sarah that Daisy has

found her a job? We shouldn't encourage her to leave school; the authorities will be after us if they find out,' Agnes said.

Meg gave a deep sigh. 'If they come hunting for us they will be doing the same to half the families in Leeds, Mam. Besides, in a few weeks, she will have officially left and at least if she goes now she's got a job to walk into. That is if she behaves herself when she gets offered it. I let her go and tell Harry her news; she can't be parted from that lad no matter what, and they are as thick as thieves, those two. He's still at work so she'll go back later. Perhaps when she goes to work at the mill in Hunslet she'll find some new friends and recognize that Harry is not the only one in the world.'

'What about your French fella, our Meg? Have you heard from him of late?' Agnes asked and saw the sadness on her daughter's face.

'No, I haven't, Mam. I don't think I'll be seeing or hearing from him again. I'm not right for him and he's not right for me. We should leave one another alone. Besides, I don't need a man in my life.' Meg gave a weak smile and pulled the covers up over her mother.

'Someday you will, my Meg. Make sure you look after yourself as well as everybody else. The best years just fly by and before you know it, your life is over and you have passed so many opportunities by. Grab life with both hands, my lass, while you can and hold your head up high. You are just as good as anyone else, and don't let anyone tell you any different.'

Agnes patted her daughter's hand and closed her eyes. She'd heard her crying downstairs. She guessed Meg's Frenchman had broken her heart, although she would never tell her that she knew, leastwise not till Meg felt she could talk to her about it.

She'd find true love, she was too bonny a lass not to and she had her head screwed on right when it came to money and life. It wasn't Meg that Agnes fretted about. It was her other daughter, strong-willed like her real father. Hopefully if she got a job she would be more settled.

21

It was Monday morning and Meg had been rushed off her feet with customers. She'd gone back to baking all her usual temptations and folk had told her all morning how they had missed the cakes and buns that they had grown used to and hoped that her mother was improving.

She looked around the closed shop and sighed. Why had she been so stupid and baked everything and anything? She should just have stuck to Ted's inedible bread and then she wouldn't be worrying about how to explain the extra money in the safe or the bills she had paid at Dinsdale's, and letting people down on his return when he didn't agree with the things she baked.

There was also the matter of the stolen shilling for laudanum. She knew he wouldn't know it had been taken, but it was laying heavy on her conscience. If she could repay it she would, and hopefully her mother would not need any more for the next day or two. If she did she'd visit a different apothecary. Mr Booth at the end of the street had looked at her strangely and started asking questions so she'd keep clear of him. She knew he was wondering how she could afford such amounts of laudanum even if he knew what its purpose was.

She pulled her accounts book from under the shelf and looked at the figures. She'd made Ted a small fortune but it was as her mother had said: he would scrutinise every penny spent and she knew he would. She looked at the invoice that George had dropped in from Dinsdale's and decided that she would pay it on her way home just in case her mother took a turn for the worse again and she hadn't got it paid before Ted's return. It was a lot, yet again, but there was more than enough money to cover it and her accounts still showed just how much money the little bakery could make if given time and love.

If only the bakery was hers, she thought, as she placed the invoice and the money to pay it in her basket. She'd give Frankie Pearson a run for his money and she'd make his fancy choux pastry if she found it would sell in her backstreet bakery. As it was, she'd soon be back to being Ted's skivvy and doing all the jobs that he didn't like doing. She'd have to remember to bring the sack of sawdust back out of the outside shed and look as if she had been using it before his return, else he'd have something to say.

She picked up her basket and closed the shop door for another day as she made her way to Dinsdale's grocery stall to pay her debts.

★ ★ ★

Joe Dinsdale was busy looking through the latest goods and catalogues with a salesman at the end of the long counter and George the young lad was running around weighing things into packages and working his way through the row of customers' shopping lists. When it was eventually Meg's turn, he looked up at her and smiled shyly.

'What can I do for you today, Miss Fairfax?' he asked. He'd started to like seeing the lass who was gaining a good reputation with customers who visited the shop.

229

'I need to pay the monthly bill for the bakery please,' Meg said and started to get out the envelope that she had placed both the invoice and the money in.

'Mr Dinsdale deals with monthly invoices and as you can see, he's a little busy at the moment. Is there anything else that I can get you until he's finished with the seller from Boston's?' George asked and looked across at the two businessmen who were oblivious to the queue of people he was dealing with as they gossiped and talked about new products and what was selling best for one another. George leaned forward and whispered. 'They are likely to be a while with one another, they both like the sound of their own voice.' He grinned.

'Oh no, there's nothing I need today. I really wanted to pay my bill but I can see you are busy.' She put the envelope and its contents on the counter.

'I tell you what: leave it with me, and I'll see that he gets it. I'll put it to one side until they have finished gassing,' George said, eager to make his queue shorter.

'Oh, thank you, I didn't want to take that amount of money home with me, just in case we get robbed. It will be safer with you,' Meg said and gave George the envelope.

'Don't worry, Miss Fairfax, I'll make sure he gets it. Now enjoy your afternoon.' George took hold of the envelope.

As soon as Joe Dinsdale had stopped gabbling, he would pass him the money that he knew he'd been waiting for. However, that would be a while yet as after they had done their business at the counter they would be going to the Bull and Calf for a drink to celebrate their deals. Usually, on the day the sales-

230

man from Boston's called on them, there was little done after the whisky or two downed by them both. He placed the money safely at the back of his till and made a mental note to pass it to Joe Dinsdale on his return from the public house.

'Thank you, I will,' Meg said and felt a weight taken from her shoulders as she walked out of the grocery store. She'd paid the last bill for the bakery, and Ted Lund had plenty of money upon his return and next month's bill would not be as much, as her larder at the bakery was quite well stocked now.

★ ★ ★

The week had been busy but now it was a warm Friday's early summer's evening, Agnes was up and sitting in her chair downstairs and Sarah was out in the street mixing with the other children of the street. Meg leaned against the side of the doorway and looked out upon the yard and looked up at the blue skies as a solitary swallow flew above her head.

Life was getting harder, and she felt near to tears as she watched Sarah talking and playing Relevo with the neighbour's children. Why was she in such a hurry to leave school and join the life of work? There was never any break from having to earn your daily bread and she would have liked her to have a better job than in a mill. It was monotonous work with little thanks and bad pay. However, she seemed happier since knowing that if Daisy worked her magic, she might secure a job at Hunslet Mill and the money she earned would be more than welcome to keep the house running.

'Penny for them?' Betsy said as she came and sat down on her doorstep with her baby on her lap, noticing Meg lost in thought.

'They aren't worth a penny,' Meg said. 'You'd not want them, Betsy, you have enough problems of your own.'

'Aye, but they always work themselves out, that's what you've got to remember. Nowt is as bad as it seems. How's your mam? Is it that you look worried to death about?' Betsy asked.

'That and a few other things. Our Sarah may have the chance of working at Hunslet Mill as a burler. But watching her now, she's still a child. I wish I could afford for us to keep her on at school longer no matter how much she hates it.'

Meg sat down on the step next to Betsy and took hold of the baby. He looked unloved, his face filthy and his nappy full by the smell of him. She immediately regretted putting him on her knee.

'You can't keep them babies forever,' Betsy told her. 'Our Harry is loving it down on the wharf. He's perhaps learning far too much from the men down there, sometimes not in a good way, but it's made him grow up. He helps out with the rent and all now. I just wish the rest of them were old enough to join him. I hear that you're doing well at the bakery; you'll be hoping Ted doesn't come back, the miserable old bugger.'

'He should be back coming back sometime next week,' Meg told her. The letter from Ted had arrived that morning. 'I'm dreading him returning because I know he'll have something to say about what I've been up to in his absence. I should have listened to him and just baked bread and not done anything more.'

'As long as he's made brass while he's away he shouldn't worry, and he must have done from what I've heard about the queues outside your bakery. You

232

must be jiggered, what with the long hours at the bakery and your mother being ill. I've heard her moaning through the walls sometimes, you must be worn down with it all. Remember you have to look after yourself as well. You are no use to anyone if you get ill.'

'I am a bit jiggered, it's true,' Meg admitted. 'Daisy Truelove has asked me to go shopping with her tomorrow, but I can't be bothered and besides I've no money. I also don't want to leave Mam or ask Sarah to sit with her because this weekend might be her last one outside of work. She deserves to enjoy it.' Meg looked across at her sister laughing with her mates as if she hadn't a care in the world.

'Well, I can sit with your mam,' Betsy offered. 'Get yourself gone, it will do you good. You can always look through those fancy windows in the Victoria Arcade and dream of what you could buy if you had the money. It costs nowt to dream. No, you go, it will get me out of the way of the rest of our house. Lord knows I get fed up of always being there for everyone all the time, stuck between them four walls. As long as I can bring the baby with me, I'd like to do that for you.' As the baby started to bawl, she reached and took him from Meg's arms.

'She'd like a bit of fresh company. I might just take you up on that, Betsy. But surely you've enough on your plate without sitting with my mam.'

'You know what they say, the devil makes work for idle hands; my Jim and my lads are all doing extra time down at the wharf on Saturday afternoon and my lodger will be at home. Perhaps I'd be best out of temptation's way, it would only cause trouble. You'd be helping me out, else I've no doubt Jim would throw me and mine out if I was tempted again.' Betsy grinned

233

and winked then grimaced as the stench from the baby wafted in her direction. 'Lordy, this one smells. No wonder he's twisty, I'd better see to him. I'll be around at two and don't argue. A half day's shopping with a good friend will do you good, and your mam and I will find plenty to talk about.'

Betsy lifted the bawling baby onto her hip and left Meg sitting on the step.

Would her mother want Betsy and the baby for the company, Meg wondered. She certainly wouldn't if the baby smelt like he just had, so she hoped that Betsy would clean him up before coming to sit with her mother. Her mother might be ill but she was still a stickler at having everything clean and fresh, no matter how down on your luck you were. Perhaps she shouldn't have said anything about the afternoon with Daisy. It had just added to her worries, the thought of Betsy coming out with all sorts about folk. She wasn't exactly tactful. But perhaps it might be the tonic her mother needed — a new face and voice. After all, she'd not seen anybody for days other than her and Sarah.

★ ★ ★

'Stop fussing, I'll be all right,' Agnes told her the next day. 'Betsy will be good company. Sarah's outside with the lass from Duke Street, she's happy, you've left me with all I want, now go and have an hour or two to yourself. You need it, you've been going around the house with a right long face of late. A bit of a natter with a good friend will do you good.' Agnes pulled her blanket over her knees and looked up at Meg. 'You've got a bit of money have you, if you'll need something?'

'I have got a penny or two. I thought I could buy Sarah a new ribbon for her hair from off the penny stall on the market. If Daisy brings news of the burlers job she'll need to look tidy when she goes to see them about it,' Meg said and picked up her handmade posy bag and hung it on her arm.

'You are always thinking of others; just go and enjoy yourself and don't bother about me. There see, Betsy is here, let her in and we'll have a good chinwag together, and as long as the baby doesn't start bawling, we'll be fine. It'll be grand to have a bit of fresh company.'

Agnes could see the worry etched on Meg's face as she opened the front door and let Betsy and a miraculously clean baby into the room.

'Hey up, Agnes, I'm here. Look, I've brought you an orange from off the docks. My Jim got his hands on a few that they said were going rotten, but some of them were all right if you cut the worst off them. I thought it would do you good.' Betsy placed the orange on the table by Agnes's side and sat down next to her, the baby on her knee wriggling to get down.

'That'll be lovely, Betsy, I'll look forward to having a bit of that. It'll be a real treat — we we can never afford oranges.' Agnes smiled at the baby, who looked as if he was teething, with bright red cheeks and dribble coming down his chin.

'Go on then, what are you standing and gawping at?' Betsy scolded. 'Your mother and me will be just grand. I'll make a brew and if she needs anything she's just to say. I'll be here until you get back.'

'You are sure you'll be all right, Mam? I can stay,' Meg said and looked at the baby who was now crawling all around the kitchen floor and exploring whatever he could find.

'Go! We will be fine. Stop worrying. Betsy and I will be just fine.' Agnes smiled as the baby tried to pull himself up by the side of her chair only to fall on his bottom. 'A baby in the house will be good entertainment. Now, get gone.'

* * *

Meg walked quickly to Daisy's home. She was looking forward to an hour with her friend but at the same time, she knew she shouldn't be out spending money they could ill afford and then there was still the shilling that she had to repay to Ted. That was weighing heavy on her mind when Daisy came to the door, dressed in her Sunday best and in a new pair of tight-laced boots that she was keen to show off.

Daisy picked up her skirts and showed Meg the ankle-length boots, tightly laced with a black frill of lace upon the top and a three-inch heel which Meg knew was not suitable for walking around the streets of Leeds that afternoon.

'What do you think? I couldn't resist them. They were in a shop window on Boar Lane. I had just got paid and they sort of said to me 'We belong on your feet' and before I knew it I'd bought them. The trouble is they rub, so I thought if I wore them around the shops today I might break them in.'

'They are bonny but you'll be crippled by the time we finish walking through the market and arcades. Don't you think you should wear something a bit more sensible?' Meg knew straight away that the answer would be no, as Daisy closed the house door behind her.

'No, I want to feel special. John has given me some money to spend on myself and my father came home drunk last night and he gave me a shilling that he'd won playing cards with his mates. He'd be cursing giving me it this morning when he got to work and remembered, but it will be too late when we have spent it. Come on, let's do the market first, I want to buy something from off the 'Don't ask the price, everything a penny' stall. They always have something good on there.' Daisy threaded her arm through Meg's and teetered off down the street, her boots rubbing her heels but she was determined not to complain to Meg.

'I need some ribbon for Sarah from the penny stall. I don't suppose you have heard any further news about the job at Hunslet Mill, have you? I mentioned it to her and both my mam and Sarah were over the moon. She'd start tomorrow if she could, she hates school so much,' Meg said as they walked across the road onto George Street where the market was at.

'Oh yes, I knew I'd something to tell you. She's to go on Monday morning to see a Mr Askew at Hunslet Mill. She's to go to the top floor where they do the burling and mending and he'll talk to her, see if he likes her. If she shows adaptability for burling she'll get the job, with a bit of luck. That'll help you and your mam a lot if she does, won't it?'

'It will. We need the money and it will keep Sarah out of mischief. I can't have her bunking off school like she has in the past and hanging around the music hall doors. My mam is taking laudanum as if it's mother's milk and I can't afford to pay for it.'

Meg sighed and made her way to the stall in the centre of the market that everybody gave their trade to.

'There's me dragging you shopping and I bet it's the last thing you want to do. Can I help? I can lend you some money. You look so down,' Daisy said as she noticed Meg pick up a bunch of ribbons and then put them back down.

'Oh Daisy, I'm enjoying my time with you but all I can think about is the money I borrowed from out of the bakery's safe,' Meg confessed. 'I only borrowed it for my mam, to get some laudanum, but now I can't afford to pay it back and Ted Lund will be back from Ireland next week. I've never stolen in my life. I might have taken the odd loaf of bread home if it was going to be left over, but not money. If he finds out, it'll be the end of my working for him . . . or even worse.'

'How much did you take? Have you no way of paying it back?' Daisy asked, thinking that Meg must have borrowed pounds by the way she looked.

'I owe him a full shilling, but that will take me a week or two to save and pay him back. He hardly pays me enough to pay the rent and bills, I never have anything spare.'

'For Lawks sake, I thought you owed him pounds.' Daisy put her hand in her purse and passed Meg the shilling that her father had given her. 'Here, take this and enjoy your day. I can either give you it or you can pay me back whenever you can afford it. I hadn't expected anything from my father and I've been saving up for weeks for my shopping spree today on top of the money John gave me. Take it and put a smile on your face.'

'I can't, Daisy, I'd owe you then and I hate owing anybody,' Meg said, although she knew the precious shilling was the answer to one of her worries.

'Then don't owe me — have it as an early birthday

present, all be it a good'en. Perhaps I've already missed it, seeing I don't know when it is. Just take it and stop your worrying.' Daisy winked at her best friend. She'd easily got the money and she'd easily lost it, but it made her friend's day better and that's all that mattered.

'Only if you are sure?' Meg put the silver shilling in her posy bag and for the first time that day, gave a genuine smile. 'What would I do without you? You've lent me this and hopefully got Sarah a job. I couldn't wish for a better friend.' Meg took Daisy's hand and squeezed it.

'Now, get your Sarah those ribbons — and then are you going to introduce me to this man of yours before we get down to serious shopping? I could treat us both to a fancy cake to take home.'

Meg's face clouded over. 'No, we'll not go there. I found out he was only using me. I don't want to ever see him again,' Meg said, the happy mood instantly gone.

'Lord, lass, you attract bad luck like honey attracts the bees. No wonder you look miserable. Now, my mission for the day is to make you enjoy yourself. Get those ribbons that caught your eye for Sarah and something for yourself and then we will go up into the arcade and look at the latest fashions. I'll treat you to a tea if we have time.' Daisy picked up some hair grips and some press studs for use on her newly made blouse.

'I'm just having a bad time, I'll get through it,' Meg smiled. 'Anyway, I said I didn't want a fella yet.'

'No, be like me, take what you can get from them but don't commit. They only break your heart, it happens every time.' Daisy grinned. 'That is until the right man does come along.'

Meg grinned back and picked the ribbons up for Sarah and a small hair clip for herself. She passed the stallholder her money, still feeling guilty that she was buying things that she could not afford and that she owed Daisy, but it was better than knowing she'd stolen from Ted Lund.

As for Frankie Pearson, she still hurt, and in the darkest moments of the night she knew he was the right man for her, and that she would still run into his arms if he knocked on her door.

She put her purchases into her posy bag and Daisy linked her arm through hers. 'Come on, lass, best foot forward. Let's enjoy ourselves! But you were right about these bloody boots — like my mam says, pride comes before a fall. I should have worn my old flat ones. Never mind, we all make mistakes!'

22

'Who can that be at my door? I never have any visitors and then when our Meg isn't here, I get them knocking on my door like woodpeckers,' Agnes said as she looked across at Betsy. She wished she and the baby would go home. Her head was splitting and Betsy didn't seem to give a damn what the baby played in or what it touched.

'I'll get it, don't you stir. Or do you want us to be quiet in case it's the tallyman, he can't see in past the curtains?' Betsy whispered and picked up the baby.

'No, it'll not be the rent man and if it is, he's paid and we are straight with him. Just go and see who it is — tell them Meg is not at home if they are wanting her.' Agnes made herself look a little more respectable as she pulled her blanket around her knees and watched as Betsy, her baby on her hip, went and opened the door.

Agnes heard a voice on the step she knew and shouted to Betsy to let her visitor in. It was Ted Lund. He'd returned early from Ireland and was now looking to pick his key for the bakery up and to speak to Meg. 'Let him in, Betsy, and thank you love, but you and the baby can go home now. Our Meg won't be long.'

Betsy opened the door wide and looked at the man who everyone knew to be a miserable tight old soul and looked across at Agnes as he walked into the house. 'Are you sure you don't need me any longer? I can stay until Meg comes back.' But Betsy watched

Ted take her chair across from Agnes and knew that she had been replaced.

'No, you're right, lass, Ted is here now. Thank you for keeping me company, now you take care.' Agnes smiled and then sat back in her chair and looked across at Ted as Betsy left with the baby starting to cry on her hip.

'Lord, I thought I'd never get rid of her,' Agnes admitted. 'She never shuts up and the baby was in the cupboards and tumbling about and she never batted an eyelid.' Agnes sighed and looked across at Ted. 'So, you are back? Have you had a good trip? It will have brought back some memories no doubt, some that perhaps should have stayed buried?'

'Aye, I'm back, more's the pity. Back to the grindstone. But I couldn't have stayed there forever. As you say, it brought back memories. We've both had our heartaches, Agnes, both left mourning when we were only relatively young and didn't bother to get remarried. A lot of folks would have looked for another to spend their lives together with but I can never forget my Eleanor and Myra and you must have been the same when you lost your old man. I think if I'd been you I'd have taken on another man — it must have been hard bringing those two lasses up by yourself.'

Ted could see that Agnes' health had failed even more while he was away. She looked frail and she constantly struggled for breath. There were dark circles under her eyes and she was a shadow of the woman that he used to know.

'I managed. You have to. It makes you stronger and it's made my lasses stronger. You'll be wanting our Meg, will you? She'll not be long. She's gone with Daisy Truelove shopping around the market and

242

arcades, not that our Meg has any money, you'll know that.'

'You're telling me that, but you've got an orange by your side, they're not cheap. I hope she hasn't been helping herself to the takings.' He had immediately wondered how Agnes could afford the luxury of the orange.

'Betsy from next door brought me it,' Agnes said sharply. 'Her fella had helped himself from some that had been going bad down at the cut. At least that's what she said, you never know with Betsy. As for Meg helping herself to the takings, you should know her better. She's a good lass. I'll have you know she's been putting every hour God sends into that bakery. I think you'll be speechless when she tells you what she's been up to.' Agnes rose quickly to Meg's defence. She'd not have the lazy miserable Ted Lund accusing her lass of anything.

'What she's been up to?' Ted repeated. 'I hope that she's just got on with her job and baked bread, bread to my standards. That's all I asked her to do when I left,' he said sharply. 'I hope she hasn't let anyone have tick or taken any notice of what that Daisy Truelove has said. She's always complaining about my bread. Saying her father doesn't like it! I doubt he'll know what he's eating some days, he's that drunk when he comes home from the cut.'

'You'd better hold your noise now, Ted, I can hear them coming. There's some giggling going on, so they must have had a good time,' Agnes said as she heard the door handle being tried and watched as Meg and Daisy waltzed into the room with grins on their faces, which soon disappeared once they realized that Ted Lund was a visitor. 'You're back then, girls, I've swapped Betsy for Ted, and he's a bit less noisy than Betsy and her baby.'

Agnes was surprised by the shock on Meg's face.

'You are back then, Mr Lund, I didn't expect to see you until next weekend,' Meg said as she placed her few bags onto the table.

'Aye, I can see that, gadding about shopping. I hope that you've kept an eye on my business because I'll know if you haven't,' Ted growled and looked hard at what bags Meg had returned with.

'Yes, I think you'll find all is in order. I've been busy while you've been away,' Meg said and felt faint at the thought of coming clean at what she had been up to.

'She has. There's been queues outside the door of a morning. Just you wait until you see what she's been up to,' Daisy piped up and Meg turned around and shook her head at her, wanting her to say no more.

'Up to?' Ted said, getting increasingly concerned at the second person to talk about this. 'I hope she's been up to nowt. Queues I never have. Queues? What have you been doing? Have you been giving my bread away? I'd better have come home to some brass in my safe, else you'll have something to answer to.'

'I'll go, Meg, you'll need to talk.' Daisy picked up her bags and gave a knowing glance to Meg. She didn't want to make things worse and as Meg saw her to the door she whispered, 'Sorry.'

Meg was left to face the music; she knew now she'd have to explain exactly what she had actually been up to while Ted had been away.

Agnes could see the worry on Meg's face. 'Now listen here, Ted Lund, I told you, my Meg has worked all the hours on God's earth for your bakery. She's done what you should have been doing for all these years that you've been feeling sorry for yourself. You've got money in your safe, of that I'm sure, not that she's ever discussed your affairs with me.' Agnes caught her breath and started coughing.

'Mam, don't get upset. It's all right, I'll tell him what I've been doing,' Meg said and stood behind her mother's chair passing her handkerchief as she coughed up the contents of her lungs. Ted pulled a face at the state of her.

Meg shut her eyes for a moment, then decided to say it all in one. The words tumbled out of her mouth, falling over themselves. 'I've been baking things that I thought folk wanted, things that I knew would sell. Scones, teacakes, a granny loaf, a Victoria Sandwich, and I were right, folk has been nearly buying me out each day. I've made you plenty of money in your absence. I know I perhaps shouldn't but it was me doing the work and it's made you good money, so I could see no wrong in it.'

Ted was silent for a moment, before growling, 'I told you just to bake bread. I'm not making work for myself at my age. How did you pay for all this? You'd need eggs and butter and the likes, how did you buy them?'

'I put them on the Dinsdale's account, it's all paid for and up to date; I've kept my own accounts book that you can have now you are back, it's in the safe. I've put every penny spent in it along with receipts and every penny made. What money is in the safe is pure profit, and it's a nice sum even though I say so myself. It's a good little business that you have, Mr Lund.'

'It is if he's prepared to work,' Agnes said quietly and sat back and looked at the anger subsiding on his face.

'I don't know why you just couldn't do what I told you to do. I want nowt with work at my age. I'll see what's what at the bakery on my way back home. You needn't come in on Monday. I'll need a day to sort the mess out you'll have left me in. Now, give me the key to the shop and safe and look after your mother instead of spending your brass with that flibbertigibbet of a Daisy Truelove. She's nothing but a gossip and is always complaining about my bread.'

Meg passed him both keys from out of the pot dresser drawer.

'Daisy got you a lot more customers from the mill,' Meg told him. 'The girls come in every morning now, they spend quite a bit on one thing and another.' Ted stood up and made for the door. 'They'll be expecting my baking on Monday morning. Are you sure you don't want me to come in? All's in order at the bakery, it's as tidy as it has ever been, you've nothing to worry about.' Maybe if it meant him missing out on money and work, perhaps he would want her as usual?

'You'd better come in then, but I'll be opening up so you don't have to come to my house and knock me up. I'll also be watching what you get up to. I suppose my bread recipe has gone out of the window?' Ted grunted and knew instantly from Meg's reaction that he was right. 'Aye, I thought so, I hope you put the price up, else we'll not be making much profit on bread, no matter what you say. I'll see you Monday morning and if things are not to my liking, you'll be looking for another job or worse.' Ted hesitated for a moment and when he spoke again, his tone was a fraction softer. 'Look after your mother, instead of trailing off. She needs you.' Then he closed the door and left a relieved Meg.

'I was dreading telling him, Mam,' Meg said. 'I didn't think he'd be back before next weekend. He's early.' Meg let out a long shuddering breath, cupped her hands, and looked up at her mother. 'Thank you for fighting my corner, I know it took it out of you.'

'Nay, that was nowt, I was tired out long before then. Betsy never shut up chittering about all sorts of rubbish, and that baby of hers was just left to crawl all over the place. I was glad when Ted Lund appeared, just to get rid of her. Now, have you and Daisy had a good day? It looked like it by the amount of parcels and bags she had, although you haven't bought much.' Agnes looked at the few packages that Meg had brought in with her.

'Yes, we had a good time, Mam. I bought Sarah some ribbons as she'll need to look tidy on Monday.'

'Why, what's so special on Monday for her?' Agnes asked.

'I've never got to tell you what with Ted being here but Sarah has hopefully got herself a job at Hunslet Mill. She's to see the manager on Monday morning. Do you think we are doing right to let her leave school early? I keep worrying about it.'

'Well, she's not learning anything at school because she's just not interested in her lessons. Happen if it's to do with sewing and she gets her first pay packet, she'll knuckle down. You were helping me with the ironing and washing at her age. It never did you any harm, and it made you grow up. I sometimes just don't know what to do with the lass.'

'I could do with going with her to see the manager on Monday morning, just to make sure she gets there and acts right in front of the manager. You know what she's like. I can't now that Ted is back, I can't be in two places at once.'

'Well, I can't take her,' Agnes said. 'I can hardly manage our stairs nowadays and Hunslet Mill is a good distance to walk. She'll have to do it every day as well if she gets the job.'

'Mam, she'd been wandering around Leeds for days without us knowing,' Meg pointed out. 'Our Sarah is a lot cannier than she lets on. She may be not quite eleven but she knows what it's like on the streets. It's just her mouth she can't control most of the time. That's why I needed to be there.'

'You can't be there for her all her life, Meg. She'll have to learn as the rest of us did. Now, I'm going to go to my bed. Let me know when it is supper time and I'll get up for the evening. I've had enough with babies, bakers and our Sarah to think about. This body is tired and I need another drop of laudanum just to keep the pain at bay. Thank the Lord that you keep getting me it, I don't know what I'd do without it.'

Agnes pulled herself up from the chair and made for the stairs, leaving Meg sat in her chair, looking at her buys from off the market. She regretted being so frivolous with her money now that Ted was back. The shilling in her posy bag would have to be replaced into the till as soon as she entered the bakery's shop, but at last, she could do it now through the help of Daisy. However, she knew that Ted would soon have something to say about what had gone on at his bakery when he learned just how much baking she had been doing.

★ ★ ★

Ted Lund strode out down the street to his bakery. He could tell things had changed in his absence straight away. The window had been changed around and the few shelves that had been in it were now covered with the lace doilies that his wife had been so happy to use, awaiting the new baking on Monday morning.

He shook his head as he turned the key in the door and looked about him. The shelves were empty and clean, cleaner than he had ever known them and everything was in place. As he walked into the bakery, he noticed all the shelves had been tidied, the baking tins put in their correct sizes and the table scrubbed to an inch of its life. He'd give Meg Fairfax her due, she'd cleaned his bakery up and not done a bad job of it, he thought, as he opened the storeroom and was taken aback by the number of ingredients stacked on the shelves. Bags of flour were on the floor and tins of syrup and jam and bags of sugar were on every one of the wooden shelves. She must have bankrupted him with the number of ingredients she had stored away ready for her use in the coming few weeks.

He cursed, mad at himself for letting a young lass run his bakery while he gallivanted about in Ireland. He should have known that she'd not do as she was told. Her mother had always been headstrong when she was younger, and obviously her daughter took after her. She could never have made any money, he thought, as he stormed over to the safe that was hidden behind a breadboard and turned the key in the lock, feeling his heart pounding at the thought of the lack of money within. She couldn't have made him any proper money, anyhow. How would she know what was a decent profit when it came to his bakery? A couple of shillings would seem a lot to that lass, she was not used to brass.

He stepped back and held his breath as he opened the safe's door to reveal cloth bags full of money and a small roll of notes. There was more money in the safe than he had made in the last year. The lass had been right and on top of the money was her accounts book, with every penny accounted for and all the invoices and receipts within it.

He couldn't believe it — she couldn't possibly have made that amount of money in such a short time. He picked up the accounts book and put it in his pocket. He'd study that in detail later but for now he'd take his stash home with him and check every penny. The lass must have baked every minute of the day. Now that could be a good thing or a bad thing, he thought, as he locked the bakery door and carried the loot back to his home.

23

Meg felt half dead as she pulled herself out of bed. She'd not slept either Saturday or Sunday night for worrying about what Ted Lund was going to say to her now that he'd returned to find his shop cleaned from top to bottom, his store cupboard stocked to the rafters and his safe well stocked with the money she had made over the weeks he was away.

She'd also felt guilty about Sarah going for her first position in the world of work without either her or her mother's support. However, Daisy had told her that Tom Askew, the manager who she would be under at the mighty Hunslet Mill, was a good man. In fact, Meg had wondered just how Daisy knew him so well but had decided that it was none of her business and took it that it was just mill talk and nothing more.

She turned around and looked at her young sister still asleep and wished that she was her age and innocent. Clean, immaculately ironed clothes were hanging up on the bedroom door ready for Sarah's interview and she only hoped that she would curtail her thoughts and words when talking to Tom Askew. Whatever pay she could bring home would be welcome, just a little relief for her, and happen just enough to pay for her mother's laudanum each week.

She kissed her own two fingers and placed them gently on Sarah's cheek and whispered, 'Good luck, my sister. Although I'd still prefer for you stay at school if we could afford to keep you there,' and then set about getting herself ready for her day at work and

251

the expected wrath of Ted Lund as he discovered just how much work she had made for him at the bakery.

★ ★ ★

The morning was fine as Meg walked along the quiet street and her mind wandered to Frankie Pearson. How she wished Brenda Jones had not told her about his shallow plans. She should have left her in blissful ignorance of his schemes. Perhaps romance could have grown out of the situation because that was how her heart had been feeling when he had kissed her. Now, she just felt empty and cheated every time she thought of him and she couldn't bear to go anywhere near the patisserie, not even to look into the window.

He was a wealthy businessman who had used her and that was all there was to it, even though her heart still yearned for his touch and would melt at the sight of him. If he had thought anything of her, he could have come and visited her at the bakery, so obviously he was not too concerned.

As she walked down the street, she noticed the bakery's shop door was open and that Ted must already have the oven lighted since smoke was coming out of the oven's chimneys. Perhaps his holidays had done him good or perhaps she had shaken him up a little by showing what money could be made if he was prepared once more to work.

'So, you've shown your face,' Ted Lund said, with more than a hint of sarcasm in his voice. 'I thought that perhaps you'd think twice about coming back this morning. When I'd seen what money had been wasted on stock that might never be used! Joe Dinsdale must have been rubbing his hands every time he

252

heard his shop bell and saw you entering his shop.'

'I know. I do feel a bit guilty about stacking your shelves so well, but you must know that I have made you good money while you have been away.' Meg watched Ted knead the bread that she usually made and hoped that he had not added the extra sawdust to his mix.

'Aye, I'll give you that, and on my walk yesterday the amount of folk who have said how good your baking's been while I've been away was nobody's business,' Ted conceded. 'So I suppose you'll be glad to know there's no sawdust in my mix this morning. I'll make the bread and you make the rest of the fancies you've been serving folk with. That will make the most sense, as I'm happier making bread than fancy cakes.'

Ted looked at his assistant and thought of the days before she arrived in his bakery. He'd been able to do what he'd wanted and had made just enough money to keep the bills paid and more besides without all the work. But he'd humour her and see how things went. 'I can't guarantee to always let you do this. I think it's madness. It's a lot of work but you've made good money, so we'll carry on until I think it's not worth the bother.'

'Thank you, Mr Lund, I enjoy baking and making people happy with what I make,' Meg said and felt the shilling in her pocket that she had to replace in the till and hoped that he had not missed it.

'That's all very well but you've made work for both of us and if it doesn't keep making me money, then it comes to an end. I still can't understand why you decided to do it. There's been no gain for you from what I can see and if you think I'll be paying you any more for your work done here, you can think again.'

253

Ted looked hard at her and shook his head as he shaped his dough and left it to rise.

'I did it because I love baking and I've always wanted to share my love,' Meg said.

'You are soft in the head, just like my Eleanor was,' Ted responded. 'Folk will support you for as long as they feel like it and then they'll desert you to go to the next best thing. We'll see just how long it lasts.'

With that, Ted went and stoked his ovens, leaving Meg to make her usual batch of baking for the day's customers.

★ ★ ★

Agnes looked at her youngest daughter with a critical eye as she sat on the edge of her bed. It was seven thirty in the morning, Meg had been gone for over two hours and now it was Sarah's turn to show herself willing for work.

'You've washed behind your ears and your nails are clean? Appearances are important when you're applying for a job. Folk doesn't want to take somebody that looks like they've been pulled through a hedge backwards,' Agnes said as she watched Sarah fasten the top button of her blouse, tie her clean cream smock-apron behind her back, and sweep her long dark hair back over her shoulders.

'They're not going to look behind my ears and yes, my nails are clean and I've got clean underwear on before you ask,' Sarah said with disdain.

'Now, there's no need to be cheeky. I'm only trying to help you get this job. It'll be a good one if you pull the line and behave yourself. You've got a lot to thank Daisy Truelove for if you manage to secure it today.'

Agnes looked at her daughter. 'Take your sampler that you've been sewing with you to show the manager. He'll be impressed with your stitching — and you take care on your walk down to Hunslet. It's not the best of places, but work is work.'

'Mam, I can look after myself, stop moidering. I know where I'm going and who to see and then if I'm in time I'll go to school as promised and if I am a bit late, I'll tell old bag Pringle why. She'll probably put the flags out when she knows she's getting rid of me. Meg will go and tell her properly though that I'm leaving, won't she? If I get the job.'

'Yes, she will, now get your bate for your dinner and get yourself gone. Else you never will get to see about your job and get to school in time,' Agnes lectured as Sarah ran down the stairs. 'And mind your manners, they cost nowt but get you a long way in this world.'

She heard Sarah grab her tin box with sandwiches in off the table and slam the door behind her.

Agnes lay back in her bed and thought about the baby of her family walking along the busy streets to the tall redbrick building on the banks of the Aire. It was a mucky place, full of the noise of the weaving that took place within its walls, but at least Sarah would be on the top floor in the well-lit room where the burlers and menders looked at each piece of material that left the building, searching out and mending the flaws in the cloth. She was thankful that she'd not be working one of the weaving machines that could damage and maim. That was a blessing, she thought, as she closed her eyes and tried to go back to sleep.

★ ★ ★

Sarah weaved in and out of the many people going to work. Nobody looked at the side she was on as she pulled the tartan ribbon that Meg had told her to wear out of her hair and shoved it in her bate tin. She wasn't a child anymore, she didn't need a ribbon in her hair. She was going for a job, but first, on her way there, she would tell Harry. She hadn't seen him all weekend and she needed to tell him her news, she thought, as she walked along the streets and made her way down to the canal docks.

The docks were heaving with early morning traffic, burly men busy unloading coal from the Tom Puds while others were unloading cargo from barges in from the distant cities of Liverpool and Manchester, loaded with everything that made Leeds the busy thriving city that it was. Sarah pushed her way past men carrying boxes, fruit and all manners of things, looking around her for Harry, following the canal and the River Aire to the district of Hunslet and her appointment.

'Sarah, what are you doing here? It's bloody early for you to be down here! Is there something wrong?' Harry jumped onto the wharf side as he turned and looked at the owner of the Tom Pud that had carried a load of coal from the coalfields from near Wakefield. 'I'm a bit busy, I daren't talk for long, else I'll get shouted at.' Harry stood in front of her, his face covered with coal dust and his hands filthy from shovelling the black coal from the sturdy barge.

'I'm on my way to Hunslet Mill. I can't stop long myself, but I wanted to tell you, I'm going there for a job. I'm to work there as a burler and mender if they take me on,' Sarah said and grinned.

'That's a right good do, although I sometimes think

256

I'd rather be back at school. Especially when I'm working as hard as I am this morning.' Harry looked with worry as the barge owner yelled his name. 'Are you walking all the way out to Hunslet? If you are quick, that Tom Pud that's just unloaded is returning up that way will take you, there's a pier directly opposite, it will save your legs.' Harry looked quickly across to the barge owner that was about to get underway. 'Hey, Tom, can you give Sarah here a lift up to Hunslet Mill? It is nowt out of your way,' he called before Sarah had time to stop him.

'Aye, if she's quick,' the owner said as the engine of the barge filled the air with the smell of paraffin from the engine as he got ready for the return trip.

'I don't know, I'd be better off walking,' Sarah said.

'Nay, get a lift, go on, you'll be there in five minutes,' Harry said and urged her forward to get her out of his way so that he could get back to work, placing his grubby coal coated hands on her clean smock without her noticing.

'All right then, I've never ridden in a barge before.'

Sarah stepped forward and took the barge holder's hand as she stepped off the quay and into the barge.

'I'll see you tonight, meet you in the shed!' Harry yelled as he watched Sarah turn and look at him as the barge with its chimney chugging out steam cleared the quayside. Thank heavens she left, she had no idea what work was like, he thought, as he watched her standing at the stern of the barge, going down the canal in the direction of Hunslet.

Sarah stood next to the owner who steered the filthy coal-covered Tom Pud barge up the canal. The smoke from the engine kept blowing in her face and hair and the owner she found was a man of few words as he kept an eye on the other traffic on the canal and concentrated on his job. She was relieved when after ten minutes she saw the large square red building that she knew was Hunslet Mill come into sight. Harry had been right, it had only taken her a few minutes to reach the mill instead of walking the full distance. Pulling up at the pier next to the mill she thanked the barge owner and climbed out of the pud, her bate box under her arm, and looked up at the hundreds of windows that shone in the sun and listened to the clatter of the weaving machines. Up there at the very top, a manager was waiting for her, one that she had to impress, and then she would be earning some money for herself to spend. She'd no longer be dependent upon Meg and her mother, she thought, as she entered the mill and asked for directions to the burling room.

The woman at the first desk looked at her and was taken aback by the sight of her. 'You've come for an interview? You are not old enough are you, and you look as if you have just come from off the streets? I don't think Mr Askew will want to see you looking like that.' She and the other women in the office looked at the coal and smoke-covered young girl. 'You can't possibly touch the clean cloth with a face and hands like that, even your clothes have coal on them.' The receptionist looked her up and down and tutted. 'Let me look. If he's expecting you, your name is in the ledger for the day. What's your name?' She consulted a large leather-bound book that was just in front of her.

'It's Sarah, Sarah Fairfax,' she said and only then looked down at herself and realized why everyone was looking at her. The crisp cream smock apron was now a dirty shade of grey and there was a smudged hand of coal dust on the side of her, where Harry had pushed her forward. She could also smell the paraffin about her that had been driving the Tom Pud. She was filthy and smelly, everything her mother and Meg had told her not to be as she had got ready for her first-ever offer of a job.

'Yes, you are down in his book to be seen. So I suppose you had better go up and see him despite your attire,' the woman said and came out from behind her desk. 'Go through these doors and keep climbing until you get to the top floor. Keep out of the way of everybody and go straight there. He'll be expecting you: he'll be on the viewing platform at the top of the burling and mending room.'

She pushed open the big wooden doors that led to the wooden stairs that reached every floor of the busy textile mill. Sarah felt her nerves set in. She felt sick, and just for once, she knew that she should never have gone near Harry. She'd been clean, tidy and respectable when she had set off that morning, now she looked like a waif and stray. With every step climbed and every door passed into the heart of the mill, she felt her stomach churning with anxiety.

She finally reached the very top and opened the door to the burling and mending room. Directly in front of her stood an immaculately dressed man in a navy suit and a pocket watch in his pocket. He turned when she pushed open the door and looked at her.

'What on earth have I got here? You can't be the Sarah Fairfax that I'm expecting, Daisy gave me such a glowing report of you. She didn't say I should expect a ragamuffin and a filthy one at that!'

'Please sir, I am Sarah Fairfax. I'm sorry, I got a

lift on a Tom Pud down the canal and didn't know that I'd got so mucky,' Sarah said, nearly in tears. 'My mam sent me out spotless, it's all my fault.' A tear dropped down her cheek making her face look even worse as a trail of coal dust trickled down her cheek and landed on the top of the once-white apron. 'I can sew and I can spot mistakes, look I did this with my mam.' Sarah pulled her sampler out of her pocket and tried to show Tom Askew.

'No doubt you can, but you are not coming any-where near our newly made linen looking like that. My girls have to be clean and spotless, we don't want dirty handprints on the cloth.'

Sarah looked down into the floor below them, where row after row of girls were mending and burling the newly spun sheets of linen which were hung up in front of them. Each one of them carefully inspected the material and took out the burrs that had been left in it or repaired the weave of the material. All were clean and well presented and Sarah started to cry in earnest as she realized that it would have been the ideal job for her. Sarah felt like a child as the man-ager looked at her and didn't know what to do.

'Daisy said that you needed this job, that your mother's ill. But you are very young, my girls on the floor are at least thirteen. Given that you have turned up looking like a lost soul, I can't test you upon your skills. I do, however, need a lass to run errands for me and the girls on the mill floor. You could start there and work your way up, providing you don't come as mucky as this every day. Now, get yourself home and cleaned up and you can start with us next Monday and we'll take it from there.

'Underneath all that grime, I'm sure a clean Sarah

Fairfax started out, but you can thank Daisy Truelove for assuring me that you would be suitable to work here. Otherwise, I would have sent you on your way with a thick ear for wasting my time.'

Tom Askew looked at the young lass that was sobbing in front of him. 'Go on, get yourself home. I'll think what to pay you when you show up on Monday.' A big smile started to emerge on Sarah's face. 'I'm too soft for my own good,' Askew mumbled to himself then adopted his original stern demeanour. 'You'll have to work hard. There will be no peace for you — the lasses will want thread and needles getting, and if you run up these stairs once a day you'll do it fifty times.'

'Thank you, I really did come all clean and tidy. Meg and my mam will kill me when they find out what I've done.' Sarah wiped her nose on her sleeve and looked at her new employer.

'And bring a handkerchief with you next time. Now go on, get gone. Monday morning seven sharp and you'll soon learn how better off you were at school. They all do when they first start here.'

Tom watched Sarah go through the doors without another word and shook his head. He shouldn't have taken the lass on, he really didn't have a job for her, but he'd find her something for her to do somewhere. It was the least he could to satisfy his lover Daisy and keep her happy.

24

'So, he's back!' Daisy whispered to Meg as she passed her the usual loaf of bread. 'Is this your making or his?' she asked as she felt its weight.

'It's all right, it's his making, but it's fine and just as good as mine.' Meg winked and then whispered another thank you for the shilling that she'd now put in the till.

'Your Sarah should know in another hour if she's got her job or not. She'll be all right working at Hunslet Mill with Tom Askew looking after her. He's a good man . . . and handsome.' Daisy had a dreamy smile on her face, that Meg was too wrapped up in Sarah's problems to notice.

'I hope she gets it. I'm dreading going home this afternoon to find that she's ruined her chance of a decent job, knowing her.' Meg wiped the counter down and listened to Ted moaning about something in the bakery.

'She'll have a job, don't you worry. Tom will have done right by her no matter what,' Daisy said and couldn't help giving Meg an all-knowing look.

This time Meg registered it. "Tom', is it? Do you know him that well?' Meg grinned.

'I may do, but don't tell his wife. It's been our secret for a while now. Now that's enough of my secrets for a morning and anyway you have another customer coming. Enjoy your day with old grumpy.'

Daisy winked and left Meg shaking her head. She could never be as carefree as Daisy and she would never be so stupid as to be a married man's mistress. She had always promised her mother to lead a pure life and to always be true to herself and the man that she would eventually marry. It would only end in tears, she thought, and then prayed that a good word from Daisy would have secured Sarah a job at the mill. No doubt she'd soon find out, however it had gone.

By noon the bakery shop had been just as busy as it had been in Ted's absence. The shop bell had never stopped ringing and Ted had never stopped moaning. He might be making money but he was also having to work harder than he had ever done and that was going down badly.

'My bloody feet are killing me, I've never sat down for a minute this morning. I think my gout is starting to play up again, I'll have to go and see Henry Booth at the apothecary's for my usual pills. It will have been brought on with all the rich food that my sister-in-law put under my nose while I was in Ireland but standing on my feet all morning has not helped.'

Ted slumped in his usual chair and Meg knew that in another few days he'd either be needing to be wakened up or she'd be left in the bakery on her own. Whichever it was, she was going to have to curtail her baking. He wouldn't want to be spending so much at Dinsdale's and he didn't like the extra work and the comments he'd overheard as she had served her customers, knowing that he had returned.

'Why don't you go and see Henry Booth now? I'll see to the shop and tidy the bakery. After all, I've been doing that while you were away,' Meg said, hoping that she didn't seem too eager to get rid of him.

'Aye, I might, I'm no good to anyone if I can't walk. We've had that many folk through the shop this morning. I must have made plenty of brass, empty me the till and I'll go to the bank at the same time.' Ted got up from his chair and passed Meg a blue cloth bag that he used for his change out of the till, which she took and emptied most of the money into.

'Mmm . . . that looks promising, but it's been bloody hard work. When I took you on, I didn't bargain for this.' Ted put the bag of money into his pocket. 'Make sure you lock up, and try to sell those last few loaves, they cost enough, now you've had your way with the ingredients, and it's a quick slope from profit to loss.'

He walked out of the bakery door and left Meg wondering if she would ever make him a happy man or if he would always see the worst in everyone and everything.

* * *

'So, you're back from wandering around Ireland are you?' Henry Booth passed Ted his gout pills and looked at the man who had an ailment whenever he couldn't be bothered with the world.

'Aye, I'm back, I'm jiggered already as well. That lass I took on before I left has had me working like an idiot. I don't think she'll be stopping much longer with me. I'm no longer my own boss in my own bakery. I can't be having that.' Ted leaned on the counter and looked at his old friend.

'Aye, I've kept hearing her being mentioned. She must have made you some money though, Ted, you seem to have had a lot of customers while you've been away,' Henry replied.

'Aye, she has, but she's spent some as well. Dinsdale's should be bending over backwards to keep me

264

happy, she's spent so much money with them,' Ted moaned.

'Aye, she's spent a bit in here with me and all. In fact, I was wondering how she could afford the laudanum she buys every week. I know it's for her mother, but it's costing her a pretty penny and if I know you, she'll not be getting paid the largest of wages.' Henry leaned on the counter and looked at his lifelong friend and saw him thinking things over.

'No, she's on the lowest pay I could get away with. She should just have enough to keep them fed and a roof over their heads,' Ted mumbled.

'Well, I'd be having a look at your takings and your books. They might be pawning stuff for the money but she's getting it from somewhere, that's all I'm saying,' Henry Booth said and left the seed of doubt to germinate in Ted's brain as he watched him walk out of the shop. He had nothing against the young lass, but he owed it to his old friend to make him aware of what might be going on behind his back.

Ted walked out of the bank after placing his money into his account and started to think what Henry Booth had said. He still thought about the orange he had noticed when visiting Meg's home and the bags that she had brought in after shopping with the loose-living Daisy Truelove. Now there was Henry telling him that she had been buying laudanum. On her wage she shouldn't be able to do all that? He'd better keep a careful eye on his employee. He could smell a rat and it was alive and smiling at him in his bakery, no matter how good her baking was.

* * *

'Just look at you! I hope that you didn't go to Hunslet Mill looking like that. They wouldn't let you in through the doors, let alone take you on. How on earth did you get so mucky?' Meg asked as she met Sarah at the school gates.

Sarah hung her head. 'I'm sorry, Meg, I went down the canal on a Tom Pud, the bargeman gave me a lift to the mill and before I knew it I was filthy with the smoke and coal. I didn't realize until the girls at the mill started smirking at me.'

'Why were you down at the canal? You should have followed the road. Let me guess — Harry! So I take it that you haven't got the job and I'm wasting my time going in to see Miss Pringle,' Meg said angrily.

'No, I got a job, but not the one I went for. Mr Askew said I was too young for it anyway but he's given me a job making sure everyone has what they need. I've got to keep the girls supplied with whatever they need and do what he wants me to do. Then he says I can work my way up.'

Sarah looked up at her older sister, praying that she'd still go in and tell Miss Pringle that she'd be finishing school.

'That's not a proper job, he's just taken pity on you. He's just made it up not knowing what to do. I don't suppose he's told you what he's going to be paying you has he?' Meg asked.

'No, but he said I'd to start on Monday at seven. It is a proper job, our Meg, I will work hard and I will get to be a burler. I don't want to keep going to school. Please, Meg, go in and see Miss Pringle.'

'We'll see what Mam says,' Meg decided. 'I'll come back tomorrow afternoon if she still thinks you can leave. It would help if we knew what he was going to pay you.' Meg shook her head. 'I knew I should have gone with you. Just for once, I thought you would keep that head screwed upon your shoulders but no, that Harry led you astray again. For Lord's sake keep out of his way, he just keeps getting you into trouble.'

Meg put her arm through her sister's and waltzed her off home to face whatever fate her mother decided for her.

★ ★ ★

Sarah sat in the corner of the shed that she and Harry had made their meeting place. She'd been sitting there most of the evening waiting for him with her news. She watched the lamplighter come and light the gas lamps at the end of the street and watched the bats creep out from the many dark places that kept them hid through the daylight hours.

It was late now, too late for Harry to be joining her. In fact, since he'd started work he didn't seem to have any time for her. She watched as Meg opened the front door and yelled out her name, the shaft of light from inside the house illuminating the dirty yard that the darkness had hidden as if it was ashamed of it.

Just like the shame she had felt when she had stood in front of Mr Askew when he looked at her with pity. He'd hopefully be good to work for. She'd soon be finding out as her mam had agreed that she could go and work at Hunslet Mill, no matter what it involved.

She knew why she'd said yes, she wasn't that daft, despite what folk whispered under their breath out of her earshot. Her mam was dying and she wanted to see her at work before she went to her maker. That was the top and bottom of it.

Sarah wiped a tear away and got to her feet. Harry would hardly ever come to her in the hut again and she too would be too tired of an evening to bother with friendships. It was time she grew up. After all, in another few weeks she would be eleven, old enough to earn her living and show some responsibility whether she wanted to or not.

25

Frankie Pearson sat back in his comfortable leather chair and folded his newspaper and breathed in deeply. It was Sunday morning, the one day he had away from his newly built business and he was going to make sure that it was his day of rest.

His housemaid came in with his mid-morning tea and bobbed after leaving it on the small table by his side. He thanked her, poured himself a cup then stood and looked out of the bay window that looked out across Headingley Park. Thank heavens his maid was about to go home. He wanted some time to himself and some peace.

The previous week had been not the best in his life. He had written to his mother requesting a meeting with her to arrange a transfer of some of his father's legacy to him. He might have been left a small fortune but it was in trust between his mother and his father's solicitor until he was twenty-one. So far she had not been bothered to reply to him, probably too busy with the numerous gentlemen friends that she entertained. He sipped his tea and thought about his past. His mother always had a string of male friends even when married to his father, which he thought as he drank, his father had permitted in their home in an attempt to keep some resemblance of a happy marriage. His grandmother, his mother's mother, had known what her daughter was like, which was why she had invested in him and his love of catering, leaving his mother with nothing, causing bad feeling between his mother and him. Especially when his father had also left him everything in his will too.

Now, he doubted that he would ever return to Paris. His mother would be all right, surrounded with washed-out artists of one kind or another. She'd not be welcoming him back with open arms, that was for sure. Besides, he wanted to concentrate more on his business. Things were beginning to pick up now his name was being talked about in society. The rich of Leeds were beginning to enjoy his pastries and things were going to plan, apart from Brenda Jones and next week he was intent on removing her from his service. He had been thinking of it for some time, and now his mind was made up.

The girls, Norah and Marie, did their jobs well; they were always pleasant and were never patronising to any of his customers. However, Brenda was a different story, he thought, as he looked out over the park and the weeping willows bending in the wind. Once or twice he'd found her looking down her nose and treating the more humble of society as if they were a piece of dirt on her shoe. He'd no time for that. Everyone was welcome in his bakery and she could not abide that.

She had to go, especially if he was going to do what he and his accountant had been discussing. She'd not like the thought of ordinary everyday tea rooms opening up above the shop. That would never do; she thought herself better than anyone else. However, the tea rooms he was planning would serve warm buttered scones, fancy cakes and plain, ordinary baking just like he had seen in the bakery where the beautiful Meg had been working.

He sighed and went to sit down in his chair and

looked at the newspaper, uninterested. Why had she not met him at the Corn Exchange and why had she not shown her face at the shop? He missed her, but the last week or two had been so busy with one thing or another he hadn't had time to go to the bakery along York Road. If only she had told him her home address he could have gone around on a day like today and stroll out with her or have tea, just to see her beautiful face and hold her tiny hands. She was everything he had ever hoped for in a woman and now she had deserted him. Perhaps he should make time and visit the bakery as soon as he could. After all, it wasn't just her face that attracted him. It was also her baking skills. Her looks and skills had him captivated.

He would have to go back and visit her soon.

★ ★ ★

Meg looked at Sarah. It was early on Monday morning and she'd asked Ted Lund if she could be late into work in order to make sure Sarah got to her new job. She now scrutinised her young sister making sure she was presentable. 'Try and keep tidy like that all day and don't answer anybody back — folk don't like you if you are lippy. I'll come in to see where you are working and then I'll leave you. I've got to get back to the bakery.' Meg straightened the ribbon yet again that Sarah kept pulling at.

'You don't have to come with me this morning; I'll go straight there, and I'm not a child anymore,' Sarah said scowling at her sister.

'You are to me and Mam. Now come on, else you'll be late and Ted Lund has already knocked my pay down, the ungrateful old bugger, after all the hours I've put in for him and all.'

The two sisters made their way through the streets and down to the canal at Hunslet and stood watching the folk flowing in through the mill doors. Men and women of all ages headed in to work long hours on little pay. The only thing that bound them all together was the comradeship of the mill. Everyone was in the same boat so it was no good complaining about their lot. Work put bread on the table and had to be endured.

Sarah and Meg stood like an island among the flow of workers. 'Don't come in with me, Meg,' Sarah said finally. 'I've got to make my own way in the world. Leave me here and I'll see you tonight.'

'Are you sure? Make sure this Mr Askew tells you your duties properly today and ask him how much he aims to pay you. He should have told you when you were here the other day.'

Meg bent forward and kissed her young sister on the brow. They didn't see eye to eye on most occasions but she did love her younger sister and she knew this was a big day for her. She watched Sarah join the crowd and shook her head when she saw her pull the ribbon that they had argued over out of her hair. She'd be all right, she was feisty enough to tackle anything, she thought, as she turned and hurried back to her work.

Worrying now that both of them were at work, would her mother manage to sort herself in a morning, and would Ted have baked proper good bread that morning if she was not there to see him do so? It was his loss, she thought. After all, it was his business if he hadn't been bothered to do so. He'd been acting stranger than usual this last week, but she had put that down to his return from his trip to Ireland, which he'd barely mentioned. Ted Lund played his cards close to his chest and nothing would ever change that.

★ ★ ★

Frankie looked across at the bakery and tried to see if he could see Meg serving on in the shop. He'd decided to visit her before he set about telling Brenda Jones exactly what he thought of her and giving her a quick shift from his employment. He'd even left his baking halfway through the usual morning's bake because Meg had been playing so much on his mind of late. It was time to tell her and ask her what he had been considering ever since he had met her.

He walked across the street and peered in through the shop's window but could not see anybody, so he opened the door and walked into the small bakery that always smelled so welcoming. The shop bell rang above his head and Frankie felt his heart pounding as he waited to see Meg. He felt like a schoolchild. He'd never felt that way before, he thought, as he heard footsteps coming through from the bakery.

'Aye, what do you want this morning?' Ted stood behind the counter in his white apron and looked his distinguished customer up and down.

'Em, I'll take a loaf of your white bread, please,' Frankie said. 'However, I wondered if Miss Fairfax is at work this morning.' He reached into his pocket for some money and waited for a reply from the stressed-looking baker who didn't look happy with his lot.

'No, she bloody well isn't. She's left me this morning making all her recipes just to make sure her sister goes to her new job. What do you want her for anyway?' Ted scowled. 'I just wanted to ask her something; it is of no consequence.' Frankie shrugged his shoulders. 'Perhaps you could tell me her home address, I need to speak to her.'

'Does she owe you money? Or perhaps she earns money another way other than working for me through the day and it's that you are asking about her for. Does she satisfy your needs up a dark alley and then take your money for your pleasures? Nothing would surprise me with that one.' Ted looked at him hard, knowing there was only one reason why such a well-dressed gentleman would be bothering his shopgirl.

'I'm sorry, I'm sure Miss Fairfax is not like that and I don't like the insinuations or your tone of voice,' Frankie said stiffly. 'I was just needing to talk to her. Her address — do you have it?' Frankie asked again, taking an instant dislike to Ted Lund.

'I don't know it, you'll have to catch her here another day if it's that important to see her. In fact, I don't know if she'll be coming back to work for me today or any day. She left in a huff and told me what to do with my job.' Ted wasn't going to give Meg's address to some fella with a foreign lisp, no matter how much a gent he looked. He was sure he was up to no good.

'That would be a shame, she is a good baker. I thank you for your time.' Frankie stopped for a second. 'If you do see her, could you tell her Mr Frankie Pearson was asking after her and that I wish her well.'

'I will, but as I say I might never see her ever again. Good morning, Mr Pearson.' Ted rubbed his hands on his apron as the fancy gent left. He recognized the

274

name — he was the owner of the fancy patisserie on the Headrow that had been the talk of the Buffalo Club. So, what had Meg Fairfax been up to with him and why was he looking for her? She was not that good at baking. It couldn't be that he was interested in her, could it?

Not long after, Meg arrived. 'A fella was asking after you when you were out,' Ted told her. 'He gave his name as Frankie Pearson, and was asking for your home address.' Ted was surprised at the shock on Meg's face as she took her shawl off and put her apron on.

'Did you give him it?' Meg asked, looking worried. She didn't want Frankie knowing where or how she lived — and after Brenda Jones had told her the truth about him, she never wanted to see him again else it would break her heart.

'No, I thought better of it. He sounded French and I didn't know what he wanted you for. Are you in bother with him? What does he want with you?' Ted pried.

'No, it isn't a case of being in bother with him. I found his card case when I was out shopping with Daisy and I took it back to his bakery. He probably called to thank me,' Meg lied and blushed and then went into the shop to serve a customer as the shop bell rang.

'And I'm a monkey's uncle,' whispered Ted to himself. Everything he'd learned since he got back made him feel Meg Fairfax was not to be trusted. She was up to something. Otherwise, how did this Pearson gent know she worked for him but not her home address? He was going to watch her like a hawk.

Meg looked and felt the bread under the counter.

She'd been right, Ted had reverted back to his old ways with her not being there. The loaves were heavy and unglazed and what cakes he had made had been given no love. She looked out of the bakery window and fought back the tears. Frankie had been looking for her, but not for the reasons she had hoped for.

Had he spoken to Ted about perhaps buying the bakery? She would be the last one to know because neither Ted nor Frankie would tell her. Whatever happened, she'd be out of work because she would no longer be taken advantage of by any man who did not appreciate her or her baking skills.

She passed the next customer one of Ted's solid loaves and knew that they would not be returning when they knew the quality had gone back to what it once was. But why should she worry? It was not her bakery and never would be.

26

It really hadn't taken Ted long to slip back into his old ways. Hard work was not in Ted's nature, Meg was soon beginning to find out, and although he liked the profits, he didn't want to work for them. Three weeks after Ted's return she was opening the bakery up by herself and had been told by him not to waste her time baking things that folk didn't appreciate and couldn't really afford.

She'd also had to give way to adding the sawdust to the bread mix. It had been that or lose her job — although Meg was beginning to think any job would be better than working for Ted Lund. However, the hours worked in her favour as her mother was getting progressively worse. Sarah didn't return from the mill until after seven in the evening so Meg was needed at home.

Sarah had fitted into mill life with relish. She enjoyed the gossip and company of the mill girls, and although Meg still didn't really know what her work involved, she seemed to enjoy it and the shilling that she brought home every week was more than welcome. Sarah was also spending less and less time with Harry, which her mam and Meg welcomed.

Meg leaned on the counter and waited for her first customer of the day. The shelves were not as full nowadays. Only the basics had been made in accordance with Ted's orders, so the shop was not as busy. Meg thought again what she could do with the business if only it was hers. What a waste, she thought, as she looked at the solid bread that nobody wanted.

'Mind the shop, George, I'll take the local invoices out today,' Joe Dinsdale said as he grabbed his overcoat and stepped out onto the wet surly streets of Leeds.

It might have been mid-summer but nobody had bothered telling the weather that, he thought, as he clutched the monthly invoices in his hands. He'd gone through the shop's books the night before and had not had slept well after realising that the young lass from Ted Lund's bakery had not paid the last month's bill, nor had Ted or her been into his shop for the last three weeks. He wondered if anything was wrong, and more to the point, was he going to get his money? He'd heard Ted was back from his trip to Ireland, so that morning he had decided to pay the baker a visit and hopefully get what was owed to him.

The rain was trickling down the back of his neck by the time he reached Ted Lund's bakery and he looked into the dimly lit shop and noticed Meg with her hands cupped around her face looking as miserable as the rain outside but soon saw her face change as he entered the bakery.

'Good morning, Mr Dinsdale, it's a wet day to be giving us a visit. What can I get for you?' Meg smiled at him but didn't get a smile back from the gruff businessman.

'Is Ted in? I need to speak to him,' Joe Dinsdale said and looked around him. The bakery had only half the baking it had a few weeks ago and there was no sign of customers.

'He's at home today. The weather has laid him low. I've opened the bakery and done what baking he said I'd to do,' Meg replied, knowing that the shelves of the shop looked pitiful now Ted was back in control. 'Can I help?'

'No, it's the organ grinder I need to speak to, not the monkey,' Joe Dinsdale said gruffly. 'I'll go and see him at his home. Good day.'

Joe left the shop and stepped out back onto the rain-sodden streets, leaving Meg wondering why he had looked so annoyed at her. It wasn't her fault that Ted was not spending any money that month at Dinsdale's. He said they'd had enough of his money and until the shelves were near but empty he wouldn't be going back. They would never be going back if it was up to him, she thought, because all they were going to be making again would be his bread of sawdust and that was not selling now his customers knew what they had been missing. He was a lazy, stupid man and didn't deserve the bakery.

★ ★ ★

'Joe, what brings you out on a day like this and to my house as well?' Ted answered the loud knock on the door that had disturbed him from writing his letter of thanks to his sister- in-law, a letter that should have been written straight after his return from her.

'It's rather a delicate matter, not one to discuss on a doorstep, no matter what the weather. May I come in?' Joe said and looked at Ted as the drips ran off his trilby.

'Aye, you better had if it is that serious.' Ted opened the door and showed Joe into his front room. 'Now, what's to do?'

Joe looked uneasy at what he was about to say. 'It's just that while you were away, the lass that you've

279

got in the shop ran up a bill each month. Which was grand, I welcomed the trade.'

The trader hesitated as Ted smirked. 'I bet you did. There's still stuff on my shelves that she bought. I want nowt with making half the stuff she makes. I want a quiet life.' Ted shook his head and looked at Joe. 'Come on then, spit it out, man.'

'Well, you answered half my question that you've enough stuff on your shelves and that's why you've not been in this month. But my bigger worry is that last month's bill was not paid. I've got the copy invoice here in my hand and it was never settled. Now, I know you've been away but it's for a good amount of money, I could do with it back in my account.'

'I'm sure she's got it down as paid in her accounts book that she made up while I was away.'

Ted looked at the invoice that Joe had hesitantly given him and went into his kitchen to pick up the accounts book that he had placed upon the other paperwork for the bakery. He brought it back and showed Joe Meg's sums for the shop. There, next to the amount owing she had written the word 'paid' quite clearly.

'Do you have a signed invoice?' Joe asked. 'Because, believe me, Ted, she's never paid me, no matter what she's put in that book. George always makes sure the payments this large are made with me and believe me, I never saw hide nor hair of her with this payment last month. This lass of yours is trying to do a fast one on you. I'd go and sort her out and I wouldn't have her in my shop on her own.'

The anger was quickly rising on Ted's face.

'I'll sort it, Joe. I'll come along later and settle this account. I'm sorry that you have had to come and

280

see me about this. I trusted her and although she's worked hard while I've been away, I've no doubt that she's also taken advantage of me.'

Ted Lund felt his hackles rising as he saw Joe to the door. Meg Fairfax had to go. She'd shown him up for the very last time and he wanted his money back!

★ ★ ★

Meg saw Ted crossing the street to her and wondered why he was coming when it was near to closing. He never showed his face at this time of day. She looked at him as he slammed the bakery door behind him and turned the sign to Closed. He had her accounts book in his hand and his face was like thunder.

'I've had Joe Dinsdale at my home this morning. I've never had a fellow trade person come chasing me for money. He says that you've never paid this bill that you've written down as paid even though you've no proof of payment. What have you to say for yourself?' Ted barked.

Meg looked at him in utter amazement. 'It was paid, I paid it just before you returned back from Ireland. I gave the money to George because Mr Dinsdale was busy with a salesperson and he put it into the till's drawer to give him later.' Her composure fled. 'I'm not lying, I'd never lie, especially when it comes to money,' she wailed, near to tears.

'I don't believe you,' Ted said bluntly. 'I think you've been taking advantage of me. It's not just Joe Dinsdale that's concerned about you. Henry Booth says you've been buying laudanum without a care in the world and I've noticed that you are living well since you started working here. I'm not having it, Meg. I'm

281

sorry but I'm sending you on your way and once I've decided what to do, you might be getting a visit from the peelers. I'll not be taken advantage of. Now get out and don't show your face in my bakery again!'

'But I didn't do it. Ask George, please ask George, he'll back me up,' Meg cried as Ted grabbed her arm and pulled her out from behind the counter and threw her protesting out of the bakery out onto the pavement, making her fall face down into the busy street.

'Get out and stay out. I don't want help like yours in my shop. I should never have taken you on. It was only because I felt sorry for your mother that I did so. You are a thief and a blatant one at that!' Ted yelled for all the passers-by to hear making Meg feel totally ashamed as she picked herself up from the gutter.

Tears ran down her face and she was trembling as she made her way home. How could Ted Lund treat her like that? She had done nothing wrong, nothing at all. She had paid the bill, and she'd watched George put the money in the till. Surely if Ted talked to George he'd realize his mistake and want her back. He'd have to! She needed the money to survive. She sobbed and made her way back home, her head hung partly in shame and partly in anger at the injustice done to her.

★ ★ ★

Ted Lund stood at the counter and handed over the money that he said was owed and looked at Joe Dinsdale. 'She says she paid young George over there, but I don't believe her. She's been spending money like water while I've been in Ireland. The bloody thief. I've sacked her anyway, I don't want her in my shop and

282

she'll be lucky if I don't call the peelers in to see her. I would if I didn't know her mother was so ill.'

'And I thought that she was a grand lass,' Joe replied. 'Everyone was speaking highly of her when you were away and her baking was the talk of these backstreets. I'm disappointed for you.'

Joe Dinsdale thought for a moment, then said, 'Just let me ask George if he knows anything about it; I didn't bother asking him when I came to see you this morning because, as I say, it is always me that sees to the monthly accounts.

'George, when you've finished serving Mrs Palmer, can you come over here please?' Joe shook his head and watched as George packed Mrs Palmers' basket and then joined them.

'Yes, Mr Dinsdale, how can I help?' George looked at both men and couldn't help noticing the anger on Ted Lund's face.

'The lass that's been working for Ted here says that she paid you for the monthly bill last month,' Joe explained. 'Now, I've never seen anything of it so it's causing a bit of a barney.'

Joe gave a searching look to his assistant who he trusted as much as his wife.

'Aye, I remember her coming in. We were rushed off our feet that day,' George said immediately. 'You were talking to the salesman from Boston's and I told her to come back later. But she didn't want to take the money home with her because it was quite a bit.' George looked at both men. 'I took both the invoice and the money that she'd placed in an envelope and put it into the back of your till, Mr Dinsdale. I did tell you when you returned from your dinner with the salesman. You must have . . . forgotten,' George said, leaving Joe in no doubt as to what he was being too polite to say.

'Well, I've never seen it and I can't remember you telling me. I wonder if that's why my till drawer has been sticking of late. I've meant to have a look at it for the last week or two.'

Joe walked over to the till and opened the drawer with a push of a button but the action was slower than usual. All eyes were on him as he crouched down and put his fingers into the very back of the drawer and felt around for what he knew now had been making his drawer stick. Right at the back and wedged underneath the drawer and the structure of the till he felt the envelope and the money within it. The coins trickled out as he pulled on the envelope but the notes came out with the torn envelope paper and were there for everyone to see.

'Well, it seems that your lass Meg was telling you the truth,' Joe said. 'I owe you an apology. I hope you've done nowt rash, Ted. She has paid me and it's me that's wrong.' Joe stood with the money in his hand feeling foolish as he watched George go back to his counter without a word.

'Well it's too late now — I accused her of being a thief and sent her on her way. I'm not going back on my words,' Ted muttered. 'I'm sure she's probably been helping herself to my money if I know her.'

Joe knew Ted was probably thankful not to be paying the bill twice, but felt the least he could do was to stand up for Meg. 'She worked every hour for you, Ted Lund, she was nicely building that bakery up again for you single-handed,' he said. 'You could do with getting her back and letting her have her own way with your business. I'm glad that I've been proven wrong even at my own embarrassment. She's an asset to whoever employs her.'

He knew it was pointless. Ted would always be a stubborn man, someone who looked at the pennies instead of the pounds.

'Aye, well, I'm not taking her back on. You can have her if you want her, I'll run my bakery as I want to run it and not how a jumped up bit of a lass thinks it's got to be run. Now, good day. I'm glad that my business here is straight with you because I'll not be coming back.'

Ted scowled across at George as he walked out of the store and back home, wishing that he had never taken Meg Fairfax on to help him in his bakery. She'd turned his world upside down and had been nothing but trouble.

285

27

'Oh lass, stop your crying. He always has been an awkward old bugger. I know that you've not taken his money. George at Dinsdale's will tell the truth, he's a good lad.'

Agnes tried to console her daughter as she sobbed in the chair across from her.

'He never gave me a chance to fight my corner. He thought the worst of me, no matter what I said. How could he, Mam? I've worked so hard, I made him so much money and I loved every minute working there when he was away.'

Her mother stood up and put her arm around her shoulders. 'He's a bitter, stupid and lazy old man, but it has given you a chance to realize what you can do if you put your mind to it. I just wish we had the money to buy his bakery; you'd be set for life then and I could go to my grave happy.' Agnes caught her breath before continuing, 'At least Sarah seems to have found happiness in her work, although she's coming home every night on her last legs. Her bit of money won't go far though.'

'I'm sorry, Mam, I've let us down. I'll try and find something else. Although if Ted Lund has blackened my name, nobody will want to take me on,' Meg said forlornly.

'You'll rise above it, if I know you. You don't let Ted Lund get the better of you. Everyone knows him for what he is. Now stop your crying, you've done nothing wrong and folk will know that. We'll just have to make do and mend until something comes along for you.'

★ ★ ★

Daisy hugged her closest friend and tried to console her. 'Well, I'm not going back and giving Ted Lund my business. His bread has always been rubbish anyway and everybody is missing you and complaining that he should take you back. I keep telling everybody that what he says is not right — and young George at Dinsdale's is sticking up for you, especially when old Dinsdale had been that drunk he'd not remembered what he'd told him. He'll not be going on any more lunchtime knees up with salesmen.'

She tried to cheer her best friend up. 'I know you probably don't want to hear this but why don't you go and see your Frankie Pearson and see if he can give you a job?' she suggested, hoping for her head not to be bitten off in reply.

'No, Brenda Jones made that as clear as crystal. I'd never fit into his world either working for him or on his arm.'

'And what did this Brenda Jones know about anything? Anyway, you're not the only one who has lost their job. I hear your Frankie has given her the push as well. She probably deserved it though, she was a snooty cow from what you told me.'

That put a small smile on Meg's face. 'He's sacked her? He said he was going to. I hated her. She thought herself so much better than anyone else and looked at me like I was scum.'

'There we are, there's still an inkling of curiosity and longing in you for that Frankie Pearson,' Daisy said. 'Why don't you go and see him? I think he genuinely had feelings for you from what you've told me. He'd give you a job as soon as look at you, I'm sure he would.' That earned Daisy a glare from Meg.

'No, I'm not being conned again. I would have given him my heart if he'd asked me for it. As it was, it wasn't me that he loved, it was what I could get and do for him. I couldn't work close to him every day knowing that I had once had feelings for him. Just leave it, Daisy, I'll make my own way in the world, I'll get myself a job. Besides my mam needs me at home at the moment.'

'All right, it's your life, I was only trying to help. I hear Sarah is settling in nicely at Hunslet Mill. At least she'll be bringing a little money in for you all,' Daisy said, admitting defeat.

'Yes, but she doesn't like parting with it and she could do with a bit better pay, you can tell your fancy man,' Meg grinned.

Daisy grinned back. 'Fancy man? I don't know what you are on about! Tom Askew and I are just casual acquaintances.'

'Well, that's one way of putting it, but I think there's a bit more to it than that.'

'You do what you have to do in this world to survive, my girl, and if me being *friends* with Tom gets me by in life, then that is what I'll do,' Daisy said firmly. 'You could do with doing the same with Frankie Pearson but I know that you are too damn proud. Now take care, my love, I'll see you at the weekend.'

Daisy smiled to herself. If Meg wouldn't see Frankie about a job for herself then she would go and see him on her behalf. Besides, she was sure that there was more than just baking and business between the two of them, no matter what the spiteful Brenda Jones had said.

* ★ *

Daisy stood on the steps of the patisserie and told Frankie the tale of Meg's downfall, watching his every reaction. 'Oh, my poor love. Is she all right?' Frankie asked immediately. 'I knew I didn't like that Ted Lund as soon as I saw him. As for what Brenda Jones told her, it is utterly wrong. Yes, I took an interest in her when I knew she shared the same passion for baking and I was worried that she was competition for my bakery. However, I grew to be fond of her and I admire her passion. I must go and see that she is all right and tell her the truth.'

'She didn't meet you when she was supposed to because her mother was ill that day and then of course Brenda Jones made her think the worst of you. It's not for me to say really, but I am sure she feels the same way about you, but daren't let her feelings show. She did speak very fondly of you and I can see you feel the same way about her, even though your meetings were brief.'

'I will go and see her, I will go this afternoon,' Frankie said. 'Would you be good enough to tell me her address, she has never given me it despite my asking her more than once. Perhaps you are wrong and she does not feel anything for me?'

'No, believe me, it's not that. She really does care for you, I know she does, her face lights up as soon as your name is mentioned. It will be that she is ashamed of where she lives. It isn't the most desired place in Leeds and I'm sure she won't mind me saying, her family is very poor. They will struggle without Meg's wages, no matter how badly Ted Lund paid her.' Daisy looked straight into Frankie's eyes. 'It would mean everything to her at this time if you were to search her out, I know it would.'

'It makes no difference to me whether she is a princess or a pauper. My heart has gone out to her and that is all that matters,' Frankie told her, to Daisy's evident delight. 'I will look after Meg, you no longer need to worry. In fact, I will go this minute. My girls can run the shop without me — once the baking is done for the day it runs like clockwork. Now please give me her address!'

Daisy did so. 'As I say, it is not the most salubrious of addresses,' she added. 'The family deserves to live in better surroundings. They have worked hard all their lives but of late they have fallen upon hard times.'

She saw the gleam in Frankie's eyes and was sure he knew what he had to do.

★ ★ ★

'Oh Lord, Mam! Who's that knocking on our door? You don't think that Ted Lund has sent the peelers, do you?' Meg stood in the shadow of the net curtains and peered out to the doorstep. She gasped when she saw Frankie standing in his best overcoat and top hat. 'Oh no, it can't be! Who's told him where I live?'

'Why, who is it, lass? You look as if you've seen a ghost,' Agnes said at the panic on Meg's face. 'It's not the peelers, is it? Ted Lund would not be that heartless, especially when he knows that you've done nothing wrong.'

'No, Mam, it's worse, it's Frankie Pearson from the patisserie. He's come to visit me. How has he found out where I live?'

She hesitated, wondering whether to open the door or not.

'Well don't just stand there, open the door. Let me see this Frenchman who seems to have gone to your head and who you have shed all these tears over. . . . Aye, I've heard you crying over him, now if you are doing that you'd better see what he has to say for himself.'

Frankie knocked again, harder this time.

Meg felt flustered, her heat thumping as loud as Frankie's knocking. She opened the door and looked at the man she knew that she had deeper feelings for than a simple friendship. She blushed as he took his hat off and looked at her with concern.

'My Meg, thank heavens that I have found you,' Frankie said and leaned forward to kiss her on the cheek. 'Daisy has been a true friend to us both and told me of your predicament, so I took it upon myself to come and declare my intentions. How that man could treat you so badly, I just don't know. You had built his business up from nothing. Besides, I have missed you so much, I hoped that you would show your face in my shop or that I would pass you on the street, but I've not seen hide nor hair of you of late.'

'Oh Frankie, it is so good to see you. I have missed you so much. But when Brenda Jones told me that I was just being used by you and that I was of no consequence to you other than wanting to get your hands on Ted Lund's bakery, I thought the worse of you. I thought I meant nothing to you.'

Frankie took her hands. '*Ma cherie*, I am not that

shallow. Brenda Jones was a wicked snob of a person. You should not listen or believe a word that she says. I knew the first time that I saw you that I was smitten. Forget the baking and bakeries, it is you that has captured my heart and I don't care where you are from or how wealthy you are. I know with every day our love will grow if given a chance. You will give us a chance, won't you, my Meg?'

'I will. I feel the same but I didn't think that you did.' Meg wrapped her arms around his neck and kissed him, forgetting that the whole world — or at least all of Sykes Yard — could see them.

'Oh my Lord, on the doorstep for all the neighbours to see. Meg, bring him in for heaven's sake!' Agnes called and watched as the couple came into her meagre home. 'So, you're the one who's stolen my lass from me and made this dying woman happy as she's listened to the words said between you both on the doorstep.' Agnes smiled at the handsome man in front of her and saw the colour in Meg's cheeks. 'I had visions of all sorts of a man courting my Meg. But you look a handsome devil. No wonder she has lost her heart to you. I ask that you look after her, no breaking her heart, she's so precious to me.'

'I will. I promise that I will always be true to your daughter, together we will conquer the world.' Frankie looked at Meg. 'Things will be all right now, I promise.'

'I hope so because I do love you,' Meg said and searched for his hand to hold as they both looked at Agnes like two children in bother.

'Well, it seems to me that you both have the same interests and that you do both care for one another, so I'm not about to stand in your way of happiness,'

Agnes said. 'Now, perhaps you should put Ted Lund in his place between you, and show him how a proper business is run.' Agnes sniggered at the thought.

'Yes, we will do that. With both of us working together, we can achieve anything,' Frankie said and held Meg tight. Meg looked at her mother and then at Frankie. She knew she was loved by both and a new life was about to begin for her and her French baker, no matter where that took her. Ted Lund and his bakery were a thing of the past. He should have trusted her, because now, with Frankie's love, she would be a true threat to his business.

Together, they would be the talk of Leeds.

Recipes

Meg's Everyday Recipes

Rock Buns

225g (8oz) self-raising flour
Pinch of salt
110g (4oz) margarine
75g (3oz) mixed dried fruit
25g (1oz) mixed peel (optional)
50g (2oz) sugar
1 egg and milk to mix

Heat the oven to 200C/400F/Gas Mark 6 and grease two baking trays.

Mix the flour and salt and rub in the margarine.

Stir in the dried fruit, mixed peel and sugar.

Mix to a stiff dough with egg and milk.

Place mixture in rough heaps on the baking tray and bake for 10–15 minutes.

Courting Cake

220g (8oz) self-raising flour
Pinch of salt
50g (2oz) sugar
50g (2oz) lard
1 egg
Raspberry jam
50g (2oz) margarine

Heat the oven to 200C/400F/Gas Mark 6.

Mix flour and salt.

Rub in the lard and margarine and stir in the sugar.

Mix to a stiff paste with the egg. Add a little milk if necessary.

Divide the mixture into two.

Place one piece on a greased baking sheet and cover with jam.

Place the other piece of the mixture on the top and nip the sides.

Bake for 15 to 20 minutes.

When cool, cut into triangles.

Granny Loaf

450g (1lb) self-raising flour
Pinch of salt
1 tsp mixed spice
50g (2oz) lard
50g (2oz) currants
50g (2oz) raisins
50g (2oz) cut peel
75g (3oz) sugar
½ pint of milk
Beaten egg

Heat the oven to 190C/375F/Gas Mark 4–5.

Mix flour, salt and spices.

Rub in the lard.

Stir in sugar, fruit and peel.

Make into a dough with the milk.

Turn onto a floured board and form into a round.

Place in a well-greased cake tin.

Brush with a beaten egg and bake for about an hour.

Victoria Sandwich Cake

100g (4oz) margarine
100g (4oz) castor sugar
2 medium eggs
100g (4oz) self-raising flour

Heat oven to 180C/350F/Gas Mark 4 and grease an 18 cm/7" sandwich tin.

Cream the margarine with the sugar until light and fluffy.

Beat in the eggs one at a time, adding a little flour with each.

Gently fold in the remaining flour.

Place in the prepared tin and bake for 40–45 minutes.

When cool, split and fill with jam or cream and lightly dust with icing sugar.

Frankie's Pastry Recipes

Choux Pastry Basic Recipe

50g (2oz) butter or margarine
150ml (¼ pint) of water
100g (4oz) plain flour
3 medium eggs, lightly beaten.

Place fat in the water and melt over a gentle heat, then bring to the boil.

Remove from the heat and stir in flour.

Return to heat, stirring until mixture forms a ball in the middle of the pan.

Transfer to a large bowl to cool.

Thoroughly beat the eggs into the cooled mixture, a little at a time with a wooden spoon or electric whisk.

Eclairs

100g (4oz) choux pastry
150ml (¼ pint) whipping cream, whipped
Melted eating chocolate

Heat oven to 220C/430F/Gas Mark 7.

Grease a baking tray, then run under a cold tap, leaving a film of water on the tray.

Place choux pastry into a piping bag with a 1cm/½ inch nozzle.

Pipe mixture into 7.5 cm (3") lengths and bake for 30 minutes.

Immediately after baking make a slit down one side of each éclair and leave to cool.

Fill with whipped cream and decorate with chocolate.

Profiteroles in Hot Chocolate Sauce

100g (4oz) choux pastry

150ml (¼ pint) whipping cream, whipped

SAUCE
150g (5oz) cooking chocolate chopped
2 x 15ml (2 tbsp) soft brown sugar
2 x 15ml (2 tbsp) water 50g (2oz) butter
1 x 15ml (1 tbsp) rum or brandy

Heat the oven to 200C/400F/Gas Mark 6.

Grease two or three baking trays, then run under cold tap leaving a film of water on trays.

Using 2 teaspoons, place walnut-sized mounds of choux pastry well-spaced out on the baking trays.

Bake for 20–25 minutes until well risen, brown, and firm. Slit sides to let the steam escape. Cool on the wire rack.

Fill choux with cream.

To make the sauce, combine chocolate, sugar and water in a heavy-based saucepan, and stir over low heat until smooth. Stir in the butter. Remove from the heat and add the rum or brandy.

Pour sauce over the buns and serve immediately.

Basic Puff Pastry Recipe

225g (8oz) plain flour
Pinch of salt
150g (5oz) lard and margarine mixed
Cold water

Mix flour and salt, add fat cut into small pieces. Stir in with a knife — do not rub in.

Mix to a stiff dough with water.

Roll out on a floured surface to a narrow strip.

Fold in three, give a quarter turn so one of the ends is towards you, and roll out again.

Cover the pastry and leave to rest about 15 minutes and then roll into the desired shape.

Slippers a la Crème

225g (8oz) puff pastry
150ml (¼ pint) of thick cream
1 tbsp of sugar
½ tsp of vanilla essence
A little cochineal or candied fruit for decoration

Heat the oven to 230C/450F/Gas Mark 8.

Roll the pastry out into a thin length of about sixteen inches.

Cut into twelve strips one inch wide.

Wet slightly one edge of each strip, grease the outside of some cream horn moulds, and wrap strips of the pastry around, allowing the wetted edges to overlap.

Brush the pastry with a little beaten egg and bake for 10 minutes, remove from the moulds and allow to cool.

Whip the cream until stiff and then add the sugar, vanilla and cochineal.

Fill each case and serve in a ring. If preferred the cream may be left white and sprinkled with candied fruit.

St Honoré Cake

Choux pastry
75g (3oz) puff pastry
75g (3oz) sugar
150ml (¼ pint) milk
3 eggs separated
1 tbsp of plain flour
1 tsp of lemon juice
Glace cherries

Roll out the puff pastry to the size of a dinner plate.

Put the choux pastry into a piping bag and then pipe a line around the edge of the pastry leaving a half-inch gap from the edge.

With the choux pastry that is left, pipe small balls on a separate baking sheet to make profiteroles.

Place in the oven and bake until both are brown and firm and then leave to cool.

Mix icing sugar and a little water and when profiteroles are cool, coat in the icing and sandwich onto the choux ring with the cherries in between.

Moisten the flour and sugar with the egg yolks and milk, add the lemon juice and then cook gently, stirring continuously until the mixture thickens, then leave to cool.

Whip the egg whites until really stiff and then stir lightly into the custard mixture.

Form into egg shapes using two large spoons and heap into the centre of the gateau.